FALLEN ANGELS: SLATER

WARRIOR ANGEL

FALLEN ANGELS AND DEMONS
BOOK TWO

ANNA LORES

Blooming Cactus Publishing, LLC

Blade's Second Fertile Virgin, Book 12

Nash's Fertile Virgin, Book 13 is coming soon…

Paranormal Romance

Werewolves and Vampires

Cursed to Love

One Night of Love

More coming soon

Fallen Angels and Demons Series

Logan: Law Angel

Slater: Warrior Angel

coming soon

For more steamy stories and to join Anna's VIP Lounge, visit
https://www.AnnaLoresAuthor.com

CONTENTS

Fallen Angel: **Slater: Warrior Angel**

Copyright © December 2025 Anna Lores

Image/art disclaimer: *Licensed material is being used for illustrative purposes only. Any person depicted in the licensed material is a model.*

eISBN: 978-1-949396-37-9

Print ISBN: 978-1-949396-38-6

Editor: Dianne Rich

Cover Artist: Sarah Marek and Benjamin Moder

Published in the United States of America

Blooming Cactus Publishing LLC

PO Box 16324

Fort Worth, Texas 76162

www.bloomingcactuspublishing.com

This book is a work of fiction. While reference might be made to actual historical events or existing locations, the names, characters, places and incidents are either the product of the author's imagination or are used fictitiously, and any resemblance to actual persons, living or dead, business establishments, events, or locales is entirely coincidental.

Warning

This print or e-book contains sexually explicit scenes and adult language and may be considered offensive to some readers. The spicy division of Blooming Cactus Publishing, LLC's print and e-books are for sale to adults ONLY, as defined by the laws of the country in which you made your purchase. Please store your files wisely, where they cannot be accessed by under-aged readers.

DISCLAIMER: *Please do not try any new sexual practice, without the guidance of an experienced practitioner. Neither Blooming Cactus Publishing LLC nor its authors will be responsible for any loss, harm, injury or death resulting from use of the information contained in any of its titles.*

ACKNOWLEDGMENTS

Thank you for buying this book. I know your time is sacred, so thank you for choosing to spend it reading Slater and Finley's story.

I wrote most of these books while I was in the throws of dealing with colon cancer and trying to beat it. There are references to God in this book and very little cursing in the series. I thought a lot about angels and demons while undergoing treatments for cancer. I thought about the fight for souls, and five stories came to me during that time for this series. It's a little different than my other novels, but it's sexy and sweet, and there remains an undercurrent of darkness that the characters struggle with in different ways.

Whatever you may be struggling with, I want you to know that I love you. And if you'd like me to pray for you, I will. Email me at Anna@annaloresauthor.com. I know many of you prayed for me while I was dealing with colon cancer. Let me tell you, I felt those prayers. Thank you for them.

As a reminder…The age for colon cancer screening is 45 — please get screened for colon cancer. It truly could save your life. I love you and I want you to live. And tell those you love and care about to get screened.

To my family, thanks for all the love and support you've given me. I love you all more than I am able to express.

To my wonderful cover artists, Sarah Marek and Benjamin Moder, thank you so much for your patience and working with me—with very little direction on my part. I trust your creativity and abilities to make a beautiful cover. I love you.

A special thanks to my editor Dianne Rich for all the prayers and support. Thank you for polishing Slater and Finley's story. Thank you for being a friend. Thank you for working with me when my world turned upside down and as I try and flip it right side up again. Thank you. :)

To: Amy Squared
Amy G. and Amy L. This one's for you!

PROLOGUE

Finley

The weekly renovations of Rager Smithson's formal dining room surprised Finley Vessel every time. The walls changed color from a crimson red to navy blue. The crown molding and the base trim remained a glossy white, but the crystal chandelier brought in from God knows where had been changed again from small pieces of sparkling crystal to pole shaped crystal spanning several feet with shiny gold mechanisms holding the magnificent piece together.

The china on the table also changed from the last time or any other dinner she'd attended with him. Today, the plates—a base of bone-white with blue and gold swirls, twisting to form an angelic halo—matching the colors of his suit and tie. The silverware changed, too. This week she held gold utensils with handles that twisted, reminding her of braided rope. The only piece in the room that remained the same was the table, and it was a magnificent table that sat at least twenty that was flown in from Texas where he and a friend designed and handcrafted it. Some weeks there was a tablecloth hiding the natural beauty of the polished wood, but he loved that table in the natural state as it looked now, and so did she.

The gold halter dress which left her upper back bare and matching shoes he'd sent her last night for today's dinner matched both his suit and the room. The man liked to dress formal for dinner and he liked those around him to be dressed appropriately for the occasion. If they were unable to afford clothes and jewelry for the dinner, then he would send them—which he did every week for her. She'd argued with him over the gifts, and lost week after week. After a few months of researching and delivering arguments on why he shouldn't send her clothes to wear during their dinners, which seemed to only get her another invitation back for another dinner the following week, she finally conceded to losing, and agreed to accept his gifts with a word of thanks and nothing else. Now she had lots of formal dresses and jewelry that would come in handy if she followed his plan for her future. But so far, she wasn't on board for the future he saw for her.

But watching the stoic man seated across the table from her release a hearty laugh made her genuinely smile. She hadn't smiled in a long time, not really. Since her apartment complex burned down, there hadn't been much to smile about.

Of course, she'd had some moments of happiness with the young children she babysat or with the older children she taught Sunday school at church, and she often giggled with her best friend Sienna Singleton-Davis. But Finley's own heart was heavy, matching the man's across from her. They both were in love with someone they couldn't have, and that unspoken knowledge connected them on an intimate level. And as usual, she knew virtually nothing about the woman he loved, but he knew everything about the man who held her heart.

Others saw her dinner partner and friend, Rager Smithson, as dangerous, distant, and impatient. But she saw the real him—a kindred spirit. A person literally dying from the inside out. A person not long for this world. A person looking for an eternal love, and to have a child born from that love. And like her, he didn't believe he'd live long enough to experience either of those things.

"Love is the ultimate winner in all things earthly and divine," she stated. "It's true. It's biblical. Are we going to spend hours on end on a discussion you know I'll win, again?"

"No, no." Rager scooted back the plush dinner chair from the table. "I've been schooled enough over the last six months in the virtues of love and its conquests. I think we can lay this argument to rest. And I don't want to move onto another subject which you have clearly been educated in since before birth."

She rolled her eyes. "I'm sure I can think of a more recent topic...maybe one from the last nine years. That would be after my tenth birthday when I moved in with Liam."

"Ah, yes. *The* Liam Hutchison Vogel from Georgia who has been relentless in his inquiries of your whereabouts, when you don't answer your phone."

"Yep. Him." *The Liam who didn't want me to move to Nevada for my higher education, but I did it anyway. You're the only person he actually likes in this town. Well, you and Sienna.*

"Are you sure you don't want to move into a room here? Liam wouldn't worry so much, if you lived here, with me." He placed his golden utensils in a diagonal across three-fourths of the meal remaining on the white with gold and blue swirls dinner plate, signaling he was done with his meal. "You could join me on the ride to the university. Your boyfriend Neeman wouldn't pick you up and drive you home anymore. You wouldn't be breaking his heart a little more every day."

"Neeman is just a friend. He's nice and interesting. Plus he drives me over to the gardens he's tending during his internship. The flowers are beautiful, and he's always bringing me new tropical flowers for my room."

"You need to tell him that you'll never think of him as more than just a friend."

"Rager, come on. He doesn't think of me as anything but a friend. If I lived with you, people would think we're more than friends. People would talk."

He grinned. "Let them talk. Some perks of living with me would be that my chef would make all your meals. We could enjoy dinner together most evenings."

"Would you eat more if I did?" she asked.

"Probably not." His blue-eyed gaze drifted to her plate with a similar amount left on it. "Would you?"

"Probably not." She let out a soft giggle, then placed her utensils across her plate like he did.

At first, he stifled a laugh, but he couldn't hold it inside, so he let it out and it filled the room with mirth, making her own inner child burst out in a similar genuine laugh, a rarity for the two.

As soon as they stopped laughing, Rager let out a long sigh. He shook his head and scrubbed his hand over the top of his short blond-hair. "Finley, Liam doesn't want you living with the Davis's anymore. He's worried about your reputation."

"So instead of me living with a big, loving family who needs me as a nanny, he thinks that moving in with a rich, eligible bachelor who is so charming and gorgeous it's sinful should be the solution to my housing issues?"

The man who never showed emotions, especially outside

his home, actually blushed at her compliment. "I am brilliant, not charming, nor gorgeous."

"I'm an observant woman, and I say you are all three of those things. I *win* yet another debate. And it's a recent topic. I'm all about winning today." She blew him a kiss and the pink tinge to his normally creamy facial color turned a bright red.

He giggled like a child. "Finley, stop it. You are too much. I can't seem to get angry with you."

"No one gets angry with me. That is, except Liam. Liam consistently gets angry with me these days." *He is tired of me living with a polyamorous family. But he should know I'm not involved intimately with any of them. I'm like an aunt to the kids. I love being part of a family, and I am a big part of Sienna's non-traditional family. I'd be lost without them. And I like to think that they need me, too.*

The man narrowed his discerning eyes. With that shift in facial movement, the blush vanished from his face, and the inquisitor within him appeared again. He just couldn't turn off the lawyer switch inside him.

He gently, but methodically skimmed his hand over the Windsor knot of his navy-blue and light shade of gold diagonally striped tie, then down, adjusting the line of the tie slightly to the left, centering over the buttons on his shirt that matched the softer gold hue in his tie. "I highly doubt Liam is ever angry with you."

"It's true," she insisted. "He threw a fit when I told him I was moving to Nevada for college."

"Now *that* I believe," he stated. "But he seems to have adjusted to the change."

"He may tell you that, but every day, he asks when I'm moving home. It's been almost three years, and he's still asking. He even uses his stern voice with me, demanding that I finish my education in Georgia. I bet he doesn't use that voice with you."

"No one talks to me like that. And I want to put on record that I'm not happy about this sudden trip he's making you take to Georgia."

"I don't want to talk about my trip home this weekend," she said. "Liam asked me to go to a family party. I'm going. End of conversation." *He's never invited me to a family party. He's never gone to a family party. I didn't think he had any family left.*

"I'd like you to reconsider traveling to Georgia on such short notice."

"No, sir. I'm going."

"Then I will go with you."

"You weren't invited. Only me. I'm going and there's nothing you can do or say to stop me."

"Well, my irritatingly obstinate friend, we need to talk about your itinerary and taking my plane and driver. I won't allow you to…" While he continued speaking, she huffed and raised her hands for him to stop. "What now?" he asked.

"I'm not taking your plane or your car and driver. Liam sent me commercial airline tickets, and I've already booked and prepaid for a car rental, with Sienna's help. Your intervention is not needed." *But I love that you want to protect me. If my heart wasn't set on Liam, I'd consider taking you up on that offer to move in with you. But then you'd attempt to control everything I do. I'd end up as an attorney and then judge. You'd take pictures of me holding a gavel and scales with a blindfold over my eyes. That would be too much. But not for you.*

"You're going on my plane," Rager stated.

"Thank you, my dearest friend in the whole world, but I have to decline your *offer.* Blade Davis, Sienna's wonderful husband, has requested I fly on his plane, instead of flying commercial." *I'm also not dressing up to get on your plane or Blade's. Although Blade doesn't have strict clothing guidelines for his planes. In fact, once in the air, clothing is optional, not that I'd ever do that, but Sienna was pretty detailed on the nudity factor during some of her private flights with Blade on his plane.*

"And you declined his offer, too, didn't you?" Rager pursed his lips together.

She didn't have to nod. The man instinctively knew the answer. "Listen, if I get into a jam with my flight, I'll figure it out. I can do this on my own. I'm an adult." *Nothing is going to go wrong.*

Rager stood and leaned forward, placing his hands on the table, glaring at her as if he were able to intimidate her. He opened his mouth.

"Before you start." She placed her hands on the edge of the table and leaned forward, mimicking him. She tipped her head down, sending blonde tendrils loose from her messy bun. Her natural wavy hair fell forward, framing her face. "You should know by now that your 'I'm a big-time attorney with more money than God and you must obey me' posturing doesn't work on me. So, don't even think you're going to bully me into something I'm not going to do. I know you. You're not going to hurt me."

"You don't know that."

"Yes, I do." She rose from her seat and tucked the hair that fell behind her ears. "I feel all the love you hide inside your heart. I love you, Rager Smithson."

"Fin, that's not fair. You can't use the "L" word and think that I'll give up. You need to—"

"Thank you for dinner and an evening filled with lively conversation," she interrupted him. "I'm going to walk over and hug you, because we both need a hug."

The long exhale that came out of his mouth seemed out of frustration, but he straightened up and stepped away from the table. He buttoned his suit jacket and opened his arms. As soon as she curled her arms around him, he wrapped her in a warm embrace. "Liam is right to worry about you. *I'm* worried about you."

"Neither of you should worry. I can take care of myself." She snuggled closer to him. Normally, she didn't like anyone touching her bare upper back, but for some reason Rager's touch took away most of the pain that was always there. She liked to think that the touch of genuine love between friends eased pain, and hoped that her touch offered him relief of at least a small portion of the suffering he carried with him.

"Don't say a word, just listen to me," he whispered.

She remained silent, waiting patiently for him to continue.

"You're going to text me every seven hours. If I don't hear from you, I will search for you. I *will* find you. I won't give up until I do. If I arrive and all is well, then I'll pretend I was in the area and decided to pop in. If something is wrong, you will have no choice but to leave with me. I will not accept your refusal. I love you too much to ever walk away from you when you need me."

She nodded and clung to him a little tighter. "I can make this trip, but I'm a little scared to go alone."

"I know," he whispered. "But I'm going to tell you a secret." He cradled the back of her head, holding her gently against his strong, muscular chest. He was the perfect man, protective, loving, smarter than anyone else she'd ever met, kind, and he loved children. He went out of his way to protect them whenever the need arose. If only there had been some kind of spark between them, or even a flutter of love that could one day lead to marriage, but there wasn't.

Maybe I'm not meant for marriage or true love or children. I miss Liam. I miss home.

"I'm going to be in Georgia while you're there," Rager said. "I'm leaving tonight and will be in a small city north of Atlanta until Monday or possibly Tuesday, maybe longer. No one is supposed to know, so this is an exercise in trust between the two of us."

She squeezed him tighter, praying for a spark of love between them. But there was nothing. Nothing but an unbreakable friendship.

"All you ever have to do is ask for my protection, and I will give it," he whispered. "You are my friend, Finley, and I have few of them. In fact, you may be the only genuine friend I have living on this earth."

"I only have you and Sienna who I'd call friends," she confessed. "I love Liam, but I don't think he's my friend." *Lately, he's been so secretive that I don't know what he feels for me.*

Rager swallowed hard, but he didn't argue, which worried her. Rager argued, often going for the jugular, when he disagreed about anything, personal or business. The subject matter remained of no concern to him. If he didn't agree with her about her statement about Liam, he would've said so.

"You know something that I don't know," she whispered.

"I know many things you don't know, Finley. One of which is that you're very kind to me, even when I don't warrant that kindness."

"Rager, that's not true." *You are the one who's been kind to me for no reason at all. Well, you do like our debates, but I like them, too.*

"It is true. And I'm thankful you've stopped sending my gifts back to me."

"You got sneaky and took off the tags on everything. You always find a way to get what you want. I can't wait to see you married and chasing a baby or two around the house. Instead of being a basic master of redirection, you, sir, will become the ultimate master of redirection for all children, which, of course, is what I am."

"Teach me your ways, ultimate master," he teased, holding her a little tighter and weaving his fingers through her hair, removing the band barely holding together her messy bun.

Her hair floated over his hand and downward to the low curve in her back. "You may tease me now, but just wait. God is going to bless you with children. And I'm going to be the only babysitter you'll ever allow to watch your children, because you know I'll love them as much as you do. I truly can't wait for that blessing to come true." *You deserve to be loved by a woman who would cherish every day she got to spend with you. I want that for you.*

While he ran his fingers through her hair like a comb, his tight embrace softened. "I love it when your hair is down. The color is more beautiful than anything I've ever seen and it's softer than the finest silk."

Liam was the only other person she ever let touch her hair like this. The sensation was soothing, calming, loving. Peace flowed through her, instead of the chaos of emotions that lived inside her—the chaos she hid from the world. But with Rager, she didn't have to hide anything. When she was with him, peace existed inside her. Sometimes, she wished he would hold her like this—caressing her back, running his hands through her hair—for hours, days.

Already they stood, holding each other for longer than most would consider appropriate between friends or even lovers.

"If I am ever blessed with a wife to truly love, and a child results from that love *and* something tragic happens to me, you will be my child's guardian. Even if my wife is still alive after I pass, my wife will have to contend with you for any type of visitation with my child. I expect you to fiercely love and protect my child or children, after my life is over."

"I'd lay down my life to protect yours or your child's, and I'd be honored to care for and love your children for as long as I live," she stated without hesitation. She placed her hand over his heart and rose on her tippy toes, giving him a kiss on the cheek. "Please, look for true love. One of us should have a happily ever after."

"That's not in the cards for me. You will be the only woman I will ever love." He retreated two steps.

She had no words for a response. He never casually threw around the "L" word. He only said what he meant, and he'd just stunned her.

"Should I have my driver take you back to the Davis's?" he asked.

She pivoted and crossed the lush Persian area rug covering the dining room floor. "I'm walking. Tell Liam I'll be in my room at Blade and Sienna's in five minutes. I'm babysitting their kids tonight and tomorrow. They need some adult time together."

"Tell Liam yourself as you enjoy your stubborn stroll down the street. My driver will follow you," Rager said.

"Whatever." She shook her head and her hair swayed back and forth across her bare back. "See you next week for dinner. I want to hear all about your boring week."

"Ditto," he said.

While she walked into the hallway, she heard his footsteps close behind her.

"Hey, what do you know about Slater Vogel?" Rager asked. He wove his arm around hers and guided her toward the front door.

"Who?" she asked.

"Slater Vogel. He lives next to the Davis's."

"Oh. He's got the same last name as Liam, but it seems to be a common surname around here," she mumbled, speaking aloud what she normally would have kept in her thoughts. "As for Slater, I don't know him very well. If it's who I think it is, he seems nice. He's got some kind of social channel? Is that right?"

"Yes, he does. What can you tell me about him?"

"I think he's got blue eyes. He helps Sienna with the triplets. Actually, I think he comes over and babysits with me sometimes, but maybe that isn't him. I don't remember ever really asking his name. Sienna talks about him. But you know me. I love the kids and they're my sole focus."

"Do you like him? Think he's handsome?"

She shrugged. "I hadn't really thought about liking him. I don't even think we've spoken more than polite niceties. As for handsome? I guess so. Why?"

"Just curious," he said. "He's been in town a lot more since you've moved into the Davis's house. He comes and goes, visiting the Davis family more often while you're there. I didn't know if there was something unspoken going on between the two of you."

She burst out laughing. "Unspoken? Oh my goodness, Rager. Really? You'd be the first person I'd tell about something *'unspoken'* going on. I'm too busy with school and helping Sienna with the kids and my other babysitting jobs to even pretend to be interested in anyone. And as far as I can tell, not that I've been looking, but not a single guy I've met is interested in me. Not one. So, I think that says it all."

"That's a bunch of bullshit, Fin. Every guy is interested in you. You're gorgeous, brilliant, ooze sex, and you're the ultimate challenge to impress. Plus, you're a virgin who love kids, and even Nash Walker trusts you to watch his niece. I'd bet he's been looking for a way to ask you to marry him since the day you showed up to babysit for him, like every other hot-blooded male to ever cross paths with you."

She rolled her eyes and blushed. "I'm only a few of those things, but I'm definitely not gorgeous or brilliant, and I do *not ooze sex.* Liam would haul my butt back to Georgia and put me in the city jail cell if he thought I was dressed sexy or acted like I wanted it or whatever, which I don't. Well, not with just anyone." She sighed. *I'd have sex with Liam. I love him so much. I want to be his wife. Why doesn't he want me to be his wife?*

"I'm a guy. You're all of those things, Fin. If I thought I had a chance with you, I'd marry you in a heartbeat."

With a tilt of her head and slight lowering of her chin, she stared at him. *You would?*

He sighed. "*So* Slater's sudden interest in staying home most of the time has nothing to do with making moves on you?"

"Mr. Blue Eyes?"

"Yes, blue-eyed Slater. The one who always wears mirrored sunglasses.

"I don't like those stupid mirrored sunglasses."

"Has he made a move or not?" he asked.

"Nope. Slater has made no moves at all. At least none that I noticed."

"*That you noticed.*" He sighed again. "I win this disagreement, because you're oblivious to the way people react to you." He stopped at the front door. "I want my driver to take you home. No arguing."

"Only this one time," she said. "But just because I'm going to get in the car with your driver does not mean you won that disagreement."

"You're killing me, Fin," he chuckled. "You can sit in the front passenger seat and chat with my chauffer if you'd like."

She knew that was a concession he rarely gave to anyone, and had told her so the first time she asked about his rules. "I would like that. Thank you."

"Enjoy your evening, Miss Vessel." He opened the door for her.

The car idled on the circular driveway in front of the house and the driver held open the passenger side door, as if he'd heard their conversation. *How did you tell your driver to open that door and not the back one? How do you always stay ten steps ahead of everyone else?*

"Thank you, Mr. Smithson. And thank you for the dress. I love it." She stepped out onto the porch and gathered the floor length golden skirt of her halter dress up a little as she descended the stairs toward the waiting car. As her golden heels hit the walkway, she glanced over her shoulder toward the door.

The gorgeous man whom she'd had dinner with every Wednesday for the last year remained inside the foyer with the door open and his hand held over his heart.

She placed her hand over her heart and smiled.

You deserve love, Rager Smithson. You deserve the kind of love from a woman that is eternal. She inhaled and turned toward the car. *Maybe we'll both find love. Maybe Liam invited me to the party this weekend because he wants to confess that he loves me as much as I love him.*

She slid into the front passenger seat and the driver closed the door. The evening had lifted her spirits, and she was ready for a night playing games and chasing all the older boys around the Davis's house and loving on Sienna's newborn triplets.

CHAPTER ONE

Finley

Standing at the car rental counter, Finley Vessel pleaded her case to the customer service representative who empathized but couldn't seem to find a solution to the problem. The fact that there were no cars on the lot for rent left her desperate with few options—options she wasn't prepared to take. Talking, begging, and crying hadn't done her any good. There was literally nothing the agent could do. He couldn't make a car appear out of thin air, and she didn't have enough money in her bank account to pay for a ride to Liam Hutchison Vogel's house—a house she used to consider her home.

In a last-ditch effort, she made eye contact with the man behind the counter. She always got her way when she let down her shields and showed her vulnerability. "Please, there has to be something you can do," she pleaded. She fluttered her lashes and pouted. "I prepaid for the car. Can't you work out something with another car rental agency?" She traced her lower lip with the tip of her tongue and glanced at the car rental counter to her right. "Could you maybe work a deal with them? They've been handing out car keys left and right."

The guy leaned over the counter and looked at the guy in the next section. "Gary, you got any cars for rent? What about your car? Could you let her borrow it?"

"Nah, Karl," Gary said. "Handed out keys to the last car on my lot a few minutes ago. Nobody has anything. But I'm expecting to have some cars tonight and tomorrow. I'd offer her a ride, but my shift doesn't end for another six hours and my mom is picking me up." He looked at Finley. "If you want to wait, my mom would be happy to take you wherever you want to go." He smiled as his gaze drifted over her chest and down her body as if he were touching her. She got the creeps so badly from his ogling that chilling goosebumps popped up all over her body.

Karl returned to his position on the other side of the counter. "I'm really sorry, Miss Vessel. I'd offer you my car if I had one. But I don't. My sister drove me to work today because my car is in the shop. I'd call her to come and take you anywhere you wanted to go, but she turns her phone off at work and that's where she is right now. So, all I can tell you is that you'll get refunded in three to ten business days. There is literally *nothing* I can do. My life sucks…" His voice trailed off as his shoulders slouched and his head tipped downward as if he were crumbling where he stood.

"Finley?" a familiar male voice asked.

"Yes?" She turned toward the voice as her mind wandered to her temporary home in Nevada. *Could you be in one of my classes?*

A tall guy wearing a black hoodie that clung to his well-developed muscles faced her. And he wasn't all chest muscles. The man before her wore dark jeans that made her internally moan. He didn't skip leg day at the gym. From the looks of him, he might spend all his extra time getting sweaty using those strong muscles to lift and lower heavy, heavy weights...*Mmm.* And he had fashion sense. His sneakers were on trend and made his casual day-look adaptable to night club ready. And he smelled good, too. Whatever cologne he wore worked for him. Everything about him worked for him.

He shifted an army green duffel bag strap across his chest. "Do you need help?"

The way she tipped her head and tried to get a better look at him, must have clued him in to the fact that she had no idea who he was, even though she recognized his velvety-smooth voice. As she gazed upward, finding gold mirrored sunglasses hiding the color of his eyes and where he was looking, she realized he'd seen her checking him out in every inappropriate way possible while still clothed.

He lowered his gold-mirrored glasses and the piercing blue eyes staring right back at her came from the same man she babysat Sienna's triplets with three days ago. Quickly, he slid the glasses up the bridge of his nose, hiding his most distinguishable feature.

In that split second, she partially wanted to die from embarrassment, but the other part jumped for joy that he stopped to help. *You're blue eyes. Mr. Blue Eyes always hiding behind those stupid mirrored sunglasses.*

"Slater Vogel, what are you doing here?" she asked.

"Not renting a car." Slater inhaled and his broad chest expanded further.

How could I have never noticed how big and sexy you are? "Ha. Ha. Not funny."

"Too soon?"

"Yeah, smartass," she said. "It's way too soon."

"Sorry. Need a ride? A walk to your rental?"

"They're out of cars. So, I actually do need a ride," she admitted. *And it's a far ride. I doubt you'll have time to take me all the way to Liam's. I don't want to call and tell him that I need him to meet me somewhere and bring me home. I promised him that I didn't need his help. I could call Rager, but I don't want to admit to him that I need his help, either.*

"I can figure something out," she added. "It's far. You're busy."

He jerked his head toward the exit, motioning her to come with him. "Follow me."

She picked up her black backpack. The familiar ache of her shoulders and back from the movement and weight of the pack in her hand pushed her to overcompensate. She swung her arm to hoist the pack up and rethought the move, stopping and nearly dropping it. She readjusted her grip and waited for the right moment to try again.

"I had a reservation but when I didn't show up on time, they rented my car to someone else," she said, biding some time to swing her pack over her shoulder. "My flight got delayed, which is why I'm late. I have the worst luck."

"All the flights got delayed out of Las Vegas. The weather was crap, and that rental agency never has enough cars in any airport I've ever been in. I got screwed by them a couple years ago. I'm sorry you had a similar experience today. I'll take you wherever you want to go." He grabbed her backpack from her hand as she was slinging it up, in another attempt to get it onto her back. Raising his arm, her pack slid onto his shoulder into place as if it was a part of him. "Let's get out of here before someone recognizes me."

CHAPTER TWO

Finley

As she walked out of the baggage claim into the confusing world of shuttles, share rides, pickup lanes, and more, she was ready to get out of the airport. She couldn't wait to be back in the small rural town where she'd grown up and lived with Liam.

For as long as she'd lived in Georgia, she'd never flown in or out of the airport. She'd never even driven to the airport to pick someone up or drop anyone off. In fact, on the long journey to the small college town in Nevada where she accepted an educational scholarship more than a year ago, she'd driven through small towns avoiding the city in the exact way Liam had instructed her to do.

Driving across the country under the watchful eyes of Liam's law enforcement friends was one thing, but landing in this airport was like arriving on another planet—everything was new and there was no safety net in place.

She slipped her hand into Slater's, needing to feel a sense of familiarity and security. Both senses washed over her at the initial spark of contact.

"Don't be scared," he said, locking her hand in his without missing a beat or a step, as if it was the most natural thing in the world to be holding her hand. "It's a gigantic airport, but I travel in and out of here a lot. We're going to take a shuttle to my car and then we'll grab breakfast on the way to wherever you need to go. I don't have to be anywhere until this evening."

He stopped, pulling her in front of him and wrapping his arms around her waist. He dropped his head and kissed her neck. Every inch of her warmed in places that usually remained room temperature or more like arctic-glacier frozen-cold.

"There's a dude looking at us," he whispered. "He's doing a terrible job trying to stealthily take a photo of us on his phone. I think he recognizes me. I don't want him to get a picture of my face. I don't want anyone knowing I'm in Georgia this weekend. Let's make sure he only sees a beautiful woman with her unrecognizable boyfriend."

You think I'm beautiful? "I didn't recognize you at first."

"That hurts." He rubbed his nose under her ear, warming more of her body. "With as much time as I've spent with you, I'd hoped to be more memorable."

"You call chasing Sienna, Emma, and Blade's kids around their backyard *spending time* together?" *You're crazy. You may have been a world-class champion at changing diapers, feeding kids, and kissing boo boos...You're actually very memorable. I don't know why I never really looked at you, until now.*

"Sure do," he whispered "All that time together made it clear that you're going to be a great mom someday. But since my time with you didn't make enough of an impression, I'll have to give you a subscription to my channel so you'll be much more likely to recognize me the next time we see each other." He kissed along her neck.

The warmth of his sweet breath seemed to awaken a deepening wish for him to continue the path of his gentle-caressing kisses to places she didn't really want to feel, let alone acknowledge. While she didn't particularly want to explore a relationship with him, she did like his attention a bit too much. Instead of ending this dangerous game of sexual awakening, she tilted her head to the side, offering his lips more of her neck to explore.

"I'd recognize you next time," she whispered. "*If* there ends up being a *next time.*"

He exhaled as he raised his head, leaving her wishing for his lips to touch her neck once more. "You smell like sweet nectar, Fin. Mmm." He slid his hand up her chest and neck to her cheek, turning her face toward his. "Dude hasn't put his phone down."

He pressed his mouth to her cheek, catching the corner of her lips.

An unexpected spark of deep desire accompanied the sweet kiss.

"I'm going to kiss you on the lips, and I need you to slip your hand over my cock and rub," Slater said. "I don't let anyone touch me, so if he's a fan, he'll think it's a case of mistaken identity and walk away. He might put it online as a fake sighting which would be awesome publicity for my chan-nel. Either way, it's a win for me. You don't have to do it. But, if you're comfortable touching me, it would help us get out of here without the need to call security."

Out of nowhere, she found herself complying with his request, secretly wishing his interest was much more than pretend.

Turning in his arms, she faced him, wanting to touch him under his clothes, too. She wanted to feel the smooth skin and hard muscles beneath his jeans and hoodie. She wanted him blowing feather-like kisses on her neck and chest and belly. She wanted—

His lips pressed against hers.

In that moment, she blocked out everything around her. Following his instructions, she caressed down his chest straight to the hard bulging package she'd eyed earlier.

He pulled her closer and moaned, deepening the kiss.

And dang...The man guided her, seemingly knowing she was entering a world she'd never known. He taught her what to do to make him moan again. And he did genuinely moan more than once more. And she wanted to hear more of that sound which seemed to come straight from deep inside him.

More and more he moaned, his hands moved from her hair to her back to gripping her bottom. He pulled her closer until she stood firm and flush against him.

In a kiss that continued to grow hotter and hotter, she finally lost all her senses. While he guided her movements, she undulated against him, rubbing along his impressive bulge, and unbuttoning his jeans. She was ready to—

In a split second, the kiss ended.

He lifted her up, pulling her legs around his waist.

She wrapped her arms around his neck, burying her face against his neck as he strode forward. With a quick glance at her surroundings, she saw everyone staring at her, their faces red and their eyes dreamy.

"You're so light," he said. "I could carry you for days."

While embarrassment and guilt set into her bones, he carried her through the airport baggage claim and onto a white shuttle bus.

"Sorry for getting a little carried away," she whispered. *More like a LOT carried away. Liam would be so disappointed in me. Thankfully, he'll never know.*

"I'm not sorry. I'd do it again in a heartbeat." He slowly

slid her down his deliciously powerful body until she stood on her own two feet. He zipped up his jeans and then handed the driver what looked like a blank business card with a few bills tucked beneath. "My flight got delayed. Sorry."

"No problem. Where is the lady going?" the driver asked.

"With me," Slater said.

"Take a seat, and I'll drive you to your car," the driver said.

Slater took off Finley's backpack and placed it on the luggage rack, then removed his duffel bag, placing it next to hers. "I see why Blade keeps you under lock and key. You're special."

That's a weird thing to say to someone you were just groping... well, more than groping. More like...kissing with intention. Are all kisses like that? If they are, I'm in trouble when I meet that special someone.

She sat next to him. "I'm not special, and Blade doesn't keep me under *lock and key.* I go wherever I want, whenever I want. Actually, he doesn't really notice me that much. I needed a place to stay until there's an available apartment in the complex where I used to live. Blade, Emma, and Sienna have been really nice to me, allowing me to live at their house while I'm between apartments."

"Why are you traveling alone? Where's your boyfriend?"

"Boyfriend?" *If I had a boyfriend, I wouldn't have kissed you.*

"The guy who picked you up yesterday morning. Gave you roses. That boyfriend."

"Neeman?"

"The one with the Corvette like Blade's?"

"That's Neeman, but he's not my boyfriend. He was sweet and brought me flowers, then dropped me off at school. He gives me flowers all the time. He's a horticulture major. Isn't that what guys in horticulture do?"

"No. They don't. They don't go out of their way to pick up girls and bring them to and from school every day."

She nearly choked on her own surprise. "You noticed?" *I've got to pay more attention to my surroundings. I never noticed you watching the house.*

"Hell, yeah, I noticed. How could I not? Part of what I do is keep an eye out for people whom I don't know that are coming in and out of the neighborhood, and you're my next-door neighbor. Plus, you're gorgeous. A man would have to be dead not to notice you."

"Slater, Neeman isn't my boyfriend. I've never had a boyfriend. I've never kissed a boy until a few minutes ago, and I've never had sex." She cringed. *And I didn't mean to tell you all that. I need to do some damage control.* "I don't have time for boys or love. Besides, I never would've kissed you if I was involved with someone else."

Liam would have a cow if he'd heard Slater even hinted that she'd been unfaithful to someone she loved. He'd lose it. Kissing was against his rules, but as far as violations went, it had always remained low on his "must not do until marriage" list. He'd forgive a kiss, but she wasn't so sure he'd forgive the public display of affection that had happened. If he found out she'd done that without a commitment behind it, she'd get grounded. Not that he could truly *ground* her anymore. She was an adult. But he was her guardian, even though she was only six years his junior. Regardless of their close ages, he seemed to be decades older than her and took his role as guardian very seriously since he'd been doing it for the last nine years. The man had earned the right to ground her, irrespective of her age or "adult" status.

And the last thing she wanted to do was embarrass him by kissing a boy in public, when he'd asked her to come back to be his "plus one" for his cousin's birthday party tonight. This party could be the catalyst to change their relationship from adult-child to husband-wife. Things had already changed for them when he'd asked her to be by his side for the family party. For as long as she'd known him, he'd never asked her to any family related anything. In fact, she had no idea that he'd kept in touch with any of his extended family after his parents passed away. She didn't think he had any cousins. Neither of his parents had siblings—or so she assumed.

"Hey." Slater rested his hand on hers. "I'm sorry. I assumed that guy was your boyfriend."

"Nope. Neeman lives in the condos across the street from my old place. The night of the fire, he saw me rushing out of the apartment and down the fire escape. He was right there at the bottom, helping me and a couple others to safety. He stood beside me as I watched the fire move through my side of the building."

She closed her eyes as the memories returned. "So much black smoke and flames. I lost everything except what I could shove into my backpack. He remained beside me as I spoke with Sienna about it. Neeman drove me to Sienna's and stayed as I retold Sienna, Emma, and Blade about the fire. Blade insisted I stay with them, and Neeman insisted I accept his offer to drive me to and from school until I had a new car or an apartment near campus."

"Neeman thinks you and he are dating," Slater stated. "I'd bet money that he is planning a dinner with the parents."

"I've already met his parents for dinner," she said. "They're nice. They're originally from North Florida, and I told them I wouldn't hold that against them—too much." She laughed, remembering the pleasant evening. "His parents should've had more children. Actually, Neeman's nanny should've had her own family. She raised Neeman while his parents traveled and worked around the world. She works for a family in the same neighborhood in North Florida. Neeman keeps in touch with her, mostly at Christmas when he visits his parents."

"You are entrenched in his life. You need to tell him you're involved with someone else, because he thinks you're his. And let's be clear about this. You are *not* his." Slater looked at her. The gravity he expressed in his stern gaze surprised her. The man was a serious as a heart attack.

"Neeman is a friend. That's all. He knows I don't have time for anything other than friendship. I'm not looking for a relationship. I'm busy." She turned her back to him. "I wouldn't lie to Neeman about being involved with anyone else. I'm not, so there is nothing to tell."

"You're involved with me," he said.

"That was a spontaneous arrangement to help you out of a special circumstance. Nothing more," she said. *Liam would skin me alive if I came home with Mr. Sexy Babysitter. But maybe he'd be jealous of Slater and finally admit his feelings for me. No. I'd be grounded and lectured about keeping my vows, which I have.* "There is nothing between you and me."

"Yes, there is," he said. "And you need to tell Neeman that you're mine."

She huffed. "Oh my goodness." Unable to hide her emotions, her cheeks heated with desire, and to her own frustration, she wished he would tell her she was his again.

She swiveled in her seat and poked him in the chest. "You have a lot of nerve. One hot kiss...well a kiss I assume is, umm, good. But I have no frame of reference to whether it is truly good or bad. Uh, whatever it was." She flattened her hand at his chest. *You are one very sexy man.* "It doesn't mean there's a relationship. A kiss doesn't." While her hand began to wander, she gazed up at his mirrored glasses and wished she could actually see his amazing blue eyes. "I'm. Uh. I'm not. Yours."

He closed his hand around hers, stopping her hand from drifting downward, caressing his abs over the thick fabric.

A spark of desire rushed through her, lighting a fire in her belly to get closer to him. *Skin to skin caresses would make me yours and you mine.*

"You *are* mine, Finley Vessel. One hundred percent mine." He brought her hand to his lips. "Did you know that I kept looking for an opening to ask you out while we were babysitting?"

She shook her head. "No," she whispered. "You're lying."

"I kept attempting small talk, but as soon as the kids were off to bed, so were you." He kissed the tip of her index finger that she'd just poked him with. "You kissed me back during that special spontaneous circumstance, and I've been trying to figure out what kind of game you've been playing since that moment."

"First. I'm not playing any games. Second—"

"I know that now." He kissed the tip of each of her fingers as he seemed to look at her behind those mirrored glasses.

"Good." The heat in her cheeks increased. "Because, uh, second, you're the one who kissed me first."

"I did kiss you. I hadn't planned on it, but I'm glad it went so well. I plan to do it again."

"I don't think so." She jerked her hand from his. "You can drop me off in front of the aquarium. You are not driving me all the way to—"

"As incredible as the aquarium is," he interrupted her. "We'll have to visit it another time. Neither of us have eaten, and food is essential to life. Let's talk more about *us* during brunch and then I'll drive you wherever you want to go. We can spend a couple days taking a roadtrip back home to Nevada, or an hour or two to wherever in Georgia, or months to anywhere in the world your heart desires to go."

While she considered his offer and her lack of options to

get to Liam's house, Slater curled his arm around her shoulders.

"I'm sorry," he whispered. "I'm used to people wanting something from me. You don't seem to have even noticed me before today, and we've spent a lot of time together on Blade Davis's property. You always seemed to look right through me as if I weren't even there. So when you looked at me today and acknowledged my presence…and the way you so easily rolled with my situation with that guy trying to take a photo…Fin, I wanted to be wrong about Neeman being your boyfriend. I'm glad I was wrong. I didn't want to explain to Neeman that you are mine now."

"Neeman isn't really my type. And I'll say it again, I'm not *yours*." She turned away from him.

I'm nobody's. Not yours. Not Neeman's. Not Liam's. I should get out of here before I do or say something I will regret. Emphasis on do, because I want to kiss him again. I don't trust myself not to.

CHAPTER THREE

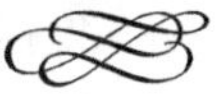

Finley

This was the most she'd ever spoken with Slater, ever.

Prior to his sudden shift to a man who thought he meant more to her than he did, the guy had moments during the times they'd babysat together when he reminded her of Liam. Slater had piercing blue eyes that shimmered with gold—like Liam—when he wasn't wearing mirrored sunglasses, which Slater always seemed to have on. And on the rare occasions Slater didn't wear mirrored sunglasses, when he looked at her with the naked eye, his irises turned so golden that the blue in them was drowned out—just like Liam's often did.

But at that moment, with her sudden affection going unchecked, if Slater took off his sunglasses and gazed at her with those golden eyes, she'd spill the fact that she'd been waiting for Liam Hutchison Vogel to get a clue and ask her to marry him. But Liam, the man who raised her for nine years, never made the slightest move on her, not even when she graduated high school. He wasn't even her real legal guardian. The man was only six years older than her. He'd taken her in when her mother disappeared, and then he'd given her a permanent home when her mother was found dead.

Ever since she could remember, Finley's mother had been prone to disappearing. Over the years, when her mother flaked out and left, Finley had gotten used to tying up loose ends in whichever town they'd lived in. When her mother remembered to come back for Finley, usually before nightfall, they'd arrive in the next small town by morning the next day or two. The pattern was consistent. Her mom *always* came back to get her, usually within a few hours of when school ended.

But the day Liam walked into Finley's life was different. The pattern of her mom's disappearance and subsequent return for Finely changed. The apartment she'd lived in with her mom for six months had already been emptied and swept clean by the time Finley arrived home from school. Still, Finley had checked with the apartment manager, making sure to be ambiguous of why she remained in town without her mom. Involving the police would put her in danger of becoming part of "the system" her mother had warned her about. And when her mom realized she'd left without Finley, the cops would probably arrest her mom for neglect or drugs or both. Finley would never let that happen. It was her and her mom making a life together, through good and bad times, forever…until it wasn't.

So, like every other time her mom disappeared, Finley handed in her key to the apartment manager as if that was what her mom had instructed her to do that day. She walked around the town square, waiting for her mom to return. Only that day, her mom didn't show up at the park—their secret meeting place—before nightfall. Her mom hadn't left Finley any money to buy a snack or dinner or anything, and she didn't call Finley or answer calls.

By the time the moon rose high in the sky that late spring day, Finley was desperate for something to drink. Food would've been nice, but it was thirst that sent her into the grocery store. Never having stolen anything in her life, nor able to think of any other legitimate scenarios to ease her thirst, she decided to take action. If she got caught, she'd have to lie about her mother's whereabouts. She'd also have to lie about her father—a man she'd never known. She wasn't sure her mom knew the man's name. With all the paranoia her mom had pumped into her head about men, women, the police, and emergency personnel, Finley literally trusted no one. So when the need to quench her thirst overrode her fear of strangers, she found the courage to do a thing she never would've done. Finley had realized that she was on her own. And this time, her mom might not be coming back.

That fateful and terrifying evening, Finley hadn't seen the man following her around the store. She hadn't realized how ragged and starved she'd looked. That the bottle of water she'd snuck into her black backpack had fallen out of the hole her mom hadn't patched.

With the pounding of her heart rushing like a waterfall in her ears, fear eliminated the sound of the water bottle hitting the floor. She hadn't seen the cameras on the ceiling watching her every desperate move to avoid attention.

An employee stopped her while she stood enthralled at the fruit drinks display. He asked her to open up the backpack housing the water she stole. In that moment, she stood ready to run, but suddenly she was blocked by the most handsome young man who appeared out of thin air. He grabbed the bottle of water from the floor and acted like he'd sent her into the store to start shopping, while he grabbed a grocery cart. The employee had apologized to him and then her, and left them alone to finish shopping.

Liam had rescued her that night. He'd become her savior in so many ways over the nine and a half years he'd cared for her. He'd always protected her. Always sheltered her. They'd grown up together, even though he'd had very little left to "grow" since he'd been sixteen the night they met. Back then, he had dirty-blond hair, like hers, and the most alluring blue eyes which sometimes morphed into the most breathtaking, shimmering gold. They looked like brother and sister, but as they aged, her hair changed to a platinum blonde while his remained that same dirty-blond. He retired his high school football jersey for a policeman's uniform, while she cheered him on and clung to him and his rules. She kept hoping that when she graduated high school or college, he'd marry her.

"Fin." Slater interrupted her thoughts. He held up her old and patched up backpack—the same one her mom had given her more than a decade ago. "Earth to Finley."

She inhaled sharply and rose from her seat. "Sorry. I was just thinking about the past." She reached for her backpack, but Slater slung it over his shoulder.

Her back and shoulders hurt to move, but she had to at least put up a little fight about carrying her backpack. Slater was being too kind, and she didn't need to form an attachment to a man Liam wouldn't approve of. If she hadn't kissed Slater in public, she still wouldn't get approval for a man who made a living as a gambler. Sure, it was a legal profession, and he didn't gamble so much now, or so she didn't think he did. But that didn't change the fact that the man was a poker genius and continued to play big games on the pro circuit. Slater Vogel wasn't an option for anything other than friendship. Besides, she was saving herself for Liam.

"I can carry my own bag," she said.

"What kind of man would I be if I allowed you to carry anything but a purse? And I'd carry a purse for you, too, if you had one." Like a gentleman, he took her hand and guided her forward, in front of him, and off the shuttle.

He tossed their bags in the back of his black luxury SUV.

While he climbed into the driver's side, he looked at her sitting in the passenger seat. "Are you okay?"

"I don't know," she mumbled. *My back hurts. As soon as Liam sees me, he's going to know the pain has gotten worse. He's going to think I've stayed away all this time to avoid going to the doctor. And he'd be kind of right. That and because I love him and keep hoping he'll come to Nevada and take me home to be his wife. So far, that hasn't happened. Honestly, I'm giving up hope that he'll ever look at me as more than the girl he rescued from a terrible situation.* "I haven't been home since I started college."

"You don't sound like you want to be here." He turned on the car and drove through the maze of vehicles in the lot toward the exit.

"I don't know whether I want to be here or not. Liam isn't the kind of guy you say 'no' to." *He's also not the kind of guy who ever asks anyone for a favor.*

"Liam?" he asked.

"My guardian. Although he isn't really my guardian. We were lucky because no one ever questioned our situation. We look similar enough—light colored hair and blue eyes— that most people thought that we were related. I was ten when my mother disappeared and Liam took me in. Then months later, my mother's body turned up deep in the woods near her crashed car. He took care of the funeral costs and told everyone that my mom had named him my guardian. No one asked him for proof or details, probably because everyone in town had watched him grow up to be an honest and trustworthy man who came from a respected family. For someone so young, he had plenty of money and a house with an extra bedroom, which became mine. He took care of me until I could take care of myself. He kept me clothed and fed and even decorated my room in his house. He required only a few things from me—honesty, straight 'A's in school, to be at home for dinner every night, and never be out later than ten in the evening unless he was with me."

"He must have been a mature eighteen-year-old to take on a homeless kid."

"Actually, he was sixteen," she said softly. "But yeah, everyone in town always joked that he was born mature."

"He sounds like a good man," Slater said.

"I'm grateful for him. I never thought I'd ever leave our town or the state of Georgia. But I got offered a great scholarship and moved to Nevada for college. It was the smart financial thing to do. But Liam was upset about it. He wanted me to go to a college closer to home, like he did. It was the first and only time I'd ever done something he didn't want me to, even though he eventually gave me permission and his blessing to go."

"You must love him," Slater said.

She nodded. "I do. I'd do anything for him. Like hop on a plane last minute because he asked. You know, he's never asked me for anything. Then out of the blue, he asked me to come home and go to a party with him. He bought me the plane tickets and everything." *He more like ordered me to come home and go with him. I would've come, even if he hadn't made it a demand.*

"What changed?" Slater asked.

"I don't know." *Liam doesn't go anywhere. He never goes to parties—birthday or otherwise. He works, works, and works some more. Plus, he lives and breathes all things Georgia, never venturing out of the state. He never leaves our county unless it has to do with learning more about the law or law enforcement. I need to find out more about why I'm here. This is too spontaneous, and Liam is NOT spontaneous. No part of this visit makes sense.*

She inhaled and refocused on the man driving the car. As often as she'd seen Slater at the Davis's house babysitting or bandaging a skinned knee or bringing pizza for movie night, they'd never really talked. She didn't know anything about him. Well, maybe she knew some, but not much. "How old are you? How did you end up being the Davis's neighbor? What do you do? Why are you here?"

The genuine grin she'd seen on his face when he'd been playing with Blade's older kids appeared, nearly blinding her with his handsomeness.

"I'm twenty-three," Slater said. "I'm from Las Vegas. I made my initial wealth from developing a sword fighting game when I was eighteen. Then I took some money and tried poker when I turned twenty-one. I found success in that arena, too. Then, about a year and a half ago, I made a bet with my best friend—and lost. He told me I had to film myself exercising. That one reel hit some kind of viral algorithm. As soon as I noticed the jump, I monetized the reel, then continued filming my daily exercise routine. Opportunities branched out from there. I started filming my everyday habits, which people seemed to be interested in seeing. I decided to monetize my endeavors in a new subscription-based online show. Rager Smithson—the man whose company handles all the security for the neighborhood—and I are friends. He told me about the house next to Blade's. Then my brother's friend Stetson Ross—who is Blade's best friend—told me the house was going up for sale. Brianna Horn, who is married to Michael Boke and lives in the neighborhood, is a real estate broker and handled the sale for me. How old are you?"

"Nineteen," she said. "I'll be twenty in a few weeks. I'm majoring in childhood education and psychology."

"I have a couple finance degrees." He handed her his phone. "Type in the address to where I'm taking you."

She typed in Liam's address, then added her name and number to his contacts—something she should have done when they'd first met a couple months ago. *I need to be more sociable. We're neighbors…at least for now.* "I'm sorry it's so far from the city."

"It's no big deal. I'm staying not far from there. It's close to the family party I'm going to tonight. I'd invite you to be my date, but you already have plans. It's really too bad you can't come. It's a formal affair, but once the music starts, the ties come off and things get crazy—a fun crazy, not a getting-arrested crazy. My family loves to celebrate anything." He zipped through airport traffic and made it onto the interstate like a professional racecar driver. "What are you doing Sunday?"

"I don't know. My flight got cancelled and rescheduled for Monday afternoon. What about you?"

"Let's watch a movie Sunday night. We'll stay at my place and fly home together on Monday. What do you say?" He turned his head, facing her with those mirrored glasses, making it impossible to interpret an expression or guess what he might be thinking.

"Stay with you?" *Liam will never go for that. He'd take one look at you in those sunglasses and even having a friendship with you would be a no-go.*

"Yeah. I thought you and Blade had a thing; otherwise, I would've asked you out within minutes of laying eyes on you," he said.

For real? Me and Blade? "Blade is like a hundred years older than me and he's married to both Emma and my best friend Sienna. Besides, that kind of relationship is Sienna's thing, not mine. Not mine by a long shot."

"Sorry. I meant Neeman, not Blade." He turned his head forward again.

Were you testing me again? Blade may have two wives, but they're happy. I'm not into that, not at all. I'm only interested in having one husband who is faithful in every way. But the more she thought about the Davis's and her living with them, the more she could see where Slater might think she'd be interested in Blade. The man was insanely wealthy and liked much younger women.

"So, should I make plans for us on Sunday?" Slater asked.

"Watching a movie with you on Sunday night sounds like fun, but I don't think Liam would be okay with me staying the night with you," she said. "But could you be my backup ride to the airport, if Liam can't drive me?"

"You're an adult. You can stay with whomever you want, whenever you want. No one owns you."

You don't know Liam. "That's overly simplified. No one may *own* me, but there is a respect factor in play here. I'm not disrespecting the man who changed his life and future to raise me, in order to have a sleepover with you." *I like you, but we're NOT having sex. I gave you the wrong idea when I groped you. I need to back off. Chill out. Stop thinking about doing things I'm only doing with my future husband.*

He sported a quick smile, then dropped it as he merged into heavy traffic.

Dang. You make me want to forget all about Liam's rules and my promises.

"I'll have my travel agent change your flight from Monday afternoon, to mine—at the crack of dawn—on Monday morning. It makes sense that we'd stay overnight together since we *are* traveling companions. Liam will understand." He shifted his gaze to hers and gave her a cocky smile as if it was inevitable that she'd be sleeping under the same roof as him. "What if you stay with me instead of with him this weekend?

I'll drop you off at his house and then pick you up after the party is over."

"How about 'no'?" *I bet you don't hear that word often.*

"Come on," he cajoled. "We'll have fun. I'm a lot of fun."

"I'll be your traveling companion—and sit next to you on the airplane Monday morning, if you pay for the flight change —but I can't sleep at your place this weekend." *Liam would definitely forbid it, and you'd chip away at my resolve until I found some kind of excuse to get so close that I'd consider doing the nasty with you. But it wouldn't be nasty. It'd be incredible. I bet it would be life-altering.*

"We're still on for a Sunday night date?" he asked.

Heck, yeah, we are. "I might have to be home by ten." She shrugged in an attempt to seem indifferent. "But I'm game if you are." *I can't believe I'm agreeing to this.*

"We'll negotiate a more reasonable curfew time." He accelerated and exited right, heading southeast, not north-west toward her final destination. "There's this restaurant that serves breakfast all day long."

"You want breakfast food?" she asked. *It's the afternoon.*

"Yeah." He sped down multiple streets and then hopped back on a highway, continuing east into the country. "I love the pancakes at this place. You're hungry, right?"

"Starved," she admitted. "But I'm broke, so—"

"Don't worry about money. It's my treat," he said. "If you like breakfast, then you can thank me with a kiss."

"I'm not kissing you." *I already kissed you and enjoyed it too much.*

"If the food makes you moan with pleasure, then you can thank me with a kiss."

She huffed inside a semi-audible laugh. *You must've enjoyed the kiss we had earlier as much as I did. Maybe I will kiss you after we eat.* "The food has to be so good that I moan as I chew."

"Oh, you'll moan," he said confidently. "Then we'll both moan."

He took a right, following the truck in front of them, onto an unmarked dirt road. "Get ready to hunker down and eat."

She swatted his arm. "How do you know anything about hunkerin' down, Mr. Big City Gambler?"

"I know plenty about plenty," he quipped.

"Yeah, I bet you do."

CHAPTER FOUR

Finley

With peach orchards on either side of the road, Finley wondered which direction within the state of Georgia they were headed. Either Slater knew exactly where they were, turning down one unmarked road onto another and then another, or the man was utterly lost and she was going to have to call Liam to find them. The irony of that potential situation wasn't lost on her. She expected at least an hour lecture about arriving home in a timely manner, even though she'd texted him about the delayed flight. She should've texted about stopping for a meal, but he would know she'd stop and eat. He knew her better than anyone else in the world.

The saving grace of Slater's tangential trip to the restaurant was that by the time she arrived at Liam's, the lecture she would receive would be delayed until morning. Liam

Hutchison Vogel wouldn't have time to thoroughly express his full disappointment in her late arrival at his house or they'd be late to the party—which is something that would make him physically sick. It was one thing for her to be late. It was quite another for her to make him late. She'd *never* do that.

The truck Slater was following slowed as the surprisingly long line of cars ahead began pulling over onto the side of the country road and parking wherever empty spaces were available. People emerged from the cars on the side of the road and walked in the same direction Slater drove.

"What is happening?" she asked. "Where are these people going? There's nothing here but peach trees."

He continued driving forward down the road as the vehicles in front of them parallel parked as other vehicles exited and drove in the opposite direction.

"They're going to the restaurant up the road," he said. "The food is so good that people literally walk from a mile away to eat there."

In the middle of an open field stood a white painted two-story, farmhouse-style restaurant with gold accents and open, oversized windows along the front and sides. An elaborate, circular geometric designed wraparound porch with outside tables and seating was filled with people eating a variety of breakfast food on simple white plates and bowls.

Patrons stood on the steps of the house, forming a line that meandered along the driveway all the way to the street, as they waited patiently for their chance to gain entrance to the restaurant.

"Is that the restaurant we're going to?" she asked, making sure she understood what she was witnessing. If people weren't standing in line, she'd never know it was a restaurant.

No sign or banner marked the building as anything other than a family home in the middle of a vast farm.

"Yes. That's the place." He switched on his blinker to turn, and people moved to allow the vehicle to roll forward onto the driveway. He turned and drove forward.

"What are you doing?" she asked.

"Parking." He continued around the circular drive and stopped feet from the entrance, near the line of people who stood on the steps. He shifted the gear into park and turned off the engine. "Let's go."

He stepped out of the vehicle and jogged to her side. He opened her door before she got over the shock of his bold move to park in the driveway where there were no other cars.

"Come on, Fin." He held out his hand to her.

She placed her hand in his and a spark of energy flew through her. With each touch of skin on skin, she wanted more. A. Lot. More.

While thoughts of a naked Slater Vogel sent a tidal wave of lust through her system, the rules Liam branded into her brain to remain pure until marriage became a lifeline. *I'm only getting a car ride from him. I might go on a date with him, but Liam will chaperone us.*

Slater rubbed his lips together and tugged her hand.

She stepped out as he stepped forward, pulling her into his arms and against his hard body.

"Slater," she said breathlessly.

Warm, soft lips pressed against her cheek. "There's something about you that makes me want to touch you all the time," he whispered. "And I want you to touch me. *Everywhere.*"

"I. Um." Her chest heaved to take in some air, but the movement pressed her breasts against him, making her too hot and aroused to function. Another spark, only stronger, pulsed through her veins. She wanted him to continue touching her, pressing those lips against hers. She wanted his kiss so badly that she turned her head toward his. Her chin tilted upward. Her lips shifted so close to his.

He captured her mouth. A moan so deep came from his lips that it vibrated into her bones as if he were claiming her from the inside out. This time, he pulled her closer as he explored her mouth.

God help her, she melted against him.

His mouth.

His tongue.

His taste.

His confidence drew her in even further.

She slipped her hands under his T-shirt and shuddered. The sparks of energy dancing frenetically in her body intensified.

"I want to fuck you right now," he mumbled, shoving his hands down the back of her jeans. "I'm so fucking hard. My balls *ache for you.*"

She stared into his mirrored glasses, seeing her blue irises shimmering with gold like they did sometimes around Liam. But her skin glowed with a pink flush which had never happened before, not with anyone, not even Liam.

"We can't stay under the same roof," she said. *I'd do things with you that I'm not doing with anyone but the man I marry.*

"Oh yeah, we can. I'm going to make sure we do. I'm not losing you to someone else." His fingers slid between her thighs and traced the wet slit along her pussy lips over her panties. "Mmm."

Her belly growled as more juices rushed onto her panties. *Why am I reacting to you like this? I don't even recognize myself.*

"I need to feed you," he mumbled. "Why did I choose this place when we could be in a hotel, ordering room service after having multiple rounds of incredible sex?"

"We're not going to have sex," she whispered.

"Hell yeah, we are, and soon." He slid his hands from inside her jeans and groaned as he released her from his embrace, but he held on tightly to her hand.

CHAPTER FIVE

Finley

With a little tug, he led her up the stairs to the entrance of the restaurant, passing the people in line. He walked inside the house and straight to the hostess stand. A gorgeous blonde hostess wearing a gold T-shirt and black shorts stepped out from behind the golden hostess table.

"Oh my goodness," the blonde hostess said with a big smile and even bigger blue eyes. "I can't believe you're here." While gazing at Slater, she held open her arms and leaned forward forming the beginnings of a hug. Then she switched gears and returned upright, dropping her arms to her side, when Slater made no effort to reciprocate the intended embrace. "Sorry. I get carried away and forget you don't like contact. Follow me."

Tamping down her excitement, the hostess flattened her

expression and led them into the middle of the open concept family room filled with diners, to a round table that could seat four but was set for two. Placed into each of the backs of two cream-colored cushioned leather chairs was a simple gold poker chip surrounded by a circle of black leather and then another larger circle of gold, framing the chip.

"We've got a treat for you," the hostess said. She suddenly glanced at Finley as if she'd just realized Slater wasn't alone. "Oh my. I'm so sorry."

The girl didn't seem sorry at all as she dismissed Finley with a bitchy smirk, then stared at Slater as though he was some kind of prince charming coming to sweep her off her feet and carry her away to his castle. But her brows raised when her gaze dropped to his hand.

As her eyelids raised, her eyes seemed to pop out with some kind of realization—probably that Slater wasn't opposed to touch, at least not by Finley.

"Is she with you?" the hostess asked.

"Yeah, she is," Slater admitted. "This is Fin. I'd like to have two of whatever the chef's special is for today."

She looked Finley over from head to toe. The blonde's jaw and mouth tightened. "Hey, *Fin.* I'm Jenn."

Returning the not-so-pleasantry with an actual real one, Finley reached out to shake her hand. "Nice to meet you."

She looked at Finley's hand and then glanced at Slater, dismissing her once more. "This is unexpected."

Finley dropped her hand to rest at her side, aware the girl had no intention of being polite. *"Nice to meet you, too,"* Finley mumbled. *She's so rude. Is the food good enough to make up for the obnoxious hostess?*

Instead of heading back to the hostess station or speaking to one of the waitresses to come over and take their order, the hostess *Jenn,* who looked somewhere between Finley's age and Slater's, walked straight to the kitchen at the back of the room.

"We didn't order," Finley whispered.

"I ordered two of the chef's specials. I'm sure Jenn is personally placing the order." Slater held out a chair for Finley. "Sit."

Finley dropped into her seat automatically, like she would've if Liam had said the same thing. Something about Slater compelled her to obey his commands. She actually liked the direct order and tone he used. *Why am I so willing to do anything you want me to? Refusing you is harder than it should be. It's as hard as it is with Liam. Possibly harder.*

He pushed her chair toward the table and seemed to float on air, as he strode around the table and sat in the chair across from her. "Jenn helped to make seating us awkward."

"It was a little weird," Finley admitted. "Do you know the chef or owner?"

"Yes. The chef and I were on the gambling circuit together. He wasn't good at gambling and lost a lot of money. I told him that if he quit gambling, I'd partner with him in a restaurant, which was his real passion. He quit. I partnered with him. He picked this property out in the middle of nowhere. I questioned him about the location. But after we talked *and* I did some research, I agreed the place had potential."

"So, is this table yours?" she asked.

"It is. The benefits of being an owner," he said.

"So I shouldn't feel bad about waltzing past everyone else who has been waiting for who knows how long to get seated?" She glanced at the people nearby. Everyone had their phones out, taking pictures of Slater.

"You shouldn't feel bad," he said. "The chef knew I was coming. I always come when I'm in the area. If you remember, Jenn did say they had a treat for me."

"And were you driving so fast because you were running late?" she asked. *How much alike are you and Liam?*

"No. I just like to drive fast." He glanced over his shoulder toward the kitchen. "What is taking so long?"

"There's two of us, not one," she said.

He faced Finley. "Good point." He traced the outside of his mirrored glasses, but kept them on. "What is it going to take for you to stay with me this weekend?"

"A miracle. You're lucky I agreed to seeing you on Sunday."

He laughed. "I'll work on that miracle. We already have a deal with a kiss on the line. I'm counting on my partner to bring us an exceptional, orgasmic-level meal."

I've never had an orgasm, so that would be interesting. "That good, huh?"

"Not quite," he admitted. "But his food commonly elicits moans. Listen and watch the other customers."

"Take off your sunglasses and I might consider staying the night with you on Sunday," Finley said. *I've got to stop encouraging him. I'm not sleeping with him or anyone. I'm saving myself for marriage.*

"I'll only take off my glasses, *if* you promise to stay overnight with me in my bed, while we're in Georgia, *and* you move out of Blade's house and into mine on as soon as we get back to Nevada."

Taken aback, she stiffened, sitting up as straight as she could manage. He seemed serious, but how could he be? They didn't know each other well enough to live together. Plus, Liam would have to give his blessing to them. And there was no way that Liam would ever give his blessing for her *and* Slater to live together.

"Are you serious?" *You can't be.*

"I'm always serious," he said. "You mentioned you were

waiting for marriage to have sex. If you're ready to get married, I'll take you to the chapel right now."

The noise that came from her mouth sounded like a nervous, half-giggle-half-croaking of a frog, instead of the laugh of disbelief she'd intended. "That's not funny." *Are you joking?* "You don't even know me."

"It's not meant to be funny, Fin. We'll get to know each other with a promise of forever and rings on our fingers. If you're not ready to make vows to me, then promise to stay overnight with me *in my bed* and move in with me. I'm easy to live with. I'll even help you study for your classes. But I'm going to fuck you like crazy, and you'll be pregnant quickly. You'll pop out a few kids before you graduate." He tilted his head to the side. "Too much, too soon?"

No. Not too much too soon. I think my ovaries are more than willing to make that happen. She rolled her eyes and shook her head as she regrouped and attempted to control her breathing, thoughts, and emotions.

Don't act flustered. He's just testing my reactions. It's a test. He doesn't really want those things. He only wants sex, not a family. "I don't even know what to think about you." *You keep saying everything I've always wanted to hear...from Liam. You remind me sooo much of him. Only you seem like you'd fight to get what you want, whereas I don't think Liam would fight for me in the same way.*

"Think about me naked," he whispered. " 'Cause I'm thinking about you naked."

She swallowed hard, trying not to think of his incredibly sexy body without any covering. *Don't moan. Don't moan.* "I'm not going to do that."

The tip of his tongue slid between his lips. "You already have, Fin."

"I bet you are one heck of a poker player," she mumbled.

His lips spread into a sexy smile. "I'm the best there is."

"Humble much?" she teased under her breath. Her stomach growled.

This is ridiculous. I am in way over my head.

I need food and I need it now. Maybe then I'll think straight, and get you out of my system.

CHAPTER SIX

Finley

After what seemed to take forever, the top of the hostess's blonde head tilted toward the table. The woman seemed to walk slower than every other employee in the restaurant. She placed a plate of plain pancakes and bacon in front of Finley and then a plate of pancakes topped with candied bananas and some kind of syrup in front of Slater. "Enjoy, Slater."

Slater looked at the blonde. "Did you tell Brock that I wanted two plates of the same special breakfast entrée?"

"He was busy," the hostess said.

Slater stood up and switched plates with Finley, making a bigger deal out of the order mix-up than necessary. "Taste this."

He lifted his chair and carried it the short distance to her side of the table and placed it next to hers. "We might have to share."

He unrolled the napkin and placed the utensils on the table. He cut a piece of the banana pancake and brought it to her lips. "Open."

Please, you have to stop doing things for me. You're turning me on so much that I don't know that I can resist you for much longer.

She parted her lips, and he fed her the delicious morsel. Dang it, she moaned as her tastebuds screamed for more.

Suddenly his mouth crushed hers. His tongue stroked her. His fingers caressed up her neck and into her hair, pulling her closer. Then his kiss softened and the soft humming rumble that he made as their lips parted did something to her that she'd only experienced with Liam when she left for college—her heart fluttered with love and longing, and she struggled to catch a breath.

"You're mine, Finley Vessel," he whispered. "And I need to get you out of here and buy you some mirrored sunglasses."

She gazed into his glasses and saw her reflection. Her irises had morphed to gold—the natural blue gone. She blinked to remove the gold that seldom appeared, except on rare occasions when she experienced strong emotions, but her golden irises remained. She blinked and blinked some more, expecting the blue to return to her irises, but they didn't.

He lowered his glasses. The piercing blue gaze that usually met her wasn't there. A deep gold filled his irises, a darker variation of hers and of Liam's. "Ready for marriage?"

"No," she whispered, lowering her gaze to the pancakes to hide the strange color of her eyes. "I'm ready for the rest of these pancakes, and for you to not kiss me like that."

"To clarify," he said, gently pressing his lips to hers. "You don't want me to kiss you like this?" He barely touched her lips, but a fire for more nearly enveloped her.

"I think kissing is dangerous with you." *But I want to. I*

want to do so much more than kiss. I want to feel you naked next to me, our bodies—

"Kissing is beautiful," he said softly. "With you, it's magical."

It is magical, although I've never kissed anyone before you. So, I don't know if it's you or if it's just kissing in general. I bet it's you.

She picked up a fork and quickly sectioned off a large piece of pancake. He remained so close to her face that as she placed the slice of deliciousness in her mouth, she ended up smearing his lips with the topping.

She chewed and the flavor burst in her mouth, sending a moan from her soul to exit from her lips. While she swallowed, she stared at the syrup on his lips. She wanted that syrup. She wanted to lick his lips. She wanted to taste him. She wanted to kiss him.

Maybe it was the pancakes or the desire to be close to him again that compelled her to curl her arms around him. The fire that rose in her bones flamed even higher.

She licked along his lower lip, gathering the syrup she'd smeared there, and traced the top with the tip of her tongue. And this time, she initiated the next kiss. She slid onto his lap, exploring his addictive mouth. And she deepened the kiss, making it shift from sweet to indecent.

Then he took over, gently easing off from her demanding kiss, teasing her with his incredible control. "This is already getting dirty, and we're in public. Lower your gaze, so people don't see your eyes. I'm leading you outside. We're leaving."

"Hey, Slater," an average sized man wearing a black chef's jacket and slacks said, standing beside the table. "You're leaving? Oh, you brought a guest. Jenn didn't tell me. I would've made something—"

"Brock, this is Finley," Slater said. "The banana pancakes were delicious."

"You barely ate them," Brock said. "What didn't you

like?" He pulled an empty chair from a table nearby and sat down. "If something was off, I need to know."

"It was good," Slater said. "It was fucking delicious. Nothing was off."

Brock looked at Finley. His eyes widened. "Holy shit, you're gorgeous." He exhaled. "Sorry. Do you like freshly picked peaches?"

"Love them," Finley said.

"Then you have to try—"

"Nope. You're not wooing her away from me with your amazing cooking," Slater said.

"Woo away," she said. "I love good food, especially fresh, off-the-tree peaches."

"We don't have time, Fin," Slater grumbled. "Brock is busy."

"I'm never too busy for you or your guests, Slater." Brock stared at her and smiled.

She found herself smiling back at him, wishing him to find love and marriage and make lots of babies. Something about the gentleness in his brown eyes made her think he'd be a great father.

"You're too busy today," Slater said. "We got one plate of my favorite pancakes, not two like I'd ordered. Jenn brought out a plate of pancakes and bacon—part of the kids' menu—for my girlfriend." He lowered his voice. "I'm angry about that. In fact, I'm furious over it. I don't bring guests with me anywhere I go, and the one time I do, my guest gets treated like dirt from the hostess. I'm trying to impress my girl, and this happens." He pointed to the plate in front of Brock. "Would I ever order that for a guest of mine?"

Brock looked down and his jaw clenched. "No. I'm sorry. I'll talk to her."

"Every patron matters. Every single fucking one," Slater whispered. "I might park where I want, walk past a long line, and sit down immediately, but this table is reserved for me. No one sits at it except me and my guest, or you and yours. It's part of our code and story which is written on the menu. No one but you and the staff know when I'm stopping by, and only you know when I'll arrive…" Slater continued on, explaining his disappointment in the staff and the treatment he received. "Brock, we didn't even get drinks."

Brock's gaze swept over the table. "Fuck." He turned around and every table within view had drinks and extra napkins and food that looked more delicious than the banana pancakes in front of her. The plates that were empty didn't leave any crumbs. The man turned and seemed to inspect Slater's table and the food. "There's no bourbon whipped cream on your pancakes. Damn it. I made it special for you. I fucking made it special, and it didn't get on your plate."

"Yeah, I noticed. That whipped cream sold me on funding your dream," Slater said. "We'll be back Sunday morning when the place opens. I expect a different experience." He shifted, and Finley rose from his lap, having forgotten she was wrapped up in his arms as though they were lovers or married. "Fin loved the pancakes. Imagine her reaction if they were made the way they were supposed to be." He stood up beside her, taking her hand.

Brock rose from his seat. "I'll fix this, and next time, I'll make a meal both you and Finley will love."

"I know you will," Slater said. "If you need help hiring or firing, I'm a phone call away."

"I got this," Brock said. "I'll see you bright and early, Sunday morning." He nodded at her. "It was nice meeting you, Finley."

"The pleasure was mine," she said.

Slater placed his hand at her back. "Time to go." He guided her forward, in front of him and out the door, not allowing her any time to acknowledge anyone around her.

Once outside, he slowed the quick pace he'd set. He halted at his SUV and opened her door.

She stepped up into the vehicle and he closed the door. Watching him as he walked around the front of the car and climbed into the driver's seat, she again wondered why she reacted so strongly to his touch. She shouldn't have reacted at all. She'd never been interested in anyone except Liam, until now.

Wasting no time, Slater started the engine and drove back the way he came, along the unmarked roads.

"I can't come here tomorrow morning," she said.

"Neither can I. I said that so the people inside who saw us kissing would come back with their friends, hoping for a sighting. Brock knows we'll be back Monday morning before the restaurant opens. It will be just us, and he'll sit down and join us."

"So no kissing during our meal?" *I shouldn't sound so disappointed.*

"We're kissing—and kissing often—during every meal," he said. "You're mine to kiss."

"Presumptuous, aren't you?"

"On occasion, but not about you," he said.

"Listen, I'm not denying the massive attraction I have for you," she admitted. "But I'm not going to—"

"Fin," he interrupted. "Once we're alone, there will be no stopping us from kissing. The kissing we will be doing will lead to sex. It's going to happen. And it will happen quickly. I'm barely able to contain myself right now. I almost lost the battle in that restaurant. I kissed you and forgot about everything happening around us. I want to pull over to the side of the road and start back up where we stopped, but I have a feeling that things will get crazy as soon as I get those clothes off you." He pointed to the glove box. "Grab a pair of sunglasses from there. It's not safe for people to see your eyes change from blue to gold."

"All eyes were on you, not me." *I hope no one took a picture of us together kissing. If Liam saw that, he'd ground me for the rest of my life. It wouldn't matter whether I was in Nevada or Georgia or halfway across the world. I'd observe any punishment he gave me. I'd do anything he required of me.* "Do you think anyone took a picture of us?"

"Yeah, they did. That kiss is going to be everywhere. Any minute, my brother will call, and I'll have to ignore him."

"Isn't he married?" she asked. *All of Stetson's friends are married.*

"Yep. Married with five kids," Slater said. "I'm going to be fielding questions about you all night from *all* my family members." He accelerated onto the highway. "I'd really like to cement this bond between us with a marriage ceremony. Let's make it legal."

"Just because there's chemistry between us doesn't mean—"

"It fucking does. It does when it's explosive like it is with us. It does when your touch is like a peaceful breeze in the middle of a chaotic storm. I *need you.* And this Liam of yours is going to either get on board with my plans to marry you, or he's going to get on fucking board with my plans to marry you."

"*Don't I* have to be ready to marry you?" she asked.

"Yep. And you will be ready by tomorrow night." He took off his sunglasses and gazed at her. "We're compatible in every way. Sex is going to be mind-blowing."

Her phone rang with Liam's ringtone. "Dang it. My phone is in my backpack." She climbed into the backseat and bent over the center into the very back, teetering with her ass in the air, and grabbed her pack. The ringtone stopped and immediately started ringing again. She unzipped the top and dug for the phone, missing the call again. But in normal Liam fashion, he called again.

Dang it. She swiped the screen. "Hey, sorry." She plopped down in the backseat and pulled down the hem of her shirt that had ridden so high it showed the bottom lace of her bra.

"What were you doing kissing some big shot poker player? It was indecent. Where are you? Why aren't you here? What took you so long to answer the phone? Are you okay? Do I need to come get you?" Liam inquired.

Oh no. You're worried, and it's my fault you're worried. "I'm fine. I'm on my way to your house. There was a problem with the flight and then the rental car. The company gave my car away and then didn't have any by the time I arrived. I'm getting a refund. Don't worry. I bummed a ride with a friend. I'll be there soonish?"

"Is the *friend* the *gam-bler*? Has he been drinking? Have you been?"

She could hear the disdain in his voice. He hated gamblers. She didn't know why he hated them, only that he did.

"He doesn't gamble much, I don't think. I'll have to ask. He never drinks and drives. I don't think he drinks, but I don't know. But we haven't been drinking. You know I don't do that. And yes, he's driving me to the house. And he's going to drive me to the airport on Monday. He might take me out on Sunday evening, but I'll be back before curfew at ten." She spoke so fast, she barely remembered what she'd said, only that she told the truth, even if she omitted some of it.

"As soon as you get home, we'll be having a conversation about respect and boys and kissing in public and so much more, Finley Vessel. Have you kept your vows?" Liam's question cut her to the quick.

You're questioning my integrity, my loyalty, my word. "Yes, I've kept my vows." *Please believe me.* "It was just a kiss."

"It was more than a kiss. Get your ass home. No more detours." Liam ended the call.

"He didn't sound happy," Slater said.

"That's an understatement." Ending her teeter-tottering climb over the center, she moved into the front seat and buckled in. She glanced at the screen in case Liam had texted an apology for being so harsh. *Nothing.* "I'm pretty sure our date on Sunday will need to be rescheduled."

"Nope. I'll talk to him," Slater said.

"That won't go over well." *He likes rules. He lives for rules, and they're good rules. He's a good man. He's the most trustworthy person I've ever known, and he doesn't like you. He REALLY doesn't like you at all.*

"He's going to love me. I'm very charming when I need to be," he said.

"No one is that charming." *He'll forbid me to date you and nothing you say or do will change his mind. I'll have to obey him. Any feelings I have for you will remain unresolved, even if I move in with you…which I won't. Not without his expressed verbal blessing which will never happen. It's marriage or nothing. Liam's rules. Liam's world.*

CHAPTER SEVEN

Finley

While rolling up the drive in Slater's SUV to Liam's two-bedroom, white brick farmhouse on his vast tract of land, Finley's palms started to sweat. *I shouldn't feel so guilty. I didn't do anything wrong. It was a kiss. I didn't break my vows.* "Thanks for the ride, Slater. You can let me out here."

"I'm walking you to the door." Slater parked next to Liam's red pickup truck. "Nice truck."

"He rarely drives it," she said. "His police vehicle is in the garage." *He knows I'm here, and he's not coming out. He's got to be furious or he'd be out here already, greeting me with a hug.*

She leaned across the center console and kissed Slater on the cheek. As soon as she'd realized what she'd done, she stiffened. *I actually have real feelings for you, not just lust. I have to move as far away from you as I can get.* "I'll call you tomorrow."

Scrambling to get out of the vehicle and away from him, she nearly fell onto the red clay and white gravel drive. She righted herself before she scraped up her hands and clothes and ran toward safety—Liam's home.

Slater stepped out of the SUV and sprinted to her, catching her hand before she could make it to the front door of the house. "Introduce me to Liam."

"Not today," she said. "He needs to cool down before he meets you."

"He's going to like me."

No, he's not. "Uh, yeah. Sure," she mumbled. "I'll introduce you another day. *Not today.*" Holding his hand, she walked to the front door and then faced him. "If you leave now, I will move into your house on Monday evening." *That did not just come out of my mouth. I'm not thinking clearly. You're so freaking handsome. I have to stop thinking about you and sex and babies. You're never meeting Liam. I don't think you're much of a rule follower.*

"Promise?" he asked.

I shouldn't promise you anything, but I have to get you out of here before Liam actually loses his patience and comes out to give you a lecture. Then the forbidding will come, and you'll get angry. You'll both argue because you both seem to have a stubborn streak. I have to make sure neither of you ever meet in person. "Yes. I promise. Please, just go."

"Okay." He grinned. "I'll call you tonight."

She nodded. *I'll figure out a way to back out of living with you.*

He kissed her lips and that fire inside her body blazed for more. "If he makes you uncomfortable, call me. I'll come and get you, then you can be my date for the party I'm going to tonight. My family is going to *love* you."

"I'll be fine. No need to meet the fam," she said. "See you later."

He seemed to want to say something, but thought better of it. Instead, he walked back to his SUV and drove away.

Inhaling, she pushed down all her feelings of desire for Slater. She turned the doorknob and swung open the door.

"I'm home," she shouted. She tried to sound happy instead of nervous, but her voice gave her away.

"I'm in the laundry room." Liam's tone held disappointment, a tone she had always avoided hearing at all costs.

While she walked toward the laundry room, she dropped her backpack on the couch. "So, what's the plan? Any carpentry jobs you need an assistant to tackle?" *Please let me help you frame a house or build a bookcase or make a treehouse for some needy kids during your down time. Heck, I'll organize your computer files at the police station. Anything. Just no talking about that kiss.*

She opened the laundry room door. Her heart fluttered the moment she saw him. The man hadn't changed at all. He remained the same gorgeous, law-abiding sheriff whom she loved above all others.

"Hey," she said softly.

He faced her wearing nothing but black compression shorts. His perfect body looked like Slater's—almost exactly like Slater's, smooth and hard and defined. His irises were golden like Slater's, only Liam's were a whiter shade of gold which looked similar to hers.

"We need to talk," he said. He turned back to the laundry basket filled with folded clothes that sat on top of the dryer. "Follow me."

She recognized the routine. He would carry the basket into his room and put away his clothes. Then she'd sit on his bed as he stood in front of her with judgement in his eyes. Once he stared at her long enough that she became uncomfortable, only then would the lecture start. His chest would expand, flexing his muscles. She'd count the rectangles of his abs—the ones she could see—while he talked about respect or rules or whatever upset him at the moment.

And this time was no different—until it was.

CHAPTER EIGHT

Finley

The man who always kept everything the same for as long as she could remember had painted the inside of the house a golden shade of white instead of the pure unadulterated white it had been. She imagined that the slight difference in color remained unnoticeable to anyone else but her.

The white fluffy comforter that he'd worn out and replaced with the exact same color and style a dozen times since she first moved in was no longer on his bed. In its stead, a handmade quilt with gold intertwining rings on a silver background lay spread out on the king-sized bed. At the head of the bed sat two pillows covered in pillow shams which matched the quilt, not the dozen white pillows of varying sizes she'd bought him every year for his birthday. The white-washed beachy themed dresser he'd had forever was replaced with an oak dresser painted with interwoven gold rings which matched the markings on his new oak sleigh bed, not the white-washed four poster bed he'd crafted with her help years ago.

At the foot of the bed, she sat on a new oak bench with the same markings as the other pieces in the room. The man had changed his entire bedroom since she'd been there last. The space didn't seem like his anymore. He wouldn't have picked out the furniture or décor in the room. Someone else had to have decorated the space. Someone who had erased all signs of Finley's existence in his home.

What aren't you telling me? Why all the changes? Do you want to erase me from your life? Have you stopped loving me?

The lack of urgency to complete his task of putting his clothes away seemed strange, too. The man always finished his tasks quickly. He wasn't acting like himself. He seemed stressed, something she wasn't used to seeing from him.

After he put the last pair of socks in the top right drawer of the dresser, he didn't even stand in front of her. He didn't enact his power stance to remind her that he remained in control and she needed to obey him or there would be consequences. Instead, he sat beside her on the bench.

This can't be good. I'll have to do a lot of apologizing for that kiss with Slater. I embarrassed you. I'm sorry.

"Listen," she said. "I know I shouldn't have—"

He held up his hand, palm up, for her to be silent.

Immediately, her mouth stopped moving and her voice shut down. It was his turn to speak and her time to listen. She lived in his world and followed his rules.

"You're an adult," he said. "But there're things you don't know about yourself. There are things you don't know about me. And this Slater guy isn't an option for you to kiss or date or do anything girls do with guys. He's a normal, arrogant dude who thinks his wealth will impress you."

"He's my friend Sienna's neighbor. He *is* arrogant, but

he's nice, too, which offsets the arrogance. Don't hate him because he made money on the poker circuit. He has some kind of online show that people subscribe to. I don't watch it, but lots of people do. I don't have time to watch stuff like that or really do anything besides read books and articles and watch educational videos to help me in my future teaching career." *Otherwise, I'd probably watch it as much as possible. Slater is sexy and handsome and that kiss was worth whatever consequences you're going to dole out to me.*

"Is he the first boy you've kissed?" Liam asked.

She nodded.

"And you haven't had sex?" he asked, in a less judgy-tone than he'd used earlier.

She shook her head. "I vowed to you that I wouldn't until I was married. I keep my promises. I never made an oath about kissing."

"I remember," he said softly.

"Are you dating anyone?" she asked. "You changed your room. It's nice, but I'm surprised."

"I don't date." The tone of his voice held a hint of something she'd never heard from him—a lie of omission.

What happened while I've been gone to make you change so much?

While he slid her onto his lap and cradled her like a little girl, not the woman she was now, she wished she could snuggle and kiss him. She wanted to comfort him like he'd comforted her so many times over the years.

"Are you okay? You don't seem like yourself," she said.

He lowered his head, resting his cheek on the top of her head. "I was contacted by a man who said he was my cousin. I didn't think I had any living relatives. At first, I didn't believe him. But he knew things that...he was very convincing. Still, I remained skeptical, until I met him. During that first meeting, we talked for hours about my parents and the extended family I knew nothing about. We talked about you, too. We actually talked a lot about you."

"It sounds like it was a good conversation. You now have family you didn't know about," she said. *Why would you talk about me? I'm not related biologically to you.* "That's good, right?"

He nodded. "Yeah, it is. He explained some things about my background, and why I'm the way I am. Why I don't like leaving Georgia. Why I don't like people who break the law or who don't follow the rules. I didn't know why both our eyes changed color to a shade of gold, sometimes. I didn't know much about my family history, until he filled in some of missing pieces."

"Like where you came from? Your family history?" *You're from Georgia, born and raised right here in this small town. You knew your parents. They loved you, and you loved them. I don't know where I was born or anything about my biological father, and until you, I moved from place to place every few months with my mom.*

"Yeah, that and more. I learned about you. In fact, he knows more about you than I do. We're not like everyone else." He rubbed his lips together.

"We're smarter." She winked at him and gave him a smirk.

He laughed. "Yeah, we are. And I can see things that other people can't. I can touch someone and feel whether they're struggling with evil or not. I can literally feel if their spirit is filled with goodness, like yours is, or if there is no redeeming quality within it. I can force evil out of people's bodies and spirits whether they want me to or not."

I believe that. You see people's auras. The minister at church explained all that to you when we asked what we should do about guardianship all those years ago. I don't see anything extra, I live by my instincts, but you're special. Everyone sees that.

"Is that why people are afraid of you? Why you're careful

about who you touch? Why you stare at some people more than others?" she asked.

"I think so. There's a certain perimeter of land area that I control, and within it, I keep the people and land safe from evil. I have a distant cousin named Logan Hutchison who lives in Texas. He is like me and can do all the things that I can and more. He isn't coming to the party tonight because his wife has some major morning sickness. It's their first child. I stayed with them for a week a couple months ago. Logan and his wife Aurora extend their regrets that they can't be there tonight, but he said they're excited to meet you."

"So Logan is the cousin who contacted you, but he's not throwing this party?" *Then who is hosting the party?*

"Actually, no. And yes. Logan isn't the relative who initially contacted me. A man named Wenzel contacted me, and it's his party we're going to tonight. He's head of the family and lives most of the time in his house in Las Vegas. He said that you're not related to us, but you're related to another special line of heavenly beings like us. My father was like Logan Hutchison and like me, a protector of the law. There is a long line of Law Angels with the surname of Hutchison. My father was a warrior like Wenzel. It's his line that connects me to him. Wenzel is great. I trust him."

"You're a *heavenly being?* Aren't all humans considered heavenly beings?" *Have you joined a cult? Have you quit our church?*

He laughed but there was a gravity underlying his tone. "Not all humans are heavenly, Fin."

"Are you a demi-god? Remember when I was in my mythology reading phase and we read about all those gods and their human children? I'm just sayin' that I'd believe you if you were. You're..." *Gorgeous and strong and I love you. You've always been larger than life. I bet you're some kind of superhero from a long line of superheroes.*

"Not a demi-god, but similar."

Raising her eyebrow, she questioned his answer. "Spit it out, Liam. Your hesitancy is off-putting." *Why are you being cryptic? You're never anything but bold and resolute.*

He inhaled. "This is going to sound crazy, but it's true. I can prove it."

"Of course, whatever you're going to tell me is true. You don't lie. I trust you implicitly. Please, just tell me." *And then you can tell me who talked you into redecorating your bedroom. And I'll tell you that I don't like her or her furniture. She can shove those gold accents up her bottom. I'll just buy you more fluffy white pillows before I leave.*

He held her tighter. "I'm a full-fledged angel."

"An angel? Like *God's angel*? Like in the Bible? Or like a motorcycle gang angel? Did you get your motorcycle driving license? I'm fine with it, if you are an angel, or in a motorcycle club. You'd look amazing on a Harley. But that would be hypocritical if you drove a motorcycle, yet forbid me to do the same." *If anyone was one of God's angels, it would be you. You're the most honorable person I've ever met. You follow every law as if your life, and mine, too, depended on it. You make rules, and we all follow them...Yep. You're an angel. That makes total sense. Unless you did join a motorcycle club. I'd hop on the back of your Harley any day of the week. We'd look great in leather—*

He kissed her forehead, interrupting her daydreams of being cuddled close, the open road ahead of them. He brought her face to his neck, holding her. "That was my line of thinking when Wenzel told me I was an angel. I even asked him, point blank, if he was part of an MC. But the man just laughed and shook his head. You're going to love him."

"If you love him, then I definitely will." She breathed in his fresh, clean-air scent. *I love you. Thank you for not making this a lecture on kissing. I'd much rather talk about your angel status and if it changes anything between us. Angels and humans can make babies, can't they? We could get married and have lots of babies. That's what I've heard and read that angels on earth do.*

"I'm serious, Fin. I'm a real angel. Wenzel is one, too."

"I believe you. So what did Wenzel say that convinced you that your lineage came directly from God?"

"The more Wenzel explained my abilities and those of my parents—the ones I remember. It was like my life suddenly made a weird kind of sense, but I was still skeptical at what he was telling me. I thought I would've known if my parents were angels, right?"

"Yeah. For sure. But maybe not. Maybe they had to hide their true identity from everyone, including you." *You were a teen when they died and the crash sparked a flame that burned so hot, nothing was left of their bodies.* "Maybe they were going to tell you when you turned eighteen? Maybe there's an angel thing where parents don't tell their kids what they are until they're about to go off on their own? Maybe there's some rite of passage that you hadn't had yet? There could be a lot of reasons why you didn't know about their angel status."

He held her a little closer, as if he needed some comforting. And she was all about being the soft place he could land, when he needed someone.

"I thought about those things, too. But right when I was about to bring all that up, Wenzel asked me if I wanted to open my wings."

She pushed out of his hold and stared at him. "No way? You have wings?"

His face softened, and he looked away. "I still wasn't sure whether I believed him or not, but I nodded. I had to know. You can't fake a set of your own wings."

In that moment, something changed between them. She felt like he was pulling away from her, that this change for him had altered their relationship and not in a way she wanted it to. She curled her arms around him and nuzzled against his neck, hoping he'd hold her closer. Hoping that this change he was going through wouldn't ruin their future together. The future she had dreamed of having with him.

His arms swept around her, and she pressed her lips against his warm skin.

"As soon as I agreed, Wenzel tapped my back and shoulders. It seemed odd that he'd do that, but the motion triggered something inside me. I had to move my shoulders and stretch out my back. My skin began to itch. The next thing I knew, my shirt ripped open in the back and freaking huge wings expanded outward. Like *insanely huge wings*. They'd been hiding inside me. It freaked me out. Then Wenzel showed me his—which freaked me out even more. But the more I looked at his, the more excited I was about mine."

He exhaled. "I've never seen anything like his feathers. They were white, but they were gold and silver, too. A portion of his feathers were made from some sort of sharp cosmic-metal, while other feathers were like baby chick feathers, so soft and light. And some feathers were…they were like wisps of air that formed into a solid structure. He said he rarely uses his wings, but when he has to fight thousands of demons, he uses them. He said some angels don't have them at all, but warrior and law angels do. And mine are like his, only not as big, and the gold in my wings are on the whiter shade of yellow gold whereas his are almost a brown-gold."

"I believe you. You'd never lie to me. I should be surprised, but I'm not."

"The thing is…I think you're an angel, too," he said.

"You think *I'm an angel*? For real?" she asked.

He nodded. "I do."

"But you know me. I'm don't think up rules and call people out who disobey them. I'm sorry to disappoint you, but *I'm no angel*." *Angels don't think about sex and babies and marriage. They think about pure things. Things I don't dwell on. My mind is in the gutter most of the time, except when I'm around children, which I am most of the time. So really my mind is on helping children and making sure they're in a safe and loving environment when I'm with them.*

"You're not an angel like me," he whispered. "But from what Wenzel described when we talked about you, I believe you're an angel, too."

"Me? Are you sure?" *Does that mean you and I could have angel babies? Are you going to propose? Are we getting married? Are we gonna have sex?*

"I'm sure you're an angel, Fin. I don't know what kind. I'm pretty sure you don't have wings, but I could be wrong. I didn't know I had wings, but I do. So far, everything he's told me makes sense. My back is supernaturally strong. In high school, I carried five guys larger than me on my back all the way past the goal line to make a touch down."

"I remember that touch down. You being an angel makes sense. You're extraordinary in every way. But me? There's nothing exceptional about me. My back always hurts. I'm not super strong or see auras or feel evil or do any of the things you do. So, what makes you think I'm an angel?" *I'm sorry to disappoint you, but you're wrong about me.*

"You're like me. We've never been sick. We're smarter and stronger than our peers."

"You're stronger. I've got normal strength. Actually, I'm weaker than the average girl. I agree that we're smarter and healthier than most, but that isn't going to convince me that I'm an angel."

"Our eyes change color—humans don't have eyes that change color. Wenzel said that only angels have eye colors that change to solid gold or solid silver or some mixture of those two colors," he said.

She looked into his blue eyes with only a meager amount

of gold in them. "My eyes rarely change and only when I'm emotional, but yours change a lot, especially when you're giving lectures to me. Everyone around here is used to your eyes being gold. I've got a good immune system. My mom was smart, and she wasn't an angel. Her blue eyes never changed color. She had no superpowers or abilities. I don't either. So our eyes are weird. It's not a supernatural ability. It just happens, and it almost never happens to mine. I'm not an angel. Sorry."

"I believe you're like me. Wenzel does, too."

"Okay, say I am an angel." She played along with his theory. "What kind of angel do you think I am?"

"I don't know."

"Is it because I have gold in my eyes that you believe I'm an angel? Is that the main factor in your belief?" *If I'm an angel because of my eye color, then Slater is an angel. And I'm pretty dang sure Slater is no angel. He's a rule-breaker, not a rule-maker. He's into sex and has probably had a lot of it. He's no virgin, like us.* "Does Wenzel know what kind of angel I might be?"

"He thinks you're a combination of two angels like I am," Liam replied. "Although, I'm a law angel, not a warrior one like Wenzel. But I do have some warrior fighting skills that come naturally, at least that's what Wenzel has told me."

"If that's the case he has to have some kind of idea what I'd be. So tell me, what types of angels does he think I might be?" she asked.

"Possibly healing and love, or maybe healing and mediating, or love and mediating angels. The combinations mentioned would make sense, but he thinks that if you're not a combination, then you might be only a healing angel. They thrive under strong leadership and straightforward laws. They're loyal and faithful. And when they make a promise, they follow through, even to their own detriment. And a healing angel's love is powerful when combined with a protector of the law." He held her. "Whether you're one or a combination doesn't matter. You're still you. But I believe that you are either a full-blooded healing angel or a combination of healing with a short list of other peaceful angel types like Wenzel suggested. There is no way you're a love angel. From what Wenzel said about them, you would've been pregnant by sixteen. He said that we'd be at odds with each other to the point where we'd have had to part ways within a week or two of meeting—which clearly hasn't happened."

"Well, I'm definitely no love angel," Finley whispered. "I'm nothing like what you described."

"Yeah," he said. "You wouldn't be a virgin if you were a love—"

"The fact that I'm a virgin, not sexy in the least, and that I'm preoccupied with school...*and* no boys have ever asked me out, precludes me from being a love angel. Well, Slater has asked me out, but he's an extrovert, focused, and determined, yet patient. I promised I'd go out with him Sunday evening, but expressed to him that I needed to be back by ten, per your curfew."

"You're not going out with him." He spoke softly, but the order left no wiggle room to question his meaning. While he gently rubbed up and down her back, irritating the pain around her shoulders and back, she tried to think of a way to change his mind.

"I promised," she said.

"He didn't even come in to meet me," he argued.

"It's good he didn't. You're barely dressed. He *doesn't* need to see you in your undies."

"They're compression shorts, not undies," he mumbled. "I hear you. You like him, but you can't be with him. You can't be with just anybody. And you need to talk to Wenzel. He said your mom wasn't your biological mother. He said the woman we buried was human, and you're *not* human. My parents' bodies scattered into the wind like ash without a trace, like law angels do when they die; whereas your mother's body decomposed naturally."

Your parents died in a crash that caught on fire. Their bodies burned with the heat of that fire. They weren't 'scattered into the wind without a trace.' "Maybe I'm part human."

"You're not."

"Maybe you're wrong, and I'm one hundred percent human with weird eyes. Maybe Wenzel hasn't seen humans with eyes like mine before. Maybe it's not just an angel thing."

"You need to talk to him. Maybe he'll touch your back and wings will emerge like they did mine."

I'm beginning to have doubts about you being an angel. I am most definitely not one. "Can you show me your wings?"

"Yeah," he whispered. "I don't have much control over them, but I can bring them out and put them back without it hurting. It was painful that first time and the second and third, but not anymore."

"Show me, please." She slid off his lap and stood, waiting for his wings to emerge. It was truth-time.

"It's a little awkward, so don't laugh at me." He stood up, facing her. He shook out his arms, circled his shoulders, and stretched his neck from side to side. He lifted his arms and rotated them around in big circles like he did in his pre-workout routine. He smiled. "Promise, no laughing."

"I won't laugh." She scooted to the edge of the bench, ready to see something magical happen, but continued to hold some doubt that any wings would appear.

While his lids closed, he dropped his chin to his chest. His shoulders rounded forward and white light burst outward, blinding her for a second.

The light softened and her sight cleared.

"Oh. My. Goodness." *This isn't real. It can't be.*

The man standing before her now had wings that rose above his head and extended several feet on either side of him, and the wings weren't even stretched to their full length. The room seemed much too small for his wings. The feathers were whiter than snow and his sun-kissed skin held a white shimmering ethereal glow.

"You *are* an angel." *And I love you so much. I love you more than you could ever love me.*

"It's kind of awesome," he said. "There's not enough room to show you the wingspan, but it's much larger than it looks. It expands and will continue to grow, as will I." He grinned. "Come here." He held out his arms. "I learned this from Wenzel."

She hurried into his arms and pressed her cheek to his chest. While she wrapped her arms around his waist, she brushed her fingers against the inside edge of the white super-soft feathers.

The wings shifted and the soft feathers morphed into some kind of golden armor that moved and curved, curling around them in a protective yet gentle hug.

"It's sound proof," Liam said. "It serves as a shield and a sword. I don't know how to use my wings in offensive measures yet, but I'm learning. Wenzel said that angels like me are drawn to protecting those who are lost or in danger, which explains why I was compelled to help you the day we first met. I knew you needed someone to protect you and that I could keep you safe."

"I love you, Liam," she whispered.

"I love you, too." He kissed the top of her head. "When I learn more about my capabilities, I'll be able to shield hundreds, maybe thousands, or possibly millions of people. I'll be able to fight, too." He squeezed her tighter. "I have a lot to learn."

"No one besides us can find out that you have wings, can

they?" *Even if I told someone, they'd think I was crazy. The people in our town in Georgia would believe me, but no one else would.*

"No," he said. "This is a secret we need to keep to ourselves, at least for now. Wenzel and Logan are going to train me, so I'm going to have to break out of my Georgia cocoon and go to Texas and Nevada for an extended time."

"That is going to be weird for you." *You hate being away from home.*

The wings rustled and then withdrew from around them until they were gone, magically hidden inside his body.

"We have to get dressed and leave soon," he said. "If Wenzel is right about you, there are some things you need to know before you meet the rest of my family."

Something about the way he spoke worried her. It was as if he knew more about her than he was letting on, and that the information he withheld was bad. Very bad.

"Just don't let anyone blindside me," she said. "If you know something, tell me. I don't like surprises."

"The only thing I know for sure about you is that since you've been gone, the pregnancy rate in our county has dropped ninety percent. And it's dropped in the surrounding counties, and overall in the state, too, by about seventy-five percent. I don't know what that means, or if it has anything to do with your leaving. But if it has nothing to do with you, it's a strange coincident."

"It doesn't have anything to do with me. The counties were booming because of the economy. People are feeling some hurt in their wallets now, so they're paying more atten-tion to contraception methods."

"Mmm. Maybe," he mumbled. "I'm sure Wenzel will figure out the reason behind the strange statistics."

"You really trust this Wenzel guy?"

"I do." He kissed the top of her head again. "You need to get dressed for tonight. Wenzel bought you a dress to wear to the party, and he wants us to arrive early so he can talk privately with you."

"I'll talk to him, but he's making a lot of assumptions based on your angel status. I'm just a normal girl who happened to get saved by an angel." She hugged him as her heart ached. She was losing him. He was moving on and this was his way of letting her go, of telling her this house wasn't her home anymore. But it was her home. He was her home.

"I'm happy for you. You finally have a family again." While she backed away, she knew she'd already lost him to a new family. He'd changed his bedroom décor for his new family...his new life. A life without her in it.

You have a family who you love so much that you will leave Georgia to visit them. You told me that you wouldn't leave Georgia for my college graduation. Sure, graduation is a year away, but I understood your physical need to remain on the land you loved. But after meeting your new family, you're suddenly okay stepping foot off of your property? You already visited this Logan and Aurora Hutchison couple and they're in Texas? Yet, still there's no words from your lips of visiting me? I thought I was your family. I thought I was more important to you than any distant cousin would ever be.

"It's pretty great to have a family again," he admitted.

I thought we were family. I guess I convinced myself you thought of me as your family. Her heart seemed to break the more he spoke about Wenzel and Logan. She closed off her emotions to avoid any more pain. "I'll be ready in a few minutes."

As she walked out of his room and down the hall, she noticed more changes to the house, and the subtle intention to erase every mark she'd ever made on his house, on him. She raced to her room, needing the comfort of something familiar.

CHAPTER NINE

Finley

When she arrived at her bedroom, tears pricked her eyes. He'd painted her room, too. All her furniture had either been moved into storage—she hoped—or tossed in the garbage. The plain, white twin-sized bed covered in furry pink linens with red hearts all over them that he'd promised would always be here for her was *gone*. A brand-new queen-sized oak, four post bed stood in its place. The choice of linens for the new bed wasn't anything she'd pick out. Instead it was covered in gold and silver threaded geometric shapes which were embroidered onto heavy white fabric making up a comforter and pillow shams.

He made it clear in the new décor that she no longer had a bedroom in his house. That she no longer had a home. He didn't want her there anymore.

A white clothing box with a red bow around it lay on the new bed. She didn't want the gift. She didn't want to go to the party anymore. But she had to. Obligation and respect for Liam forced her to untie the red bow and open the lid. It pained her to place the lid and bow on the shelf of the new oak armoire, not the missing white, six-drawer dresser Liam had made her for her birthday, the first year she moved in with him.

If she'd known he'd get rid of all the memories they'd made together in this house, she never would've left Georgia. Regret worked its way into her system.

I never should've left home to go to college. You were right. It was a mistake. This is my home. I should've come home more. I should've asked for help paying for flights to visit. You would've given it. Pride stopped me. Pride, and the hope you'd come for me stopped me from asking. I stupidly hoped you'd miss me enough to leave Georgia to come visit. You never came. Not for family day. Not for any of the awards I won. Not even for a football game.

She unfolded the red tissue paper and found a small envelope lying on top of a white silk dress. She pulled a card from the envelope.

Finley,

This dress is special. It will change color with your emotions. Liam said that you keep your emotions to yourself and hide your true feelings. This fabric will make it more difficult – if not impossible – to conceal those feelings.

I am looking forward to meeting you.

~Wenzel

P.S. You're not compatible with Liam. I won't allow you to stand in the way of his happiness anymore.

SHE REREAD the note again and again.

You don't know if I'm compatible with Liam. If you're right, and I'm an angel, I could be the only woman alive who is compatible with Liam. You don't know me or him. I'm not standing in the way of his happiness. I love him. Screw you, Wenzel. You probably did all this redecorating to my room and my home. I hate you.

She touched the fabric of the dress and it turned a murky bronze. *What the heck is that about?*

As soon as she lifted her hand from the dress, the murky bronze morphed to white. *This is too weird. The dress is probably rigged to turn colors near Liam. You want to make sure he will never look at me like a lover, like a mate, like a wife.*

She walked into the bathroom and stopped at the vanity, turning on the faucet at the sink and wetting her face. *I need to calm down. That note doesn't mean anything. Wenzel is testing me. Trying to get me to show my feelings in colors only he could interpret. I'm going to show him. I'm going to numb my heart. That mystical dress won't tell him anything. I'll screw up this power play for him. He won't know what hit him when this dress remains white the entire night.*

She inhaled and exhaled, trying to let go of the ridiculousness of that man's note and the strange color of the dress from her touch.

I'm worked up over that stupid note, and Liam just showed me his wings. The most important person in my life has freaking amazing wings that can do magical things, and here I am stressed over a redecorated house and the words of a man who doesn't even know me.

Liam is happy. I make him happy. He loves me. Wenzel doesn't know shit. I'm going to wear jeans and a bikini top just to be difficult. Take that, Wenzel, you mean, distant cousin to my Liam.

Exhaling, she rethought her decision to wear something inappropriate. Liam would give her a lecture about being an adult, which meant that she couldn't throw a tantrum because she wasn't getting her way. *Think like Rager would think. Beat your opponent at their own game by making them play yours. I got this, Rager. I have so much I need to talk to you about. I don't know what to do about Liam or Slater or this asshole Wenzel.*

She took off her T-shirt and jeans, peeled off her wet

panties, and wiped between her legs, removing all the desire that the kisses with Slater had produced.

I hope Wenzel added white panties with that dress or I'm going to wear my little lamb undies. Liam's new family will get a good look at the bright pink and green baby lambs doing yoga poses all over my panties.

Walking to the bed, she eyed the dress in the box. *Dude paid a fortune for that dress. Whatever he had done to it to make it change color like a mood ring had to have added an extra-hefty fee.*

She stopped and gazed at the fabric, examining it for anything out of the ordinary.

Did the man line the dress with some kind of poison? That note seemed like a battle cry. Do you want a fight, Wenzel? Do you want me out of the picture? You know I'm only human but you're filling Liam's head with visions of me being some kind of hybrid healing angel. If I were a healing angel, I'd heal my back. I'd heal every child in the world. I'd go into the medical field and work in hospitals to save babies and children and ease the pain of women in labor. There are so many things I'd do, if I had that ability. But I don't. Wenzel knows I'm not an angel. That's why I'm not compatible with Liam. That's why he wrote that note. This dress is to prove to Liam that I'm not like him. It's mean, but it's honest.

With a heavy sigh, she abandoned all the nefarious ideas that Wenzel wanted to kill her off and picked up the dress. She flicked the dress, holding onto the top, and saw the silk billow outward as it caught air. Sure enough, an almost nonexistent pair of white panties floated to the carpet at her feet.

Thanks for thinking of lingerie. But where's the bra?

The dress lengthened and shortened the more she handled it. She flicked her wrist, the dress expanded and lengthened, and the delicate scent of lavender and rose spread through the room, calming her.

She stepped into the dress and pulled it up over her

breasts, sliding the wide straps of white silk upward, covering her shoulders. The fabric tightened around her chest and waist. The material over her shoulders thinned to the size of a strand of yarn. The skirt of the dress expanded and then constricted, lengthened, and then shortened in what seemed like a blur of confusion.

Finley grabbed the panties from the floor and ran to the bathroom, watching the rise and fall of fabric in the mirror as the dress changed shape and dimension as if an invisible tailor was designing a one-of-a-kind dress in that very moment. She slid the panties up her legs as the dress continued to morph into a skimpier and skimpier version of the original one. The panties molded to her, covering only the barest of essentials.

She bent over and the panties parted to either side of her nether lips, as if she'd allow a man easy access to that part of her.

The length of the dress rose from her feet up her legs, stopping at a point that was higher up her thighs than any dress she'd ever considered wearing. She tugged at the skirt, attempting to force it down to cover more than a half-inch of her thighs, but it wouldn't budge.

A heavy sigh accompanied her thoughts. *Liam is not going to like this. He's going to be angry. But this isn't my fault. It's Wenzel's stupid dress. I had nothing to do with this. The thing barely covers my ass. I can't bend over. No one near me will be able to pick something off the floor without seeing parts of me that aren't allowed to be seen by anyone other than my future husband.*

While she worked through her fury and embarrassment, she gazed for any color changes in the fabric, but it remained white. *Maybe this dress won't show my emotions, because I'm so furious right now that the dress should be red and orange to represent the flames of hell—a place I'd like to send Wenzel.*

"Fin, are you ready?" Liam called.

"Yeah, but you're not going to like this dress your cousin gave me," she said.

"I bet you look beautiful," he replied.

"I don't think you're going to say that when you take a look at me. I've never worn anything this tight and short and revealing." She strode out of the bathroom and opened the door to the bedroom.

Standing in the hallway, Liam looked more handsome than he did in his police uniform—and that was saying something. When he got all dressed up in his kick ass SWAT gear, ready to help out his fellow officers on a raid in the bigger cities nearby, she melted into a hot mess of love and lust. The black tuxedo looked downright sinful on him. S-i-n-f-u-l.

"You look so gorgeous." She swallowed and dropped her gaze to her hands at her waist, seeing the color of the dress shift from white to a light pink and then return to white.

He cleared his throat. "Thanks. That dress is really…uh—"

"Revealing. Whore-like."

"You don't look like a whore. You're beautiful. It's just not what I expected. It's tiny, like you."

The dress is made for a child, not an adult with curves. I hate this. I'm embarrassed to be seen in it. I look like I should be selling myself on a corner, not going to a family birthday event.

"I don't have shoes and I really want out of this dress, but I think I'd need scissors to get out of this thing."

"You're not supposed to wear any shoes," he said. "Wenzel will give you anything else you need for the party."

"Like a new dress that covers my ass? Maybe makeup and hairstylist, too?"

"I don't know about the new dress, but he'll probably have stylists there. It's an important day. Come on. We don't want to be late."

"Yeah. God forbid we're late," she mumbled. *I can't make*

Wenzel wait while I put on a real dress that actually covers my girlie parts. "Where do I put my phone?" She'd already texted Rager that she'd arrived safely and not to expect a call until tomorrow night. But she also felt a bit uneasy about this party and might need a backup or an escape plan. Wenzel's note had her worried and the changes in Liam's behavior made her uneasy. She might be giving Rager Smithson a text to come get her before midnight.

He held out his hand. "Give it to me."

She placed it in his hand. *Then I am coming home with you. You wouldn't take my phone and abandon me.*

He placed it on the bed. "You don't need it. You're with me." He wove his fingers between hers. "If you're uncomfortable, we can leave early. It's important that you meet Wenzel and my family."

Yes. Your family, not mine. I'm dressed to embarrass you. It's just another reason to cut me out of your life. Tonight is going to be a nightmare.

"How about I not go?" She tugged at the thin straps on her shoulders, but the thin thread-like material seemed glued to her skin. She continued fidgeting with the hem of the dress that seemed to continue to shorten, showing the bottom of her panties.

"Stop that." Liam's tone came as a warning—no more complaining or she'd be grounded. "You're going. This is important to me."

It's not important to me. "Yes, sir. I'm sorry."

"Follow my rules, and we'll be back home eating popcorn and watching a movie on the couch in an hour."

She nodded. "I like your plan."

This party is a mistake.

Nothing good will come of tonight.

CHAPTER TEN

Finley

The man she didn't want to meet had invited her to an area of the state that she didn't know well. A newly built cream-colored mansion with golden accents stood on property that extended into two counties west of theirs. Liam insisted on parking in the garage on the west side of the house, even though she expressed concern that they'd get blocked in once guests arrived. He seemed intent on obstructing all of her exit strategies.

Since she'd moved to Nevada and met Sienna, she'd been in big houses. In fact, she'd thought Sienna lived in an enormous house, but this mansion made Sienna's twenty-bedroom suite home look like a doll house in comparison. This place was more on the same comparable rating as the size of Rager Smithson's, who also lived in Sienna's neighborhood. But Rager's house seemed to discourage people from entering with its darker exterior than the mansion she stood inside. But Rager's house held a warm, inviting interior whereas this mansion looked and felt like it had the opposite intention.

"I don't like this place," she whispered. Shivers ran down her spine and goosebumps rose on the flesh of her arms and legs. "I want to go home." *This is not a safe place for me.*

"It's fine. I've been here a lot recently. Don't worry."

She blew out a frustrated exhale. "I don't trust your cousin or the safety of this house."

"You don't trust anything or anyone. You never have."

"I trust people," she retorted.

"That's such bullcrap, Fin. You don't trust anyone. Sometimes I wonder if you trust me."

"Why would you say something like that to me? I trust you more than I trust anyone else in the world. I don't question your judgement." *I love you. Don't you know that I only love the people I trust? I love you and only you.*

"You're questioning my decisions now." He slid his arm around her back and tucked her against his side. "You're safe. I'm here. You have nothing to worry about."

"Hmm," she grumbled. "I don't feel safe. I feel like a sitting duck that is going to be the main course at dinner." She glanced down at her shrinking dress. *White. Yep. No one is going to know my true feelings. I don't feel safe here. I don't like this place. I want to leave. I want to leave now. If you don't bring me home soon, I'm calling Rager. Shoot. I don't have my phone. I'll have to borrow one. No. I can't do that. Rager's number is private for a reason. I can't let anyone else have it in their contacts. I'll have to figure out something on my own.*

"You're being ridiculous," he whispered.

"Where is this Wenzel dude?" she asked. "Why didn't he meet us at the side door? This place is gigantic. I could live here for years and still get lost in this maze of a house. There are doors and more doors that all seem to be there to confuse guests. This place is a labyrinth for people to get lost in." She looked up, noticing the ceiling cameras with laser green lights that seemed to track their movements.

"It's okay. Once you meet Wenzel, you'll calm down. He's great."

"Great to you. You're his family. I'm the outsider." *I'm always the outsider. I freaking hate it here. Something bad is going to happen.* "He doesn't give a rip about me." *He's probably going to tell me to my face to get out of your life. That I'm a loser and standing in the way of your angelic mission to save the world.*

Liam stopped in front of a gold door.

"Is that real gold?" she asked.

"Yes," Liam replied. He turned the gold knob on the door.

The door swung open and he strode forward, tugging her into an enormous room that held seven clearly defined sections. A large, black gym mat marked one section at the far end of the room that was separated by a painted white line down the middle. Exercise equipment, an office area, a changing space with lockers and benches, different styles of armor hanging from hooks in the ceiling in a separate section, and several cots for sleeping finished up the space.

The weapons on walls, tables, in glass-encased displays, and beside full suits of golden armor sent her senses on full-alert. This was not a place for someone like her—someone human. There weren't enough men like Liam to protect her in a place like this. And no matter how much she wished to the contrary, she couldn't protect herself in this room, in this house, or on this property. She doubted she could fake enough confidence to stand up to the man who would have a room like this in his house.

I'm screwed.

"My back hurts more than usual. I need to lie down," she said. "Let's go before someone notices we're here."

"I'm here," a man's confident voice sounded from behind her.

She spun around and retreated several steps. "What the heck is wrong with you?" She hadn't meant to say that aloud, but for some reason her internal dialog that had helped her control her emotions for her entire life flew out from her mouth.

A brown-haired man wearing a black tuxedo took a step forward and stood shoulder to shoulder with Liam. His irises swirled with ribbons of gold, sometimes drowning out the calming sparkles of emerald green. The man was gorgeous and he knew it.

Power and confidence rolled off him in such a strong current that fear filled every inch of her body. He didn't look much older than Liam, but if she didn't know better, she would gauge his age at more than a millennium, not two and a half-ish decades. They had similar features and looked like they could be brothers. They were most definitely family. And she was most definitely *not*.

The man laughed. "You're very controlled, Finley Vessel. I thought I'd elicit some emotional fluctuation from you, but nope. Even under duress, your dress shows no signs of your stress, only the purity of a calm spirit. You're a rare one."

He stepped toward her, but she retreated.

"I'm Wenzel Vogel," he said. "I'm a warrior angel and the head of the Vogel family."

You're too close. "Nice to meet you, Mr. Vogel." *I don't like you. I wonder if you know Slater. No. Slater wouldn't be friends with someone like you. He wouldn't be related to someone like you, not even a distant cousin. Slater is definitely no angel. He gambles. There is probably something in angel DNA that doesn't allow for one to gamble for a living. Besides, Vogel is a popular name in this area of Georgia. And it's super popular in Nevada. I must have met at least three dozen students at college with the same last name. None of them were angels.*

She lifted her hand and waved. *No way am I getting close enough for you to touch me. No freaking way.* "Thank you for the note and the dress."

"You're welcome." Wenzel patted Liam on the back. "You can wait for us in the hall."

"Oh no," she said. "Liam isn't going anywhere."

"Yes, he is," Wenzel stated. "I'm going to speak to you candidly, and you're going to listen without any distractions. Liam, leave us."

The tone and energy that accompanied the man's words were final. There would be consequences for disobeying his commands, and the way her gut knotted, those consequences would be dire.

Without the slightest hesitation, Liam followed the man's commands, walking out the door and leaving her alone with the warrior angel to fend for herself.

The door closed and then she heard a locking mechanism.

No. No. No. I'm freaking locked in with this guy? What happened to Liam keeping me safe? I'm going to die. Liam will have to hide the truth from the world. He'd do that for family…for his new family.

She stared into Wenzel's strange colored eyes, pretending to be confident in her ability to survive this encounter. She wasn't confident in the least, but she'd follow Liam's rules and those rules kept her alive and safe for the last nine years. The only problem was that Liam's rules didn't take precedent in this place. Wenzel's rules were the only rules that mattered, and she had no idea what kind of rules governed his home, his land, his life. And she wasn't so sure she wanted to find out.

"What is the purpose of this dress, and why am I here?"

While he walked toward her, she attempted to keep a fair distance from him. He moved toward her. She retreated, looking for some kind of advantage in this strange game of chess.

He continued forward, driving her movements toward the back southern corner.

"I'm not here to play games," he said. "I'm walking to the mat. We're going to either stand or sit on the mat and talk honestly in a calm and respectful manner."

She circled him to the north of the room, giving him lots of room in the direction he'd been heading. Somehow, he'd managed to guide her onto the edge of the mat with her back to the only exit that she knew of, while he stood in the best possible spot to see the majority of the room and close the gap between them whenever it was most advantageous for him to do so.

She stopped, recognizing her error in switching direction and truly losing the benefit of sight. She realized that she'd lost before he ever announced their meeting was a battle that preceded a war.

"I'm going to be straight with you," Wenzel said. "You're not going to like what I have to say, but my words are the truth."

Drawing her hand to her hips, she inhaled, waiting for whatever bomb he would drop next. "Say whatever you're going to say, and then let me leave."

"Wow, you don't even flinch when I flex my power. Your emotions are so hidden that I wonder if they'll show at all while you're here."

She shrugged. *No, they won't. I'm not giving you any piece of me. I'm using my fear to keep my emotions in check. I'm Liam's plus one. I'm not family, but I know where I stand in the hierarchy of your world. I'm at the bottom. I'm the one you want to scare so I never come back to Georgia. Here's a news alert—I'm coming back whenever I want. It's a free country, and you mean nothing to me.*

"First, Liam is off-limits to you," he said.

She rolled her eyes. "Is that all?"

"You can visit him on rare occasions when I allow it, but you're not sleeping in his house or attempting to seduce him. I have alternate sleeping arrangements for you here, in my home."

"I'm not sleeping here. And if Liam doesn't want me in his house, he can tell me that himself. I'll find another place to stay, if need be." *Liam will never kick me out of the only real home I've ever had.*

"Don't make Liam tell you that you're not welcome to sleep in his home. It will hurt him, and I don't want his feelings hurt over something so trivial and unnecessary."

Trivial? Trivial my ass. "Maybe *it is necessary,*" she said.

"Maybe it is for you," he said. "But not for him. He's done a lot for you. He's sacrificed the last nine years to care for you. Save him some pain, Finley."

You're the one hurting him, not me. "What else do you have to tell me?" she asked.

"Will nothing elicit an emotional response from you?" Wenzel asked.

"Nope."

"How old are you?" he asked.

"Almost twenty," she said.

"You're still a virgin?"

"That's none of your business."

He grinned. "You are. That's quite the accomplishment."

"If I am, it wouldn't be that difficult," she stated. "Boys are boring. School is fun and interesting."

He let out an obnoxiously confident belly laugh. "Boys are boring?" He nodded and laughed again. "Angels of Law are boring and strict. Warrior Angels are anything but boring. We fight and fuck and party in between. No one has ever called *me* boring."

"I wouldn't know. I don't know you."

"Ahh." Wenzel nodded his head and then sat down on the black mat with his legs extended in front of him. "Come here."

She felt no compulsion to follow his order or be polite. "No."

"Finley Vessel, *please*, come join me." He patted the mat. "Come on. I'm not going to touch you without your permission. I'm not going to hurt you physically. Some of the things I am about to tell you will hurt emotionally, and I'm sorry about that. But now that I've met you, I believe you can handle a blunt conversation. I believe you'll think about what I say and come to the same conclusion—Maybe not right away, but it won't take you long."

"Don't attempt to touch me," she said.

"There will be no touching without your permission," he stated.

"There better not be or I'm leaving with or without your permission." She walked toward him, but kept more of a distance than he seemed to want. She carefully lowered to the floor, attempting some manner of modesty. Sitting on her heels, she met his gaze.

"Thank you," he said.

She nodded.

"I thought you might be a combination of healer and mediation angels or even possibly a healer and music angel. The other combinations would've been extremely rare, such as a healer and love angel or a healer and messenger angel. But you're none of those combinations."

"Yes. I know. I'm human. One hundred percent normal, a run-of-the-mill female human."

"No. You're not human. You're so rare that there is only one of you in existence."

"Dude, I don't have any powers. You've got me confused

with someone else." She lifted her hips from her heels, ready to rise.

"Stop," he ordered. "Stay where you are and listen to what I am telling you."

She exhaled and slowly lowered her bottom back down. *"Listening."*

"You're the last of your kind. You're a full-fledged Love Angel. I haven't seen one of your kind in centuries, possibly longer. I have no idea who your parents are or how they died and ascended to Heaven. You are so rare in our world, so very rare. I want to say that about sixteen or so years ago, I received news that all Love Angels were extinct. The last community was eliminated, not even half-breeds were left alive."

"I knew my mother, and she was no angel. She was every bit human with human problems."

He frowned. "That was not your mother. Love angels have wings that span almost as wide as mine. Do your shoulders ever itch when you're around children?"

I'm going to humor you in this and then tell Liam that you're insane. She shrugged. *Not that I've ever noticed.*

"You're not going to offer any information to me, are you?"

She shrugged. *No. I'm not. I don't like you.*

"O-kay. Let's talk about my favorite subject—me." He leaned back on his elbows as if he had all the time in the world to talk and relax. "I look and tell people I'm thirty, but I'm more than seven thousand years old. My father and step-mother are alive. My stepmother who I call 'Mom' is a mixed breed. She's three-quarters warrior angel and a quarter healing angel. She's a pain in my ass, but I love her. My father is a warrior angel, although he's pretty much done fighting demons. He stepped down as head of the family a couple millennia ago. I'm not sure of the exact date. It's been a while."

"Why am I here?" she asked. "Whose birthday party is this, and are we going to actually attend it?

"I lied to get you here. We're not celebrating anyone's birthday today. You're here because I'm going to attempt to find you a suitable husband from the men in my family."

She huffed. "I don't think so. I'm not—"

"You need real protection. You need a husband from my warrior angels, not a law angel." He sat up and glared at her. "You're rare. You're more beautiful than anyone I've ever met in all the years I've been on earth. I bet you're dying for sex. You *want* and *need* to procreate."

"You're wrong about the sex and the beauty and the protecting and the *procreating*. I'm average looking at best. I'm fine on my own. And I almost never think about sex or having children."

I only think about it when I'm with Slater. So, there. Well, I think about it at night. I think about being with Liam and snuggling and kissing him. But that's it. Well, I think about having children, but only when I'm with kids, which is a lot. Actually, I'm surrounded by kids at Sienna's house so I think about having a family of my own all the time. I think about being a mom more than I care to admit.

"You're just flat out wrong about me," she said.

"You're delusional," he said. "I usually like delusional, but not when the stakes are this high." He softened his glare. "Would you like to expand your wings? Let them out?"

She shook her head. *Do I?* "Why are love angels so rare?"

"They've been hunted, I thought, to extinction, but then you appeared alive and well in my house. They're usually easy to pick out in a crowd because their emotions are so chaotic and loud they make epic public scenes. Think extra-extreme diva drama from a jealous goddess and those are typically love angels. Liam has good instincts and kept you safe all these years. You don't date or engage in social activities. You hide your emotions almost as well as Liam does. I don't know how you're managing that. It's not natural for angels like you. And you are so beautiful, I almost want to take you as my wife, and keep you for myself."

"Take me? Keep me? *You wish*," she huffed as her heart hammered in her chest so hard that she thought the action might break a rib. *I would fight you, and you'd kill me easily. I can't defend myself. I can't fight. I'd try. I'd do my best. I'd die trying, but you'd win. Then you'd realize that I'm a boring human. Easily broken. Easily killed.*

"I wouldn't take or keep you without your desire matching my own, but that doesn't mean I don't appreciate you. You are extraordinary. Your hair is almost the color of pure spun gold. I haven't seen strands of that color since..." He sighed. "I don't think I've ever seen hair as beautiful as yours before. I don't think I've ever seen a woman as beautiful as you in all the years I've lived, in any continent in the world."

He seemed to look off into nothing. "I don't know who your parents were. They wouldn't have left you or given you to someone else to raise. They must be dead. Everyone in your line must be dead. How did you survive?" The question seemed hypothetical, but she couldn't have answered it even if she wanted to.

She had no idea how she ended up traveling with her mother from one rural town in Georgia to another. But something about that question made her think that there might have been truth to some of what he'd said. Not about being a love angel. That was clearly wishful thinking on his part. But maybe that her mother wasn't really her mother. They didn't look anything alike. She was as black as Finley was white. She was very tall whereas Finley was average height at best. They did have similar colored blue eyes, although Finley's were as blue as the summer sky and her mother's was more of a bluish-green like pictures of the waters of the tropics. Actually, the color of their eyes didn't really look anything alike. Maybe her mother picked her up on the side of the road. Her mother was kind, loving, and a wanderer.

Finley didn't know whether to believe him or not. Maybe the man was playing games, telling her a truth within many lies. She couldn't see auras like Liam. She only had her gut as a lie detector, and it wasn't so skilled in that area because it wasn't tying in knots like it usually did when people lied to her. Maybe Wenzel believed he was telling the truth. But the real truth was that he was dead wrong about her. Any way she looked at it, she wasn't an angel. She had no angel powers. She thought about sex about as much as the average person. She was no love angel. She wasn't an angel at all.

The dress remained white which seemed to perturb him. Maybe part of the testing was with the dress. Maybe he couldn't see auras either and the dress was some kind of lie detector. She'd seen it change color twice, but that could've been in her imagination, thinking she saw something that wasn't there. Maybe her desire to be special, even though she wasn't, pulled her closer into believing his lies. Maybe her wish to have Liam think she was beautiful, even though she knew the opposite to be true, kept her ears open to Wenzel's lies. Maybe her hope that she'd be a special angel like Liam, even though it was impossible, held her seated in position until the truth of her humanity became undeniable.

I'm human. Everything he's telling me is subjective. He might think I'm pretty, but others don't. If I were a love angel, everyone would fall in love with me. Liam wouldn't be able to resist me and he has. He does. Proving I'm only human.

He shifted his hips, adjusted the big bulge in his pants, and turned his focus back on her. "I'll keep searching for information on you. Do you have any questions?"

"If I have wings, why haven't they come out on their

own? Why would I need you to help me if they're as big as you say they are? And if I were to allow you to bring out these *wings* you say I have, what would the implications be to my normal life?"

"I can help you manage the pain of the first time your wings expand. You don't need me to help you bring them out. They will come out on their own at some point. Usually, they exit your body and expand when desire wars with a promise, or to protect a child or a person you love. The implications of expanding your wings..." He sighed. "You'll start searching for a male to love and have sex and babies with. You'll emit a scent that will be so alluring, men will fight to have you." He tapped his fingers on the mat as if he was missing something. "What else? What else?"

Tap. Tap. Tap.

"Your natural complexion will have a sexy pink *just fucked* glow when you meet your mate. That's about it. The dress you're wearing won't be affected. It won't tear or anything when the wings expand from their hiding place. Both the dress and your wings are magical."

"I'll let whatever happens, happen naturally," she said.

"The first time is going to be rough."

"I don't care." She rose from the mat and tried to tug the hem of the dress down, but it didn't budge. In fact, the skirt of the dress shortened once more, turning into a short ruffle at her waist.

"You are a rule follower," he said.

"I like rules." While facing him, she retreated toward the door she'd entered with Liam so he wouldn't see her ass hanging out of her panties "Are we done here?"

"Yeah," Wenzel said. "We can head to the party now."

I don't think so. There will be no matchmaking at this gathering. "I'm going home."

"No, you're not. You're going to be polite and make small

talk with all the single men who have come from all over the world for one heck of a party honoring you. If your dress changes to an appropriate color stating interest, you are going to spend time getting to know that person or persons. If no one here interests you, then you'll be living with me and attending more of my parties, meeting single men multiple times a week until you find one whom you'd like to settle down with and marry."

"You can't force me to do that." *What kind of crazy person are you?*

"I can. *I don't want to force you.* But I'm the only one on this earth who can not only force you to come to my magnificent and fun parties, but I can put a time-limit on the search for an appropriate mate for you. Believe me, when word of you gets out, and it will, angels will be coming in droves from every corner of the world to marry you. I'd prefer you to be with a warrior angel, but I'll accept other angels as potential matchings—if that dress's color changes to the correct color."

"And what color do you think that will be?" she asked.

"Crimson. Until then, you're mine."

"Who do you think you are? You're nothing to me."

"I'm Wenzel Vogel, head of the Vogel family. Liam handed you over to me, and now I am your guardian. You will follow my orders. You will live where I tell you to live, and you will walk by my side into the party I organized for *you,*" he shouted.

"I'm walking out of here, and you're not going to stop me." She ran to the exit. As soon as she touched the golden knob, the mechanism that locked the door unlocked it. She flung the door open.

Liam stood in the hallway. "What did he say?"

"That I'm not allowed to stay with you. That you're no longer my guardian. That I have to obey *him.*" She grabbed

Liam's hand. "I listened to him like you asked. Now, please, take me home."

"You can't leave," Liam said. "You have to meet my family. I know he said more than you're telling me. Learning you're an angel is a lot to process, but please, don't make me leave so soon."

"I know you're an angel," she said. "I thought you were a god the day we met and then every day since. I'm healthy and fit and maybe that's why I never get sick. I probably just have exceptional genetics, but I'm not what he thinks I am. I'm not an angel, Liam. I'm sorry to disappoint you, but I'm just not that special."

He pulled her against him, hugging her. "Fin, you are that special. But forget about all that angel stuff. I want you to meet everyone. You're going to fit in like you wouldn't believe. You're one of us and you'll know it as soon as you meet everyone."

"Dude wants to marry me off to some rando at the party," she whispered. "That's freaking nuts. I think he's clinically insane."

"He's not insane. He's brilliant. Let's go to the party and mingle." Liam kissed the top of her head. "Please *do this for me*."

"I don't like this place. There's so much hostility," she whispered. "I feel stressed. I need to go home."

"You don't look stressed. You look more beautiful now than you did when we got here. Please, Fin," he pleaded. "I want to introduce you to my family. This is important to me."

"Fine, I'll stay, but only for a few minutes. I'm not a piece of meat for someone to buy."

"Liam," Wenzel said. "She's walking in with me."

She glared at Wenzel. "I won't go inside without Liam beside me. And I will not live or remain under this roof with you."

"Then you'll walk between us. What you do with Liam, you'll do with me. If you hold his hand, you must hold mine, too. If you hug him, you'll hug me. You're not leaving until either you find a match or I leave. You're my responsibility now." He held out his hand.

Dang it, she stepped out of the safety of Liam's arms and took Wenzel's hand. As soon as she realized what she'd done, she held out her other hand to Liam. "This is a one time—"

"Quiet," Wenzel ordered. "Be respectful, Finley."

She closed her eyes and inhaled. *You're not going to get me to reveal my feelings. I can control my emotions. I do it every day. All day long.*

While she exhaled, she opened her eyes and smiled at Wenzel. "My dress might not change, but I'm letting you know that I hate you, Wenzel Vogel. You don't rule over me. You will *never* rule over me."

"You're so cute," Wenzel said. "I love your spirit. Now, let's find you a husband."

CHAPTER ELEVEN

Finley

"This is Finley Vessel," Wenzel said, introducing her to yet another good-looking single man wearing a tuxedo who was approximately her age. The guy was a warrior angel in Wenzel's family.

She shook the guy's hand. "It's nice to meet you." *You're gorgeous like all the rest of the men I've met today.* But she'd experienced no spark. No interest. No nothing. "I'll see you around the dance floor." She glanced at Wenzel and his jaw clenched.

"Save me a dance?" the guy asked.

She smiled and shrugged, turning her back on that guy and toward the back of another blond in a black tux with a killer bod. *I would totally do you. Your ass is fine. And your shoulders…You're stronger than the others.*

Her heart fluttered and she grabbed onto Wenzel's hand for balance.

The man turned around, and she couldn't breathe.

She couldn't believe her eyes.

A cocky smile filled Slater's lips and his blue eyes instantly turned gold. "How did you crash this party?"

"I should be asking you the same thing," she said.

"Come here, beautiful." Slater held out his hand and without thinking she reached for it.

She shuddered as the spark of energy from the touch of his hand hit her like a mountain of rock.

He pulled her close and his mouth landed on hers in less than a millisecond.

She parted her lips and he dove inside, stroking her tongue, drawing her into a dance of raw need. The desire to touch more of him sent her hands under his jacket, pulling out his shirt, touching his skin.

"Oh fucking yes," Slater moaned. "Fin...we need to fuck now. Right fucking now."

She gripped the back of his waistband. "Yeah. No." She let go and retreated so fast that she fell straight backward into Wenzel's front. "I can't."

"And we've got a winner," Wenzel said. "It's wedding time. I love weddings."

"No," Liam said. "He's *not* marrying her."

"Yes, he is," Wenzel said. "Look at her. That dress is so fucking red it's practically dripping with love and desire. She's chosen and he's one hundred percent worthy." He took her hand and placed it in Slater's. "Slater Vogel, do you take Finley Vessel to be your lawfully wedded wife?"

"I do," Slater said. "Fin, I love you."

Liam stepped forward. "No. She's not marrying—"

Suddenly, she stood enclosed within Wenzel's golden wings with him and Slater.

"Do you, Finley Vessel, take Slater Vogel to be your lawfully wedded husband?" Wenzel asked.

"I…" *Slater Vogel? How are you related to this asshole?*

"I love you, Fin." Slater took off his jacket and bow tie. "I will protect and love you for the rest of my life, and I promise we're going to have a ton of kids." He unbuttoned his shirt.

Her tongue traced her lips, wetting them while she watched him take off his shirt and undershirt, revealing utter masculine perfection.

"Slater…" *Dang, you're handsome. I want you.* She labored to breathe. "I can't just…I want to…"

He placed her palm to his heart. "My heart beats for you."

He placed his palm at her heart. "Your heart beats for me. Don't you feel the thumping of our hearts beating in the same rhythm?"

"I do," she whispered.

"I now pronounce you husband and wife," Wenzel said.

"But I didn't—"

"Take her forearm," Wenzel said.

Slater grabbed her forearm. "This is an honor."

Wenzel slid his hand into his jacket pocket and took out two golden bracelets that nestled together.

"What's happening?" she asked. "I didn't agree to anything. I'm not—"

"Did I tell you how beautiful you look tonight?" Slater whispered. "That dress…" He made a low rumbling sound that warmed her belly.

She bit her bottom lip and gazed up at him, batting her lashes. "You like it?"

"Oh yeah," he mumbled. "Red is my favorite color."

Wenzel pulled the bracelets apart and suddenly the thick bands widened and grew spikes on the inside.

Slater's arm curled around her back. "This is a Vogel wedding bracelet. It tests our compatibility and decides whether our marriage is blessed by God."

Wenzel moved so quickly that she had no time to react.

He slammed the spikes into their forearms. An initial shock of pain shifted her focus from Wenzel back to Slater. The desire for Slater intensified. The bracelet acted like a living, breathing entity as it snaked around her forearm and melted into her pores until it vanished inside her.

"A perfect pairing," Wenzel said softly. "Congratulations. Slater, you may kiss your bride."

"Wait," she said. "What would've happened if the bracelets decided we weren't compatible?"

"You and Slater would've died," Wenzel said. "The bracelets would've killed you both. But that didn't happen." Wenzel smiled. "Congratulations. You're married and alive. There's much to celebrate."

Whether it was the look on her face or the sudden thrust of her hands against Slater's chest which alerted them to her displeasure she didn't know, but they moved quickly, sandwiching her between them so she couldn't move.

"I don't want this," she shouted. "You tricked me. I'm not one of you. I'm not who you think I am."

"You are exactly who I think you are," Wenzel said.

"Slater, I never agreed to marriage," she said. "I never..."

Slater leaned back and cupped her face. "You don't want to marry me?"

Gazing into his golden eyes, her heart fluttered and desire to feel more of him came roaring back to life. "I, uh, do, but..." She curled her arms around his neck. "You haven't met Liam. We don't know if we like the same things. Just because we're..." She slid her tongue over her lips, wetting them. "We have chemistry but that doesn't mean we're ready for marriage. You're the only man I've ever kissed. I've never kissed anyone before today, before we kissed at the airport. This isn't how this happens. We're supposed to date and then you're supposed to meet Liam and ask his permission to marry me. This is all wrong. It's happening out of order. I'm not even supposed to be dating. Liam forbade me to—"

"She's a virgin," Wenzel said. "She just found out she's a love angel. Lots of firsts for her today. If her wings sprout during sex, that's a good sign. Once I retract my wings, don't go straight to your bedroom for sex. Dance first. And be nice to Liam. He loves her, and he's family."

Slater grabbed her ass and lifted her up.

She wrapped her legs around his waist. "You know we're not married."

"We're married," Slater mumbled. "Two months of wanting you…"

"Two months?" Wenzel asked. "She's the one living at Blade Davis's house?"

"The one and only," Slater said. "My balls are swollen. So screw the dance floor, I'm—" His mouth was on hers and then she was moaning so loud in a tone she didn't recognize.

"Welcome Mrs. Slater Vogel to the family," Wenzel shouted.

She broke the kiss and inhaled as the room erupted in shouts and whoops of congratulatory celebration.

"Oh my God, what have I done?" She slid down Slater's sexy body. Guilt racked her bones. *How could I have made such a huge mistake?* She looked for Liam, searching the smiling crowd for her true love. "I need to talk to Liam."

"Don't be long," Slater said. "Wenzel is right. We need to dance and visit. Then I'm taking you to my place, and we're staying in bed until we leave for the airport."

She didn't answer.

She couldn't think. *Liam, please be here.*

She pulled away from Slater.

Where are you? Where are you? She spotted Liam, finding him staring emotionless at her.

As she raced toward him, he turned his back on her.

Finley

Grabbing Liam's arm, she stopped his exit.

"Take me home with you," she begged. "*Please.* I didn't marry him. I didn't agree to it. I agreed that his heartbeat was in rhythm with mine. Wenzel tricked me."

He turned around, facing her. "Fin, I'd never met Slater before. I didn't know he was one of us."

She clung to him. "You shouldn't have brought me here. I want to go home. Please, take me home."

"I can't take you home. I asked about him while you were..." He dropped his gaze down, avoiding hers. "He's young and powerful. He's second in command over all of us, over all angels of light. He plans our war strategy. I overheard people saying that his parents gave guardianship of him to a human family the day before they went into battle. They hadn't expected to survive, but wanted him to be loved the way they loved him, if they didn't come back. Wenzel tried to make the human family give him guardianship of Slater. They refused, but did offer open visitation, which Wenzel accepted. Wenzel trained him from the time Slater was a baby."

"I don't care how powerful anyone is. I have rights. I want to go home with you. I'm not married. I never agreed to spend the rest of my life with him. Why can't you just take me home? I don't do well in crowds. You know that," she said, frantically. "I panic." *I'm panicking now. I'm freaking out. This is bad. Really bad.* "Take me home, Liam. I want to go home."

"You *are* married." Liam grabbed her hands and pulled them from his arm. "You're wearing the Vogel marriage bracelets. I can't take you anywhere without Slater's permission. I can't hold you, comfort you, touch you without his permission." He exhaled a sad sigh. "I love you, Fin. I thought I'd be walking you down the aisle in a church with everyone in town attending. I thought the man you loved would ask my blessing..." He choked up. "This is not what I envisioned for you. You're not even wearing a wedding dress. You'd never pick this kind of dress to wear outside or even as pajamas. If I had any indication that this would happen, I never would've agreed to bring you. I swear, I thought Wenzel was going to introduce you to everyone, then you'd pick a few guys to date and in a couple weeks to months, you'd plan a wedding. But you took one look at Slater and that dress turned such a crimson red that there was no doubt in anyone's mind that you wanted him."

Her heart broke. *You love me like a father. You've always loved me like a father, and I've foolishly loved you like a...I thought we were meant for each other.* "It's lust, not love with Slater."

"It's love, Fin. It's okay that it's love. You don't have to deny it. That dress won't let you deny it." He turned his gaze toward the door.

"I'm not ready for love. I'm not. I promised that I wouldn't date unless I told you. You had to approve him. You don't approve. This is—"

He dropped to one knee and gazed into her eyes. "Breathe with me." He inhaled and she inhaled with him like she'd done a bazillion times over the years when her emotions overwhelmed her. It had been years since she needed him to calm her.

"Repeat after me, Fin," he said softly. "I'm safe."

"I don't feel safe," she replied.

"You're safe or I wouldn't leave. And *I'm going to leave you with him.*"

The air whooshed from her lungs. *No. No. You can't leave.* "Please, don't leave me." She sounded desperate. *This was not how this night was supposed to end.*

"Fin, I raised you to tell the truth and you're not being honest," he said. The blue in his eyes glittered with gold. "You told me earlier today that you wanted to date him. I've accepted the fact that you love him. It's time for *you* to admit you love him."

Her chin quivered as she shook her head.

"Inhale, Fin." He took in a deep breath, and she followed his lead inhaling with him as she'd done so many times before, since she'd met him. "You're married, Fin. The bracelets bond you for life to him and..." He closed his eyes and rubbed his lips together. "I can't take you home with me. But I love you, Fin. I love you more than I ever imagined possible."

"I didn't come for this. I came for you. I came to support you. I came because you asked and because I love you. I came for no other reason—not for a husband, not for someone to replace you as my guardian or protector."

He glanced to his left and then at her. "This is what you came here for—a husband who will love and protect you, and

Slater Vogel will do both. He has the ability to protect you in ways I never will."

"But I'm not one of you. I don't need special protecting. I'm not magical. I'm not—"

"Stop."

She sat down on his thigh and wrapped her arms around him, clinging to him. "There's been a huge mistake. I can't do this. I can't lose you. Tell them there's been a mistake. They'll listen to you. If you take me home, I won't go back to college. I'll go to the local college here, in town. I'll never leave our state, our county, our town. I promise, I'll do anything you want as long as you take me home and promise we'll always be family. Always."

"You married my distant cousin. You *married* into my family, and will therefore, always be my family." He whispered into her ear, "There is nothing I can do, and everyone is watching us. If you don't pull it together, I'll be forbidden to see you. If that happens, I will have to comply. Please, breathe, and then introduce me to your husband. Follow my breathing pattern and we'll both get through this—together."

While she pressed her chest against his, she followed his breathing pattern until she could feel the beat of his heart matching her own. "I feel out of control."

"But you're hiding it now," he whispered. "Remember, you can be chaotic inside, but calm outside. It's a good chaos, not bad—and I know the difference."

"I don't know that I can do that."

"I have faith in you. Now, introduce me to your husband." He squeezed her tightly. "You can do this. Tell me something about Slater as you stand up."

Her chin quivered as she rose. "Slater lives in the house next door to my friend Sienna Singleton Davis—the one I'm living with. I told you about Sienna. She is the one I always volunteer with during the holidays. She has triplets and invited me to live with her after the fire destroyed my apartment."

Liam stood and smiled like he did the first day he dropped her off at her new school, having reminded her that she had nothing to worry about because she was under his protection. "Sienna is really nice. So that means you'd met Slater before today?"

"Yes. We've babysat Sienna's kids together," she said softly, almost losing the battle with her emotions to grab onto him and never let him go. "This afternoon, he walked me to your door to introduce himself to you, but I made him leave. You were angry with me, and I thought you needed a little time to process the video or reel or whatever it was that went viral. I'm sorry I made him leave. He didn't want to upset you. He was planning to talk with you tomorrow. Is it okay if I properly introduce you to him now?"

"I'd like that," he said.

She couldn't tell whether he really wanted to officially meet him or if all of it was for appearances. "Okay."

She turned and noticed what Liam had seen all along— the entire Vogel family was staring at her and Liam. Slater held no expression, but Wenzel had the biggest grin on his face that she'd seen on him yet. The jerk was too pleased with himself. He'd gotten everything he'd wanted, everything he'd brought her here to accomplish.

Taking Liam's hand, she led him straight to Slater.

"Hey," she said softly.

The men to the sides and back of Slater retreated one step in unison, as if they were telling her and Liam that they had Slater's back, not theirs. Sides had been chosen and they were most definitely on Slater's side, not hers or Liam's. She'd always been an outsider, but Liam hadn't. The man had lost his family, and now he'd found one with these people. She didn't want to ruin that for him. As much as she didn't like the way things went down that evening, she didn't want Liam to suffer because of it.

Slater looked at her and then Liam. His gaze dropped to her hand in Liam's and frowned.

"Slater, this is Liam," she announced. "Liam, this is the guy I was telling you about earlier today...Um, the poker player who has an exercise channel thing that I don't subscribe to."

Slater held out his hand. "I've heard a lot about you, Liam. I'm sorry we started off on the wrong foot. And what I'm about to ask has been made kind of a moot point since we're married, but I'd be honored if you'd give me your blessing to marry Fin."

Liam let go of her hand and shook Slater's. "Of course, you have my blessing. I am happy for the both of you. If you ever need anything, just let me know, and I'll be there."

Slater pulled Liam into a man hug and let him go. "Thanks, man. When you're in Vegas training with Wenzel, call me. I'll come down and join in on the fun. I won't be visiting you in Texas when you're training with Logan. Logan isn't fun, but he might be your kind of fun. Fin and I will come to Georgia to visit after you complete all your training. You'll have to tell us about the laws you've learned from your time with Logan, and how you intend to keep people on the right side of it. You've done a great job already—Fin is proof of that."

"Logan is my kind of fun," Liam mumbled. "Fin might like to visit Logan's ranch in Exorcise, Texas. Logan's wife Aurora is sweet and would get along well with Fin. Y'all should reconsider visiting while I'm there. They have several guest houses now."

"We'll consider it," Slater said in a tone that told her and

Liam that visiting Texas wouldn't be on her agenda, ever. "We're about to get on the dance floor. Are you gonna mix it up and party like the rest of us?"

"I'm too wet behind the ears for Vogel partying. I still have a lot to learn about warrior angels. So, I'm gonna take a step back and sit this one out." Liam placed his hand at Finley's back.

She leaned into him before she realized what she was doing.

Slater's gaze turned hard. The look he gave Liam seemed to be one of murder—a slow and tortured murder.

A shiver ran down her spine. Quickly, she righted herself to the stiffest and straightest standing position she could muster, hoping to heal some of the damage she'd done between the two men she loved.

Slater's gaze softened, but only slightly.

Her loyalty had always been with Liam, and that loyalty remained strong, but bruised. She had to convince Liam that her feelings for Slater were lust, nothing more. That she wasn't going to be intimate with Slater. That she'd fight for him, even if he wouldn't fight for her. "Maybe I'll si—"

"Go dance with your husband," Liam insisted. "And let me be the proud honorary dad."

Dad? Why would you say that? Do you really feel that way? Did Wenzel put that crap in your head? I've loved you forever and you love me. You love me…as your honorary daughter?

She hugged him even though his words struck her heart. "I know we—"

"You're newlyweds and need some time alone together," Liam interrupted her. "Have fun tonight, but let me know you're safe at home every night, like usual, so I won't worry."

"You never have to worry about *my wife*," Slater said. "I'm a warrior angel. I will destroy anyone who attempts to separate me from Finely. She's *mine*. She doesn't need anyone else."

"She *needs* me," Liam said. "A daughter always needs her father."

"You have a lot to learn, *cousin*," Slater said. "Fin, come on. I know you can dance. I loved watching you get your groove on in the evenings."

She cringed. "I don't call dancing before bedtime with the kids at Sienna's house *getting my groove on.*"

Slater held both his hands out to her and smiled that sexy smile which elicited butterflies to flutter and fly in her belly. "I'm not talking about that."

She placed her hands in his. "Then what are you talking about?"

He smiled and swayed from side-to-side. "Baby, I'm talking about the nights when you lose yourself to the music and forget I'm there. Seeing you dance under the light of the moon and stars, like you're calling out for a partner, waiting for your true love to come." He gently tugged and she landed in his arms, pressed against his front. "I'm your true love, Fin. I'm your dance partner for life." He kissed her cheek. "You're mine, Finley Vogel, and no one will take you from me."

"Wow, her dress changed to crimson again," someone said.

Finley stiffened and backed away from Slater. "I want to go home." She looked at Liam. "I want to go home. Now. Right. Freaking. Now."

No one moved to help her. Not one person.

"We're not leaving, yet," Slater stated as if she had to obey his decision.

Glancing around the room, she noted everyone's eyes seemed to be glued on her. But it was Wenzel's gaze and smug grin that drew her in, held her still, and sent her off kilter. *You got what you wanted from me. But you're the one who's going to feel my wrath for taking my Liam from me.*

While her mind was set on a time delay, her body ran at warp speed toward Wenzel. The two parts of her split into chaos, ready to attack and fight.

Suddenly, someone grabbed her from behind, lifted her up, stopping her from reaching the man who ruined her life.

CHAPTER THIRTEEN

Finley

"**C**alm down," Slater said softly in her ear.

Since when has those two words ever effectively calmed anyone down who was fired up and out for blood? Never. And it didn't calm her down one iota. In fact, it riled her up even more.

Kicking her legs, she attempted to somehow injure Wenzel. But the more she flailed, the more frustrated and angrier she became. She screamed at the top of her lungs. "I fucking hate you, Wenzel Vogel. You tricked me. You ruined my fucking life. I hate you. I fucking hate you!"

Wenzel smiled, seemingly pleased at her outburst. "Take her home, Slater. I'll bring breakfast tomorrow and see if she still *fucking hates me* after you've fucked out all of her sexual frustrations."

"I will never stop hating you," she screamed. "I don't ever want to see your face again."

His smile broadened, infuriating her further.

"That's going to be tough to make happen, since we're family," he said. "And because I'm head of the family. When I call, I expect you to *come running*."

"I'm not running anywhere for you," she shouted. "I'd rather die than obey you."

"She's going to be great in bed, Slater," Wenzel said. "You're a lucky man…a very lucky man."

Slater carried her out of the room and through hallways and gathering halls and more hallways and corridors until they exited to the outside in the cool night air.

"If I put you down, are you going to run back inside to attack Wenzel again?" Slater asked.

"I might," she grumbled. The farther they were from Wenzel and his home the calmer she became. Not that she was calm. She wasn't. Not by a long shot. But she felt sprinkles of calm here and there softening the chaos roaring inside her to be let out.

"Then I better get you home before you can turn around." He carried her to his SUV and buckled her into the passenger seat. He closed the door and swiftly ran to the other side as another round of fury and chaos swept through her. While he started the car and zipped out of the parking space and out onto the private road, she fumbled with the seatbelt.

While she continued to press the button and pull the belt, her hands shook with so much rage that she couldn't release herself from the confinement.

"Wenzel—"

"Don't even mention his name," she yelled. "He tricked me. I didn't give permission. I didn't agree to the bracelets. I didn't even agree to marrying you. I answered *your* question, not his."

She grabbed the hem of her skirt and tried to cover more of her legs. "I want to go back to this morning. I want to go on a date with you. I want to take it slow. I want to be normal. I want Liam to be Liam, not an angel with wings. I want him to be my overly protective Liam who everyone is afraid of. I want him to be angry with me for coming in one minute late for dinner." She tugged as hard as she could on the soft fabric that should've ripped long ago, but not only did it not rip, it didn't stretch either. "This might never come off."

"It will disintegrate as soon as we have sex. It's a traditional virgin Love Angel's wedding dress. I've only read about magical dresses, but never seen one until tonight. I recognized it immediately. I wasn't one of the first to meet you because I didn't know you were the special guest. It's a damn good thing you weren't hot for any of my cousins or I'd have to kill them," Slater said. "And don't think I didn't notice your moment with Liam. You're not going to have another one of those. You won't be seeing him anytime soon."

"I left my backpack and phone at Liam's house. You're going to drive me there tonight. Or I'll drive myself." *I'm calling Rager to come and get me. He'll come. I know he will.*

"You're not going there. The man I'm not supposed to mention will bring your clothes and phone tomorrow. He'll make sure you have everything you need. And you'll need to be prepared for a lecture from him about apologies and forgiveness. He's going to throw us a real wedding party at his home in Vegas. He's big on celebrations of any kind." He glanced at her. "Ah shit. You're so angry you can't hide it. Your dress does show more than love colors, and so does your aura. You've kept it all bottled up until now."

"I'm not angry." *I'm so freaking pissed I want to cry.* She closed her eyes and tried to think of Liam and the breathing techniques he'd taught her. Only now, their connection seemed to be severed.

"You are angry, but I don't understand why. You were

going to move in with me when we got back to Nevada," Slater said. "We would've gotten married by Monday night at the latest. I'd wager we would've gone to a chapel and married tomorrow. It doesn't matter that we got married today. The fact is that a marriage between us was inevitable."

She shook her head. "I didn't agree to marry you. I didn't agree to those bracelets. And that ceremony—whatever strange illusion all that was—made me lose the only person who I ever fully trusted. I lost the only family I've ever had. Now, I have no one."

"You have me."

She nodded and wiped the tears from her eyes. "Yeah." *You're not Liam. He promised to protect me and he didn't. He let Wenzel pimp me out—*

"You have both of my families," Slater said. "Our kids will have human grandparents and an aunt and uncle and cousins, and then the entire Vogel family of angels. You and our future children will have the best of both worlds."

Tears continued falling down her cheeks as quickly as she wiped them away. "Uh huh."

"You haven't really lost Liam," Slater said. "He's still your family. He's related to me. He'll be at all the family gatherings, although you'll have limited exposure to him."

"You don't understand. Liam took that jerk's side over mine." *Liam chose Wenzel instead of me. He lied to me. I can't believe he lied to me.*

"Liam did, as he should've. Sometimes it takes a while to understand why Wenzel does what he does. Wenzel looks at things long-term—as in thousands of years, not in days, weeks, months, or five-year increments. I don't know what he said to you prior to the party, but whatever it was, take the time to analyze it with as little emotion as possible."

"Yeah." *You'd take his side over mine, too.*

"I don't want you to be sad or angry," he said.

"I'm fine."

"Oh no. I know the *I'm fine* comment. That means you're not even close to *fine*. When my mom would say that to my dad…" He whistled. "We were all in trouble."

She couldn't even find it in her to offer a half-hearted laugh, and he was funny. So she shifted, facing the door, showing him more of her back as she continued to think of ways to circumvent Wenzel and Slater's plans to keep Liam away.

"Baby," he said softly. "We're almost home."

"Home?"

"I bought it a couple years ago when I opened up Brock's restaurant. I stay in it when I need to get away or when I have private discussions with Wenzel, or when I need to check in on Brock, which is much more frequently than I had originally planned. I have a house in Vegas near Wenzel's, too. I'm just going to get this hard conversation out of the way. Wenzel and I spend a lot of time together. He's my best friend, so you're going to see him often. It's important that whatever animosity you have toward him be resolved soon."

"No." Sobs broke out between each of her staggered breaths.

"Sex isn't gonna happen tonight, is it?"

She sniffled. "You can go and snuggle with *Wenzel*. I'm off limits—for the rest of my life."

"I don't know who to be angry with—Liam or Wenzel or you. I want you to be happy and begging for my cock, not crying and ready to rip it off." He drove down a gravel drive that led to a white cement driveway and a beautiful south-western style ranch home with a huge empty porch.

The hangar of the garage opened and he drove inside. "It's a five bedroom, five bath house with media and exercise rooms along with an office and sunroom. There's a heated pool in the backyard. Our room is on the opposite end of the house from the others. There are a lot of weapons inside which, I assume, is not something you're used to. I'm acknowledging that fact as something you'll have to deal with as my wife. I will try and be sensitive about your anxiety with all the change that is being thrown at you."

"Yeah, you're *super sensitive*. You've shown off that side of you this evening." She managed to push the button on the buckle lock and pull the belt in just the right way that her shaky hands released the strap holding her hostage. She wiped the last of the tears that had fallen down her cheeks.

Her bare feet hit the smooth, immaculately clean floor of the six-car garage. "Do you hire a cleaning crew or do it yourself?"

"I do my own cleaning. But if you want, you can take over that duty. My human mom and dad raised me to pick up after myself *and* my older siblings because they're slobs."

"Hmph."

"Come on, baby," he cooed. "Give me a break. You love me. I love you. Let's make love and babies and live happily ever after."

She closed the door to the SUV and walked to the door to the house, meeting him.

"You're not going to make this easy, are you?" he asked.

She shrugged. "I got blindsided and then—"

"Will you at least admit that your issue is not with me?" He stood facing her in front of the door to the house.

She nodded. "But we're not married. I never—"

"We're married. It's a fact." He swept her up into his arms, cradling her.

"What are you doing?" She tried for a tone of outrage, but it came out more like a needy plead for love.

"I'm carrying you over the threshold. It's what husbands do." He stepped inside.

She curled her arms around him, and she liked that he

bounced her up enough she caught air and dropped down, floating softly back in his arms. His muscles flexed and her insides melted enough that it took her a few moments to remember she was upset.

Gazing up into his golden eyes, the memory of their first kiss sent heat waves through her. She hadn't been this emotionally unstable since she started puberty. Her world had turned upside down during that phase of her life, but Liam had been there to help calm her, control her urges. It was then that she pledged to remain a virgin until marriage. It was then that she learned to focus on children, ignoring her sexual desires.

But she couldn't ignore her desire for Slater much longer. She wanted him and as much as she wanted to deny those feelings, she couldn't. Because the truth of matter remained. She would've either stayed in Georgia with Liam or gone back to Nevada and married Slater, and she couldn't deny that fact any longer.

For self-preservation, more like emotional stability, she broke eye contact with him and gave a sweeping glance around the large hallway. On each side of the huge foyer, glass cases filled with ornate sheaths with equally beautifully crafted swords and daggers were displayed and extended along the entire length and height of the walls.

"You weren't kidding about the weapons," she mumbled.

"I've told you this before; I'm serious about everything, Fin. Absolutely everything."

CHAPTER FOURTEEN

Slater

While he walked the cream halls and rooms of his house telling Finley about where he acquired the different types of weapons and their significance in history and to him personally, he liked the way she shifted in his arms, pushing her perky breasts closer to his chest. She didn't ask any questions, but he could tell she was listening intently.

The exercise room that rivaled Wenzel's seemed to impress and settle whatever nerves she'd had about being alone in his house with him. Maybe it was her fighting spirit that kept her unfazed by the rest of the weaponry in the house and steadied her breathing. Or it could've been just being in his arms. Whichever it was, or if it was something else entirely, he didn't care. As long as she remained compliant and on her way to happy again, he held hope that the night wasn't lost to newlywed bliss.

The closer he moved toward the bedroom, the more his body ached to empty his seed inside her. He'd wait until she was ready to consummate the marriage, but he hoped he wouldn't have to wait much longer. He hurt inside and out from wanting her so badly. If he could make her forget about Wenzel and Liam, he was confident that he could seduce her.

For being a full-fledged love angel, she wasn't in a rush to jump into bed. And he worried that Wenzel had screwed him over in marrying them on the spot—a marriage that would've happened with Liam's blessing within a couple days anyway.

"Would you like something to drink?" he asked.

"Mmm." She rubbed her nose against his neck. "No thanks. I like your house. I feel safe here."

"You are safe here." He stepped into the bedroom.

She lifted her little nose from his neck and looked around. "This is *nice*."

"You like it?" *Maybe all isn't lost. If you'll just let me kiss you, really kiss you, we'll be stripping…I'll be stripping and your dress will disintegrate as we make love.*

"I love it," she said in a sultry and seductive drawl.

He swallowed hard at the sound of her voice. *You're the sexiest woman in the entire world and you're all mine.*

"I love your cream-colored, fluffy duvet," she said in that same sexy voice.

Every inch of his skin heated with a need to be naked with her under him. "Yeah?" *We are so gonna make babies tonight.*

"And the midnight-blue stained wood of the bed is beautiful. The frame looks sturdy…uh, big…um…" She rubbed her lips together. "I like that the wall color is a pinkish-cream. The pillows are so pretty. I love pillows. I love being surrounded by so much fluffy softness in a coating of such strength."

I've not even shown you my wings and you're describing them as pillows. I don't know whether to throw you on my bed and start fucking you or continue to talk and see if you soften some more. I need you to want me as much as I want you.

"My mom decorated the bedroom," he said. "Mom said that I needed a bedroom oasis with a touch of femininity to balance the extreme masculinity of the rest of the house. I told her to do whatever she wanted. She'll be glad to hear you love it."

"I love this room," she mumbled.

I want you to do whatever you want in this room, like part your legs and let me into that untouched pussy. "Thanks."

"Your mom did a wonderful job," she whispered.

I don't want to talk about my mom anymore. I want you to be tilting your chin up for a kiss so we can get to the good stuff. "I'll tell her you said that. I probably need to tell her I married you."

She drew a little of her bottom lip into her mouth and held it with her teeth, then slid her tongue across it and closed her mouth. "Is she going to be upset?"

"A little," he admitted. *She's going to be furious, and I don't care.* "But she called me about the kiss that went viral. I told her that I convinced you to move in with me, and that I'd marry you the minute I got the chance." *And she said I better not elope or there'd be hell to pay.*

The dress Finley wore turned a beautiful crimson. He hoped she was thinking about that kiss in the restaurant because he sure was.

He tilted his head toward her, praying she would give in to the inevitable.

She lifted her chin and her lips met his in a tender, chaste kiss.

"I love you, Fin," he said.

She tightened her hold on him as he climbed onto the bed and gently placed her on top of the covers. With her under him, he kissed her softly.

Her hands caressed his chest and back. Sparks of energy and love with each touch of her skin sent his desire soaring to new heights.

She unzipped his pants. "We're not going to…I just want to…um…do…"

"What do you want to do?" *Tell me you want me to make love to you.* "It's all up to you, Fin. There's no rush." *I'm in a rush. Don't make me wait.*

She pushed his pants and boxer briefs over his ass. "Mmm. You feel so good."

With his cock free, he rocked forward. The magical fabric of her panties opened for the tip of his cock. He parted her wet folds. Juices lubricated the head of his cock. Her walls softened as his cock dipped into her pussy.

"Wait. I'm not ready," she whispered in a sultry tone that seemed in opposition to her words. The crimson color of her dress flashed white before shifting back to crimson.

Maybe you're not ready. But you want to be with me. He shifted back and lifted his cock up on her belly. "I promise, there's no rush." *There's not going to be any sex tonight. I need to just accept it and do a full seduction tomorrow. One more day of blue balls isn't going to kill me.*

The most alluring shimmering pink flush appeared on her skin. "I want to, it's just…this dress. This night. This situation."

"Talk to me. How can I make this better for you?"

"I want to change into something pretty. This dress makes me feel dirty. I can't stop thinking about the way everyone at the party looked at me. I'm comfortable naked, but this…it's like there was just enough fabric to cover the barest of essentials but not enough to make it acceptable to wear in public."

"The only way to get the dress off you is for us to make love. The dress will literally disintegrate as soon as we both climax. I'm sorry, but the minute you put it on, the only way it was coming off was marriage followed by sex."

The sound of her gasp surprised him.

"So if you weren't there, I would've been stuck wearing this thing until you eventually showed up?" she asked.

"Yes. Or if someone else interested you."

She rolled her eyes. "As if anyone would."

"Good answer," he said.

Her cheeks reddened, but she glanced away. The way her brows crinkled and her golden eyes morphed to a summer sky blue, she seemed to be in a mental battle of her own.

Since the day he met her, he'd been playing the long game. He knew she was like him, but he didn't know which angel DNA claimed her lineage. He hadn't cared. He wanted her, and he'd wait as long as needed in order to have her. Now was no exception. The woman had denied her body for years, and for a love angel—from what he'd read—that wasn't normal. But she was an exceptional woman. So, if she needed time, then he would give it to her.

"What if I put a dress over this one?" she asked.

"From what I've read." He rolled over onto his back and slid his arm under her neck. With a little nudge of his finger, he encouraged her to snuggle him.

Sweet, caressing fingers glided across his chest and downward. "What have you read?"

"Part of my training was to learn about the different kinds of angels. Wenzel has thousands of scrolls about the origins of the angels who followed Lucifer and fell to earth with him, and of those angels who have come and were born to combat the evil those fallen angels of Lucifer generate. Love angels have hundreds of scrolls dedicated to their history, rituals, practices, and abilities. The wedding dress is among the rituals. If it is mistakenly given to a non-love angel, then the dress will adjust to that angel's modesty. It will slip on and off like a normal dress. But when put on a female love angel, it fuses with the angel's cosmic being. It shifts to make an ideal fit on the love angel, not for her, but for the man who loves her. The dress you're wearing is my fantasy. In a perfect world, it's what I would have you wear at our wedding."

"This?" she asked. "You'd want me to wear this in front of your family and friends?"

"Yeah," he mumbled. "I hope someone got a picture of us."

Instead of rolling toward him, she rolled away, her back facing his side. "This is lingerie, not a wedding dress." She swung her legs forward and over the edge of the bed and bolted upright. She spun around and faced him lounging on the bed. Her cheeks flushed a glorious reddish-pink. "Slater Vogel, you're going to…"

Staring at her didn't seem to make her finish her sentence. The pause she extended well past acceptable silence continued. Her cheeks grew more red than pink and the flush extended over her torso.

While he watched her decide what to say next or whether to continue with the sentence at all, her irises morphed from blue to gold and back, again and again. Her gaze never left his, but her normally light sugary scent became heavy, like a thick honey. He couldn't help but flare his nostrils to smell more of her aroma with each inhalation.

"Slater," she whispered.

"Yeah?" *What have you decided to do, beautiful?*

"I'm not an angel. I don't have wings. I don't understand what is going on here, but whatever it is…" She tilted her head slightly to the side and wistfully smiled. "Part of me wants this all to be true. But it's not. This dress is some kind of illusion. This whole night has to be some kind of crazy dream. If I give in and make love to you, I'm going to wake up right before climax. But if this isn't a dream…" She made a noise that sounded a lot like a moan. "And we do make love…" She rubbed her lips together and he wanted those lips wrapped around his cock. "I will have broken a promise. I don't break promises."

"What promise will you have broken?" *I'll take care of this right now, and we'll be back on track to having a real honeymoon.*

"No sex before marriage."

"We're married, Fin. It's legal in both the earthly court system and the heavenly one, too."

"But I never agreed. I answered your question. I didn't answer Wenzel's. It's not real."

"Do you love me?"

"Yes," she said so softly, he could barely hear her.

"Do you want me to call someone here so we can have another marriage ceremony where you explicitly tell the officiate that you take me as your husband? Would that make this legal for you?"

She nodded.

"Wenzel marries everyone in the family. Everyone. There are no exceptions to this hard and fast rule. But he's already married us, so I could call someone outside the family to marry us. But they might not be appreciative of the way that dress fits you."

"Stetson Ross could marry us. He wouldn't have a problem with my dress. Sienna could be our witness."

"No. If Stetson marries us, my mom and dad would need to be there and they wouldn't appreciate a love angel's wedding dress, and they know what I am. We'd have to invite Wenzel over to—"

"No." She turned her back on him and walked into the bathroom, closed the door, and locked it.

Fuck. Fuckity. Fuck. He bolted out of bed and stopped at the door with his hand on the doorknob, ready to rip the thing off its hinges. Instead, he closed his eyes and inhaled. *I don't want her to hate me. Keep it together. It's the chaos in her that sent her in there.*

"Let's compromise," he said.

"How?"

"Accept that we're married and have sex so your dress isn't an issue anymore. Then we buy a wedding dress that you pick out. We call everyone—my human family, Sienna, Blade, their friends and kids, Liam and Wenzel, too. We go to Vegas and exchange vows in a church with a human officiate. We take pictures and have a reception and do the whole thing this weekend."

"I don't want Wenzel anywhere near me," she stated.

"If Wenzel isn't there, then Liam can't be there. Wenzel is my best friend, Fin. He would have to be my best man. It would be an insult to both me and him, if he weren't there."

"Fine. Whatever. Have a nice night," she said.

"Fin, please don't be like this." *It's Wenzel I need to blame for her being in there.*

"Leave me alone. There will be no sex tonight, tomorrow, or ever. I'll find my own ride to the airport Monday. And I'm not moving in with you."

Fury like he'd never known before rose within him. He wanted to destroy something. Anything. He needed to fight, to battle, to win. Mostly, he needed to calm down enough to think clearly. He needed the woman on the other side of the door to be reasonable, which was an impossibility with a love angel. Chaos ruled them. Fin might be able to hide the chaos, but it was there, would always be there, waiting patiently for the right time to come out. This wasn't the right time.

Instead of saying something he'd instantly regret, he needed to call in the big guns.

There was no other option.

If this didn't work. Nothing would.

CHAPTER FIFTEEN

Slater

Slater strode to the nightstand next to his bed and opened the drawer. He grabbed his phone. His fingers flew over the screen. His wings came out and enclosed him to give him total privacy as he heard the first ring.

"What's wrong?" his mom answered.

"Finley. I don't know what to do. Wenzel upset her. She's locked herself in the bathroom and refuses to come out."

"You eloped, didn't you?" she said in the accusing tone he expected.

"Yeah."

"And you're not sorry?" she used that same tone.

"Nope. Wenzel and I kind of tricked her into the marriage."

The noise she made produced the guilty response she'd

instilled in him. Then she amped up the guilt with her next words. "He eloped and Wenzel was involved."

"Oh no," Dad mumbled. "You should talk to Finley, honey. Woman to woman. You can rail on Wenzel with her. You now have someone you can complain to about him."

"Tell Dad that complaining about Wenzel is not going to help. I don't need her angrier than she already is. I want her out of the damn bathroom and in my bed."

"Give her the phone," Mom said. "But know that I'm getting a wedding out of this. If you had listened to me, then she wouldn't be cock blocking you right now. Think on that, while I fix this for you. Now give her the fucking phone, Slater. I may not be the *Supreme Guardian Angel Wenzel Vogel*, but do not fuck with Mama Bear."

"This is on you," Dad shouted. "Mom is going to save you from your blue balls, son. You better thank her with a celebrity wedding she can invite all her friends to that will make them jealous. And you're making Wenzel pay for all Mom's friends' and families' flights. And it better be this Saturday!"

Mom started with soft laughter which increased to full belly, struggling to breathe laughs. "Yes. Wenzel better send his planes, because I'm inviting everyone—even your cousin Jenny and her girlfriend who live in France."

"You're going to make my life miserable, aren't you?" he grumbled.

"Yes, Slater. I most certainly am. Now give your lovely wife the phone," she said in the sickly-sweet tone she used as her battle cry. The woman fought and won against Wenzel Vogel. She even gained the man's respect in the process.

"Yes, ma'am." His wings receded inside his back as he walked to the bathroom door. He knocked. "Fin?"

"I'm not coming out," Finley said.

"My mom is on the phone. Will you please talk to her?" he said.

"What did you say to her?" she asked.

He couldn't tell, but she sounded panicked. "That we eloped, and Wenzel was involved, and that you won't come out of the bathroom."

"You told her that I'm in the dang bathroom? That we're fighting?" She gasped. "What the heck is wrong with you? Oh my goodness. Now she's going to hate me. Slater Vogel, I'm so..." She made a high pitch scream very much like his mom did when she was frustrated with his dad.

Slater's mom cleared her throat. In the softest and most gentle voice he'd ever heard come from his mom's mouth, she whispered, "You were supposed to protect her from Wenzel and you didn't. She's scared, Slater. She feels alone and vulnerable, and honestly, she is. Slide the phone under the door so I can talk to her."

His heart ached. The one thing about his mom that he could always count on was the honest truth, whether it hurt or not. He hadn't protected Finley from Wenzel. He'd found a way to get what he wanted, and he used Wenzel as much as Wenzel used him in the surprise wedding ceremony. He wanted Liam out of the picture and Wenzel did, too. He and Wenzel never disagreed on anything because their goals were clear. Do everything in their power to ensure the balance of power tipped on the side of good. Marrying Finley, the love of his life, tipped that balance even farther. It ensured their warrior numbers would increase. She wanted him as much as he wanted her, but he should've held off. He should've explained the details of the dress. He should've told her about the bracelets. He didn't.

Crouching down, he slid the phone under the door. "I'm sorry, Fin."

"Mrs. Vogel?" Finley asked. "Oh, sorry. Um, I didn't know he had a different last name."

She really didn't listen to anything I ever told her when we babysat. I've dug a deep hole, Mom. Help me get out of it.

Finley

Sitting on the cushioned chair in the corner of the bathroom, near the closet, she listened to Slater's mom—Noelle Tarington.

"Slater has been talking about you for months," Noelle said. "I knew he was in love the minute he told me he was babysitting for Blade. Don't get me wrong. He loves kids. He's an incredible uncle and has changed tons of diapers. He will drop everything to babysit his niece and nephew, but other kids…he's not going to volunteer for diaper duty. So, I asked who the girl was that would be babysitting with him."

Finley laughed. "He seemed so enthusiastic about taking care of the kids."

"He enjoys taking care of Blade's boys. They run around and play, but Slater's mind is always working on levels I can't comprehend. He moves the kids into place for battles and competitions and watches what they instinctively do. So playing is one thing, but staying the night or watching them for a couple days? He would never volunteer for that if he wasn't trying to impress a girl—something I've never actually seen him ever make an effort to do. Girls try to impress him, never the other way around."

"I honestly never noticed what he was doing, only that the kids were safe and happy. The boys get rough when they play. Slater handled all the cuts and scrapes. He was great at redirection to distract them. And he is king of changing diapers."

Noelle laughed and her laughter made Finley laugh, too. "I told him to ask you on a date, but he said that he never got the chance, until today. And I'm sorry that the wedding ceremony sucked. Slater will be making that up to you *and* to me. I made him promise me that there would be a wedding in Vegas on Saturday, along with a reception..." She continued telling Finley about Wenzel paying for flights for everyone and shelling out a lot of money for a wedding and reception fit for royalty. She offered ideas to make Wenzel's life miserable with details of the wedding.

What the women didn't realize was that Wenzel loved a big celebration and could probably pull something off like what Noelle wanted in hours, not days. And that Wenzel would remain in control. He'd tell Liam when and where he would be, who he could talk to and about what. That any sign of her affection toward Liam would have some kind of consequence that would end in her never seeing him again.

The more excited Noelle got about the wedding, the more depressed Finley became.

"That sounds wonderful," Finley said.

"What's wrong? Are the diamond earrings for all the guests, too much?" Noelle asked.

"Oh gosh, no. I'd throw in diamond necklaces for all the guests, too. We'll set a carat minimum."

"Now we're talking." Noelle didn't say anything, and so Finley remained quiet, too.

Silence.

Silence.

"Well, it was—"

"Finley, I'm sorry Slater didn't protect you from Wenzel," Noelle said.

"There was no protection needed. Wenzel wasn't a threat. He's big and strong and handsome, and he likes to get his way, but I was never in danger. I didn't need protecting from anyone," Finley said. "I love your son. Wenzel was aware of my feelings and—"

"He forced you into a wedding ceremony. He probably turned your reasons for not getting married into reasons *to* get married. And because he's the only person allowed to marry anyone in his family, he got everyone at the party to cheer him on. The next thing you know, you're married to my son when you wanted a beautiful dress and to walk down an aisle with your friends and family in attendance. I've learned a lot about the type of ceremonies that the Vogel side of Slater's family perform. Certain words need to be used. They don't have to be said at the same time. Much of the reasoning for that is so that the type of people Wenzel and all his family are can keep their identities and their rituals secret."

"I'm not sure what you mean. I wasn't—"

"When I was fighting to keep custody of Slater from Wenzel, there were many secret conversations that I had with Wenzel. One of which was about the wedding ceremony that Slater would one day have. Slater was less than six weeks old when we had the discussion. But Wenzel laid it out for me. He said that once Slater met the girl he fell in love with, he'd give him two months to get the girl to agree to marriage and then get it done within a week of that agreement. If Slater didn't make it happen, then Wenzel would get involved. He'd isolate the girl and Slater in the old ways—whatever that means—and marry them. The key words to make the two husband and wife were 'I do' during any point of the isolation period. Those two words bind the couple in matrimony. The words don't even need to come out at the same time. An 'I' and a 'do' could be in two separate sentences. So, if you said either of those words, your marriage is considered official. My son knows it. Wenzel and all the Vogels know it, too."

Finley had no words. Slater had tricked her into marrying him. *No. He didn't trick me. He wouldn't.* "Slater wouldn't—"

"I know my son. He would've. He's head-over-heels in love with you. He's been desperate for you to notice him for months. I'm sure he'd told Wenzel all about you. I'm also sure that Wenzel vetted you and found at least one way to get close to a family member or friend or both. Slater might not know the lengths to which Wenzel will make sure he complies with their laws, but he might. My son is a good man. He's also just like Wenzel and will do things the rest of us wouldn't in order to keep us safe, and that would include marrying you, *by any means necessary*."

Finley swallowed hard.

"I'm going to tell you a few things about Slater that you need to know, but you might not like hearing or knowing, or maybe you will. I don't know."

"Uh huh," Finley mumbled. *You've already said a lot of things I didn't want to hear.*

"He dated a girl when he was a teen. She wanted to have sex. He did not. She set him up to make it look like they were sexually active. There was a lot of inappropriate touching. They did not have sex. She ended up pregnant and told everyone it was his in an attempt to force him into marriage. Wenzel got involved. The truth came out that she was having sex with a guy who graduated the year before. Slater hasn't touched a woman since then. He doesn't even offer a handshake to anyone who isn't family. So when that kiss you and Slater shared appeared in my social media feed, I had a feeling that either the fates aligned for my son to finally get what he wanted or Wenzel had somehow orchestrated a situation which would force you to notice my son and show your interest in him as your husband."

"Okay?" *What do you want from me?*

"My son is a virgin."

"Uh, all right?"

"He's honorable, and he's been hurt by women."

"Yes, ma'am." *He distances himself from women, except for me. I do like that about him.*

"I need you to go out there and show my son not all women are liars and cheats. I need you to show him that you love him. That you want him. That you want *his* children. That there is nothing on this planet that matters more than the love between a wife and her husband. That no matter what happens in his or your life that love will conquer all obstacles, even the greatest of all obstacles—Wenzel Vogel."

I believe in love, too. Finley cracked open the door. "You're a great mom, Mrs. Tarington. Slater is lucky to have been raised by you. I'm going to hand him the phone." She opened the door wide enough to slip her hand through.

"I'll handle Wenzel. I can't wait to meet you on Saturday for the wedding ceremony you and my son and I deserve."

"See you Saturday." Finley opened the door wider as her heart gained another wound.

While she gazed at her handsome husband standing before her nude and hopeful, she handed him the phone.

He placed his hand under hers and stepped forward as he raised her hand holding the phone to his ear. "I love you, Mom."

"Make me some grandchildren," his mother said. "She's lovely. You're lucky to have her."

He gazed into Finley's eyes. "I am lucky to have her. She's everything I've ever wanted and needed. She's my true mate. My soulmate. My life. My love. My world."

"Make sure to tell her that every day. I love you. Congratulations." She ended the call.

"You shouldn't have gotten your mom involved in our marriage." Finley remained in the bathroom but didn't try to remove her hand from his.

"I love you. I just didn't know what else to do." He stepped closer and her dress shrunk into a bra. The panties shrunk, too.

"Are you doing that to my dress?" she asked.

He nodded. "I can't stop myself." He flicked his wrist and the phone flew from her hand, landing on the bed near his nightstand. "Please tell me you need me like I need you." He let go of her hand and cupped the back of her head and the other landed at the base of her spine, dipping her backward. One thigh pushed between hers.

Heat burst through her body, making her skin flush pink. Her breasts pressed against his chest. Juices flooded her panties, wetting his thigh. Her breath hitched from the assault of desire she withheld from him. The truth remained clear—she needed to make love to him as much as he needed to make love to her.

"I promise to love, honor, and obey you, my husband, for the rest of my life." She hadn't known where the words came from or why she was compelled to say them at that precise moment, but those words changed everything.

"*Yes*," he said on a breathless whisper.

She wrapped her legs around his hips. "Don't think for an instant that I've forgiven you."

"I..." His golden eyes shimmered with what she recognized as a deep, profound love. He carried her to the bed and climbed onto the mattress, placing her under him. "We can't make love until you forgive me."

"I'm not forgiving you."

He crawled down her body. His lips pressed a kiss between her legs. "I'm going to torture you until you forgive me."

You're a virgin. What do you know about sexual torture? "Give it your best shot. You're going to lose."

"I don't lose, Finley. I *always* win."

CHAPTER SEVENTEEN

Slater

The scent of her drove him mad. The more he kissed and licked and sucked her clit, the more control he seemed to lose. Her taste. Her moan. Her movements. They all came together as one enormous seduction.

"Why did I fall in love with a love angel?" he mumbled.

"I'm no angel, Slater. I'm human." She gasped.

He was getting close to making her forgive him. A little more. He had to keep himself under control for a little while longer. He slid a finger into her sex and searched for that special spot he'd read about in one of the many love angel scrolls detailing sexual pleasure. He curled his finger slightly and she trembled. *Found it.*

"Forgive me, Fin," he cooed. "Forgive me and I'll make love to you." He glided his finger in circles, on and off the spot, teasing her more and more. Her body trembled and she started making the sexiest sounds he'd ever heard.

"Feels so good," she moaned. "So good."

He withdrew his finger and kissed her drenched pussy.

"No, no, no. Please. Keep doing that," she begged.

"This?" He glided his finger back into position and rubbed the spot.

She spread her legs and her aroma surrounded him like a warm coating of sugary caramel and chocolate. He wanted to please her, to bring her to orgasm. He wanted to stop leaking cum and start sending it up into her channel to make a baby. He wanted to end this torture for both of them.

"Yes. Right there, my love." She shifted her hips, guiding his finger deeper. "I'm going to…Oh, Slater."

He pulled his finger from within her. "Forgive me."

"I want you. Now. Please, make love to me," she pleaded.

So close to giving in. He rose up and rubbed the helmet of his cock up and down along her slit. "Forgive me, and I'll fuck you any way you want me to."

She lifted her hips up off the covers and pushed against his cock. "Do it. Please. Do it."

"Say that you forgive me," he demanded.

"I forgive you," she whispered in a sexy sultry drawl that made him want to give her the world, yet dominate her in the most primal ways.

This is it. You're mine. He thrust his hips gently, testing her tight pussy for ease of entry. She felt so good. She was soft and beautiful and juicy and finally ready.

She arched her back, moving with him instead of countering and trying to take his cock all the way into her. Then she tilted her hips.

This was it. He was going to finally take her. She was his. All his. Forever.

He thrust harder and his entire cockhead pushed into her, opening her for more.

"Slater." She moaned as she grabbed his shoulders. "More."

Unable to do anything but take what he wanted, he thrust into her.

She welcomed him, sucking his entire length inside her virgin channel.

"Give. Me. *More*," she cried out.

He'd never felt so good in his life as he did with his cock buried deep in her pussy. She was his home, and he'd be damned if Liam or Wenzel ever screwed things up for him ever again.

With her under him, snug and needy, he slowly rocked back and forth, getting her used to his length, his girth, his rhythm. Everything described in the scrolls of love angel pleasure was true. Every line. Every word.

Her pussy sucked him in and squeezed him hard, then softened.

The more he continued the gentle rhythm of making love, the closer he came to easing her into the kind of sex he wanted to give her—the all-encompassing sexual experience he'd read about and Wenzel had told him only comes with the blessing of the Vogel Marriage Bracelets.

She squeezed and softened those pussy walls, like she was working the seed up his shaft, needing his sperm as much as he needed to give it to her. His balls were clenched and ready to unload every ounce of seed, ready to crack through the shield of her eggs and create life.

As he held back from giving in to his needs, the sparks that filled him with her touch turned into bombs of ecstasy. He couldn't hold back any longer. It didn't matter that she was a virgin. Heck, he was, too. They both needed more, and he planned to give her everything she ever wanted. He'd waited months for this moment. He wasn't waiting any longer.

As he let out his wings, he grabbed the metal enforced wooden headboard so he wouldn't go crashing through the wall. Heck, he might go crashing through the brick wall, ending up outside, anyway, with the intense amount of power coursing through every inch of his body.

He thrust and she cinched his waist with her thighs, caressing the feathers of his wings with her toes. The sexy purr that came from her mouth had him nearly coming undone. Then her fingers stroked along the inside of his wings. His desire rose ten-fold.

He shifted his hand grip, grabbing the metal rungs attached to the studs in the wall, anchoring the bed in place for making love.

She dropped her hips in one quick motion, gliding down onto his shaft to the base.

He shuddered.

Gold and white light exploded around them. His cock vibrated with so much need to create life that nothing else mattered. He pounded into her with a ferocity he couldn't contain.

"Yes," she shouted. "Yes."

She countered his moves, stroking his cock with the muscles of her channel. The gentleness of her fingers and toes caressing his wings took his need to a new level.

His wings fluttered and expanded as more pleasure rose within his body and soul. With his balls loaded with months of waiting sperm, he thrust again and gave in to the pleasure. "Mine!"

She shuddered.

"I love you," she mumbled.

His seed filled her womb while his wings wrapped around her, cradling them in softness while protecting them from the outside world.

She moaned softly as her vaginal walls squeezed his cock,

milking his rod of all its seed. Rocking her hips, she reached behind her and massaged his balls, sending the remnants of his sperm flowing from his shaft into her.

He kissed her lips softly. "I love you, Fin."

"That was not what I thought it'd be. There was no pain. It was *all pleasure*." She pulled in her bottom lip and closed her eyes. "Mmm."

Her pussy vibrated and clenched around his cock, making him instantly hard. "I need you to..." She opened her eyelids and her eyes were solid gold. She panted as she parted her lips to talk and then closed them and moaned.

"What do you need?" He barely recognized his own voice, the tone deep and sensual.

Her pussy began clenching and relaxing around his shaft. "I need you to do. That. Again."

She didn't have to ask twice. He'd make love to her for days. He'd been ready and willing for far too long.

He gripped her hips and this time, the feathers of his wings caught air as he pumped in and out of her body. His wings had never taken over control, but they did this time, seemingly knowing instinctively what to do.

"Yeah. That." She moaned, sliding her knees up his sides.

Between the beautiful vibrations from her pussy squeezing his cock and the blissful stroking of his feathers from her hands and legs and feet along the length of his wings, love, pleasure, and peace filled every inch of his body and spirit.

"I'm coming again." She arched her back and rubbed her chest against his. She parted her legs and ground her clit against him. "Please, come with me."

His balls drew up, sending sperm into his shaft so fast that his orgasm came in a mad dash to victory. His entire body tingled and shook with each incredible spurting release.

"Yes," she whispered on an exhale. She drew her knees in

toward her sides and then straightened them along the sides of his chest until her adorable little toes wiggled against the upper portion of his wings. "You're so freaking sexy. And your wings...mmm...I love them."

Without thinking, he spread his wings to show off their enormity and impress her.

"Oh shit." He curled his arms around her, squeezing her tightly as the night wind pushed against their bodies, attempting to separate them.

"You fly," she gasped.

"Not supposed to be flying right now," he mumbled. *This is not good.* "Hang onto me."

She gripped the back of his neck, clinging to him, as he got his bearings.

He flapped his wings, shifting his course from plummeting to the ground to rising toward the stars and back to the house. The light illuminating from his wings shined so brightly that all the angels in the area and probably across the country would be alerted to the fact that a male warrior angel pleasured his wife so thoroughly he couldn't contain his pride—something Wenzel warned the family against doing.

With his course set, he curled his wings around her and dove toward home. Wenzel would be calling or stopping by soon to reprimand him.

The man was on his way because Slater could hear on the airstream Wenzel's lecture starting already, *"Don't lose control of your wings. Don't use them to fly unless you're fighting demons. Control your emotions and you control your wings. Lose control of your emotions and your wings will take control and fly."*

The airstream shifted at the end of Wenzel's sentence, alerting him to slow his descent. He opened his wings, adjusting the angle of his feathers to ease the impending landing. Slowly he lowered his feet to the ground in on the lush grass in his backyard. As his wings retracted, he maneuvered Fin until her legs clenched around his waist. While their bodies were still connected intimately, he strode to the back door and swept his hand across the deadbolt, unlocking the mechanism with the power of the wind.

He strode toward the bedroom, listening for his phone to ring.

"Is everything okay?" she asked.

"Yeah. I lost control and…" He lifted her off his cock and placed her on her feet in the hallway. "There is damage to the bedroom. I may have to do some construction tonight to fix the outside of the house. It's a rule that we immediately fix what we break, when these things happen."

She walked into the room as Slater followed.

Wenzel, holding a piece of sheetrock and a box of screws, stood next to a large hole in the wall. The remnants of a broken bed were pushed to the middle of the room. The headboard had been torn off and was nowhere to be seen. The frame of the bed had been broken into large pieces. The duvet and sheets were ripped to shreds. Pillow fluff was everywhere. The room looked like a disaster zone.

Finley covered her breasts and ran to the bathroom.

"Sorry," Slater said. *She's not getting over this tonight.*

"I expected it," Wenzel replied, as if the apology was geared toward him. "Two months of wanting a love angel who clearly wanted you isn't something to be taken lightly. The victory of a long-fought conquest."

Wenzel raised his brows and an amused smile crossed his lips for a moment before it was gone. "And the creation of a child between two angels is bound to bring a huge light show and some damage to a house. Congratulations are in order, which is why I'm not going to continue my lecture tonight. I think you've heard enough. The good news is that we'll probably have a bunch of babies come due in the next nine months or so because of your display of libido. The bad news is that you've got me as the only help to fix this, and it must be fixed tonight. We don't need more attention coming your way tomorrow than is absolutely necessary."

"I'll put on some clothes and take over," Slater said.

"Did you know Liam worked as a carpenter on when he wasn't at the police department? Finley was his assistant for many years. She's going to join me in fixing this wall, while you brick up the outside. I've got all the supplies and tools out there waiting for you."

"Fin might not—"

"She *will* assist me," Wenzel stated. "She has no choice in the matter, and neither do you."

Like so many other times in his life, when Wenzel ordered, Slater obeyed, whether he wanted to or not. He walked into the bathroom and found Finley in the shower crying.

"Don't cry," he said. "We've just got to fix the hole. It's not a big deal. We'll sleep in one of the other rooms."

"I don't want *him* here." She sobbed.

"He's not leaving until you come out and help him patch up the hole on the inside. I'll grab you one of my T-shirts to wear. He'll leave when it's finished." *He must want to repair your friendship with him, or possibly have you apologize to him. I don't think you'll ever apologize or be genuine in any apology you offer him. Come to think of it, this could end up being a problem.*

"I'm not helping him do anything. I'll do it myself," she screamed. "I freaking hate him." From the looks of her, she was planning to attack Wenzel again, and that battle wouldn't turn out well for her.

"Please, just help him fix the sheetrock while I brick the outside. Then he'll be gone, and we'll be making love for the rest of the weekend."

"Screw you," she screamed.

"I'm grabbing you a shirt. Put it on or go out there naked.

It's your choice. But you're not getting out of working with him," he stated. "The sooner you get out there, the sooner he leaves."

He didn't like that Wenzel was in his bedroom either, but he wasn't throwing a tantrum over it. He pulled on jeans and a T-shirt, then grabbed a shirt and a pair of shower slides for her.

The spray from the shower stopped.

He strode into the bathroom and placed the shirt and slides on the vanity counter. "It will take me longer to brick up the hole outside than it will take you and Wenzel to repair the sheetrock. You can do this, Fin. Take a deep breath and —" He stopped as the lack of movement from her made him turn all his attention on her.

The stillness of her body and the steady intake and exhale of air in her lungs worried him. She was too calm. She was so calm that she reminded him of his pre-battle tranquility.

"Are you ready?" he asked. *I can't call my mom to bail me out again. You won't accept it, and she'll be furious with me for letting Wenzel screw things up, again.*

She wrung out her hair and reached around him, grabbing the shirt without touching him. No words left her mouth as she slipped it over her head and smoothed down the front which fell to mid-thigh. She walked into the bedroom without the shower slides that would've been way too big for her anyway.

He followed her, watching for any looming sign of attack on Wenzel.

"I brought several different sizes of drywall tape," Wenzel said. "Do you have a preference?" He gazed at her, waiting for a reply.

She shrugged, not saying a word.

Wenzel glanced at Slater. "Leave us. You have a lot of work to do outside."

"Yes, sir." Slater walked to her and kissed her cheek. "I love you."

She didn't say a word, nor did she look at him. Her focus remained solely on Wenzel.

Wenzel's attention never wavered from hers. He'd never seen Wenzel look at anyone like he did her. The man who, outside the Vogel family, people thought was unpredictable and insane, looked at Slater's wife as though he had no idea what she was capable of. And although Slater wasn't scared of her, he too had no clue what she was thinking of doing. But he did know, without a doubt, she was formulating a plan to do something.

"Well, okay, I'll be outside if either of you need me," Slater said.

"Don't come back inside until I call for you," Wenzel stated. "No matter what you hear, do not come inside, Slater."

"Yes, Slater," Fin said in a tone so flat that it sent cold shivers down Slater's spine. "Don't come inside. Wenzel seems to want to flex his power and have me cower in a corner. I have nothing to lose, since he's taken away my only family and makes all those related to him his subjects to rule over. So, please, don't return until the head of the Vogel family requires your attendance. My request means nothing, as I'm nothing but a peasant."

Her golden gaze seemed as icy as her tone. "Actually, he considers me to be less important than a peasant. I'm a bug who crawls on the floor, ready to be stomped to death—or some lesser being that, with a swipe of his finger, disintegrates like the dress I was tricked into wearing to the party I agreed to go to under false pretenses."

"I don't know that I should leave," Slater said. *She's going to attack you, Wenzel.*

"Leave," she said in that same flat, emotionless tone. "I don't need you. I don't *need* anyone."

"Baby, you love me." Slater reached to take her hand, but she turned away, leaving him to grab air.

"Love has nothing to do with what happened tonight," she said. "Go away, Slater. Your master and I have to fix a hole in your bedroom."

"Oh fuck," Slater mumbled on an exhale. *What do I do?* "Wenzel, let's not do whatever you have planned to do tonight. I'll fix my house."

"Listen to your wife," Wenzel said. "The longer you procrastinate in repairing the outside, the longer you'll have to wait to make love to your love angel."

"Fin, if you need me, call my name and I'll come."

She shrugged. "*Whatever.*"

"I will come," Slater promised. "You're mine."

She ignored him, but she didn't ignore Wenzel. Her gaze narrowed in on the man.

While Slater walked out of the bedroom, he prayed that Wenzel knew what he was doing. Slater didn't want Fin to hate Wenzel, but he felt like it was a possibility with the standoff the two most important people in his life—Finley and Wenzel—remained in.

CHAPTER EIGHTEEN

Finley

Standing in the destroyed bedroom and staring at Wenzel Vogel, Finley tried to soothe the fury that wouldn't leave, no matter how many deep breaths she took. She'd always been able to calm herself, to control her emotions, until tonight. Everything went to shit so fast...too fast.

But as soon as Slater carried her into his house, the fury pumping inside her veins began to dissipate until there was none of it left. Then he upset her and the call with his mom soothed enough of her anger to send her into a position of vulnerability. And everything shifted to wonderful. She'd been in his arms, surrounded by his hard body and soft wings. She'd never experienced safety like she had while enclosed in his wings. It was the best experience of her entire life. Nothing else even came close. Well, sex in that cocoon... that might have been better by just a little.

And when he placed her down and she smelled his wonderful sweet scent cascading off the land and his home. That sexy, confident energy and aroma rose around her with every step toward the house. Her body and soul responded with desire for the man who turned her on and gave her that first real kiss in the airport. Then that kiss at the restaurant. It was like every breath she took after they had sex was a gift of love from him. A complete sense of security enveloped her. No one would ever harm her as long as she was here, in his home. And even though she'd lost Liam, being with Slater soothed enough of that loss that she found herself giving in to the desire to be closer to him. To be intimate with him. To do anything and everything he wanted.

When she made love to him, she gave in to her most vulnerable emotions and felt a kind of connection that rivaled the one she'd had with Liam. It was a different connection, but the depth of it was the same. Slater was as much hers as Liam had been. Wenzel took Liam away from her. And he could take Slater from her, too. *Wenzel ruined everything.*

With Wenzel suddenly in the mix again, the same sense of loneliness and danger she'd experienced earlier came raging back. Slater didn't love her like she loved him. Liam didn't love her like she loved him. She would forever be alone because of Wenzel and his trickery. And the one thing she felt not only on a visceral level, but a spiritual one, too, was that she needed to belong to someone who would protect and love her. And Wenzel wasn't here to protect her, no matter what he said. He was a liar. And she didn't trust liars.

"Hand me that drill," Wenzel said.

"That wouldn't be wise for me to do right now," she said.

"Do it anyway," Wenzel said.

Don't attack him. Don't try and kill him. She grabbed the drill from the charger on the floor and handed it to him. "Here. I still *hate* you."

"Thank you. You can hate me all you want, but I'm still going to love and protect you." The man drilled a screw into the sheetrock like a pro. He didn't need her help. He could fix the wall all by himself.

He continued drilling screws into the sheetrock, securing each section to the studs, then handed her the drill. "Put this on the charger."

She obeyed his order, taking the drill and placing it on the charger. "Now go away."

"What made you lose control at my house? I have to admit that it's been thousands of years since someone tried to attack me in my own home. And it's never been an angel, only demons that I allowed inside so that I could kill them. So, what was it that pushed you to the point of attack?" He leaned against the wall. The man seemed in no rush to leave.

She inhaled, attempting to remain calm, but the man's scent overrode Slater's. Every breath was like breathing in Wenzel Vogel, the man who took Liam away from her.

"I can't really talk about it," she said. "I'm hanging on by a thread. I want to grab that spear on the wall and shove it up your ass. I don't like the energy in your house. I didn't want to be there and then you took the one person in this world I could count on away from—" She clenched her jaw and held her tongue as she pointed her index finger in his direction. "I hate you so much." Her entire body shook with so much fury that it took every bit of control not to attack him, again.

She backed up toward the bathroom, moving farther away from him to get some breathing room. She didn't trust herself to refrain from grabbing that spear off the wall and trying to kill him. She was close to becoming unhinged. She'd never been this close to totally losing it, except for the day Liam came to her rescue at the grocery store.

"You're not alone," Wenzel said. "You're not reacting like a love angel. They assimilate into families. Becoming part of my family is an ideal situation for any love angel. And you are definitely a love angel. Yet, you went after me like I was your enemy, instead of your family. I'm not your enemy, Finley. I will never be your enemy."

"You're not my family. And you're definitely not my friend," she said. "So what does that make you?"

"Grab the spear and come at me. Let's get the fight out of the way," he said. "You *are my family.* And *I love my family. I love you.* Everyone else in the family is happy and ready to party and celebrate, except you. So, come at me. Let's fight so we can make up and find the love that is there." He pushed away from the wall, motioning with his hands for her to attack him.

She didn't move.

He waited. "Come on. Tell me how much you hate me and grab that spear, *sweetheart.*"

She wanted to hurt him like he'd hurt her. But she didn't want to give him the satisfaction of doing what he wanted, knowing she couldn't win. She would lose. And she didn't want to lose, not against him.

He sighed. "You're actually the first love angel I've ever known or heard of that went on the offensive. It's really interesting because your kind, prior to you, only use defensive techniques in fighting. You went straight for the jugular at my house. What happened to you before you met Liam?"

"Answer me this," she said. "Why would I tell you anything when you tricked me into wearing that dress? Tricked me into going to a fake party? Tricked me into a marriage that I didn't even…" She inhaled Slater's scent and a rush of hot desire pulsed through her. She stumbled backward, hitting the doorframe of the bathroom. "What just happened?"

"Slater is worried about you," Wenzel said. "He's flexing his power by expanding his energy and scent to cover you. He owns this land and house, and he's staked more than one very public claiming of you. He'd fight me for you. He'd lose, but he'd put forth a valiant effort."

Would he really fight you for me? Would he choose me over you? Is this just another trick to get me to trust you?

"What are you thinking, Finley Vogel? I genuinely want to know. I kind of wish you hadn't fucked Slater. That dress came in handy in reading you—the tugging of the skirt, the slight almost indiscernible notes of color within the white fabric hinting of your emotional status, then the moments of vibrant color that you couldn't contain...Such a young angel with an unusually rare ability to control your aura, your emotions, your tongue, your actions. Tell me, Finley, are you still hanging on by a thread? Are you strategizing the best means of attack? Are you analyzing my next move? Looking for my end game?"

"What do you want from me?" *I don't know why you tricked me. I don't know why you'd bring me to your house under false pretenses. I don't know why Liam would allow it.*

"Did Liam know you wanted to marry me off? Did he know there was no real family party? Did he know the gathering was for me?"

"I want you to love being a part of my family," he said as if that was the sole reason for inviting her to his house in the first place. "And yes, Liam knew why you were coming. He knew the dress you wore was a wedding dress. He knew the party was to celebrate your marriage to one of my warriors, not for a family gathering to celebrate being Vogels. What else would you like to know?"

She glanced at the spear on the wall. *I don't believe you.* "Did you tell Liam not to tell me?"

"Yes. I ordered him not to tell you. He's young. He's a rule follower. He's a good soldier as were his parents. He does what he's told. What else?"

"Why don't you want me staying with Liam ever again?"

"You're married. I knew you'd be married to one of my warriors. I assumed you'd go for someone who never colors outside the lines. But I was wrong. You picked my right-hand man, my best friend. You picked my fiercest warrior. You picked a man who straddles the line of the law and often finds loopholes to circumvent it, when it suits him. You picked a mini-me."

"I'm not married. In order to be married, wouldn't I have to apply for a marriage license? Sign documents?"

"Not really. The marriage license is already filed and approved. A copy is on my desk in my house and a second copy is on Slater's desk in this very house. I also have the documents from the wedding ceremony which I performed. Your signature is on it and so is Slater's. It was witnessed by the entire Vogel family. Your show of the consummation of your marriage in the sky tonight completed the requirements. And yes, I forged your signature. You were kind of busy after you left my house." He turned his back to her and picked up a roll of drywall tape. "Ask me anything, Finley. Was it Liam's disinterest in you as a lover that sent you on the offen—"

She raced across the room, grabbing the spear off the wall, and brought her arm back to stab him in the—

He moved so fast that she didn't see him take her down to the floor until her back hit the carpet and the wind was knocked out of her. The spear somehow ended up back on the wall where she'd taken it.

"Liam loves you, just not the way you want him to love you. He's a Hutchison, even though he has warrior blood running through his veins and his last name is Vogel. He's not ever going to party with us. He's going to watch from a distance and make sure no one breaks any laws. It's what angels of the law do. He is *not*—and I will repeat this until it sinks in—he is *not* in any form compatible with you. There is *no universe* where Liam Hutchison Vogel would ever want you as a lover or wife. He desires to protect you from harm, that's it. *Nothing more.* He doesn't want to shove his cock inside you or he already would've a million times. If he wanted you as his wife, he wouldn't have let you move away. Once an angel of the law chooses a wife, he's in close proximity with her twenty-four hours a day, seven days a week, every day of the year, barring the most unforeseen circumstances. It's who they are. There is little to no separation between an angel of the law and their spouse."

"I fucking hate you," she shouted. "I fucking hate you."

"Was Liam the only person to ever protect you?" he asked.

Tears filled her eyes. "I fucking hate you. Stop talking about him."

"Oh…He said you were alone when he found you. Were you always on your own? Didn't your human guardian protect you? Love you?"

She forced the tears to stop and compartmentalized her emotions, shoving them into the back of her mind and locking them away. With a steady voice, she said, "Please, release me."

He kept her pinned down. "Answer me, and I'll let you go."

"I wasn't alone. My mom would leave, but she always came back for me until…" *Liam saved my life. He loved me. He protected me. He cared for me, until I was capable of caring for myself. He gave me a loving home.*

"I'm sorry," he whispered. "These feelings you have for him aren't as a husband. Your feelings for Liam are as a father, but you don't remember ever having a real father, do you?"

He held her wrists as he shifted over and off her. He

pulled her forward by her wrists until they sat upright face-to-face. He didn't let go of her wrists, but he did release enough pressure that she could move within his grasp.

He seemed to choose his next words carefully. "Fathers protect and love their children. Slater is going to be a great father. He's loyal and faithful, and he brings the party with him. Fin, he's so much fun. He's a great guy. But listen carefully to me…"

She didn't want to, but curiosity got the better of her. She leaned forward, closer to the man she hated, so she wouldn't miss a single word.

"Husbands protect and love their wives, but it's more than that," he said. "They need to touch each other. They need to kiss, and I'm not talking about a kiss on the top of the head or the forehead or cheek. There's a fire inside that comes out when they touch. It's a touch that starts with a spark that burns into a four-alarm fire. And that fire rages out of control until it has run its course. It's primal. There's nothing sweet about it until after they've been sexually satisfied. The love of a father is sweet. The love of a husband is hot and sexy and demanding and all-encompassing."

Tears slid down her cheeks. *I wish you'd shut up. I don't want to listen to you anymore.*

"You don't love Liam like a husband," he said. "You may have fantasized about him. Dreamed of him as your husband. But it was because he is the standard you compare every other man to. That's a high standard, which explains why you turned your nose up at every one of my warriors, except Slater." He loosened his grip on her wrists, but continued to hold them. "While at my house, I could've been more sensitive to your feelings, but I had a job to do. I apologize for being harsher than necessary. I hadn't been expecting a love angel. Actually, you weren't even on my radar as one."

The tears started again and she couldn't stop them from sliding down her cheeks. *I still hate you. No apology will undo what you've done to me. You've taken away my Liam. I'll never forgive you.*

"This is where you accept my apology," he said. "And possibly offer an apology to me."

She nodded. *I'll never, never, never forgive you.*

"Think about what I've said. Think about the difference between the way you feel about Slater and the way you feel about Liam."

She nodded. *Leave me alone. Go away. I don't want to listen to you anymore.*

"I've talked to Slater's mom, and we've planned the wedding for this Friday instead of Saturday. Invitations will be sent by personal messenger in the morning to all the guests. I've booked a wedding venue, and we're having the reception at my house in Vegas. I'm doing my part to apologize and give you the wedding you wanted. I'm even allowing Liam to attend and walk you down the aisle."

While the tears continued falling, she nodded. *You're terrible at apologies. The wedding isn't even for me. It's for Slater's mom. She deserves to have a wedding for the son she fought for and raised. She deserves a wedding she'll be able to celebrate and remember forever. You're acting like dangling Liam like a carrot in front of me makes what you did okay. It doesn't.*

"I'm not convinced you're accepting my apology." He continued staring at her.

She remained silent, rubbing her cheek on her arm.

"I'm rolling the dice on this one," he said. "I'm going to let go of your wrists. You don't have to attack me. And at the moment, you don't have to apologize to me for this incident or the one at my house." He released her wrists and held his hands up in surrender. "I'm going to finish fixing the wall. Think about what I said."

She looked at the spear on the wall. *I'm too slow to kill him. I'm not strong enough to fight and win.*

"I'm one of your protectors, Finley." He glanced at the spear and then at her. "Your wings are your best weapon. When you're ready to learn how to use them to protect your children, I will teach you."

"Baby?" Slater said.

She looked at the bedroom entrance and Slater stood at the threshold, gazing at her

"You okay?" he asked again.

No. I'm far from okay. She nodded. "Yes."

"You don't look okay." He strode in.

Rising from the floor, she swiped the tears from her eyes. She inhaled and ran to him.

He opened his arms, and she rushed right in, hugging him as he hugged her. "I've got you, Fin. You're safe."

"Are you done outside?" she sniffled.

"Almost."

"I'm done in here," Wenzel said. "I'll finish the outside for you. Take care of her, but no more flying tonight."

"Thanks, Wenzel," Slater said.

"I'll see you both tomorrow for brunch with the family at my house," Wenzel said. "It's mandatory. Get there before noon, and expect to stay the night."

She didn't see him leave, but sensed the energy shift in the room and her excessive emotions dive down in the compartment they typically remained in, far from the surface. "I'm not going to his house tomorrow."

"You have to," Slater said. "It's what we do."

"It's not what *I* do."

"This isn't worth battling over. Fight for something worth fighting for. A meal with the family isn't worth a mini-war with Wenzel."

It is to me. "I have no clothes."

"I'll have Liam drop off your backpack."

"I'm not going." *If I have to, I'll call Rager for help getting to the airport and flying home tomorrow. You'll be at Wenzel's, and I'll be on my way back to Nevada. Maybe I'll sneak out tonight and get my backpack at Liam's. Dang it. I don't have a freaking phone. Rager will come, if I don't check in again with him in the morning. He'll come and find me.*

"We'll discuss this in the morning." He squatted and scooped her up into his arms. "We need to pick a room to sleep in. Or we could sleep outside under the moon and stars."

I could take your car while you sleep. You might not hear me leave. But you'd hear the tires on the gravel road. You wouldn't hear that from inside the house. Maybe you would, but it wouldn't be as loud. I could tire you out with sex. You won't hear anything after I'm done with you.

"I don't care where we sleep as long as Wenzel isn't with us."

CHAPTER NINETEEN

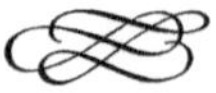

Slater

While Finley slumbered, Slater snuck out of the bedroom and called Wenzel.

"Has she tried to leave?" Wenzel asked.

"No, but I'm pretty sure that was the plan. She's sleeping, finally."

"She's refusing to come to my house?"

"Yeah. She's back to calling you a 'fucker'. Your strategy with her isn't working."

"I did some digging into her elementary school records. She'd gone home with a rotating list of teachers, when her mother didn't pick her up at school—which was often. And she and her mother moved when the school threatened to report her mom for neglect, which I found to be, on average, every two to four months. Finley had lived like that from age three until Liam brought her home to live with him at the age of ten."

"I can't imagine living like that," Slater said.

"It's not a good life for a love angel. Love angels aren't nomadic. They find a place and set down roots that last for generations. Love angels have been mostly wiped out of existence because they congregate in one area and *never, no matter what happens, leave*. When demons find a community of them, they go in and kill all of them. Love angels don't attack, they defend and sacrifice to save their children. I think Finley's entire family, probably more than a thousand love angels were murdered in front of her as a child. I don't know where she came from or how she survived, even with Liam as her guardian. Love angels always withered and died when they were left alone or too far from other love angels. They need family to survive. It's actually more important than food or water or shelter to them."

"Can you call some love angels you know and see about having her visit and learn from them? Give her a family of love angels to contact, so she doesn't feel so vulnerable, so alone?"

"Slater, there are no other full-fledged love angels. I couldn't believe my eyes when I walked into the room and saw her. There are only mixed love angels living on earth, and they're few and far between. I only know of three, and they're healing angels whose DNA is less than one percent love angel. Finley wouldn't consider them family at all. Finley needs a *family* connection. Your wife is the very last of her kind. There are *none* like her. At least not that I'm aware of and I've been looking since I found out about the catastrophic decimation of the last living colony by demons that caused their extinction sixteen years ago. I never thought to look for one sole love angel. They only survive in twos or more. They don't survive alone. They die. She shouldn't be alive. She's an anomaly of epic proportions."

"I didn't think you were serious about her being the last

one. But if she's the last one, then how would you know to give her the dress?" *She can't be the last one. There has to be more. She needs to be surrounded by her kind to thrive. I love her so much, I'd do anything to find another love angel.*

"Liam's description of her actions didn't jive with a full-fledged love angel. I thought she was a healing angel with a portion of love angel in her lineage. The dress would've adjusted to her body as a healer, making a modest dress that covered her from her neck to her ankles. Believe me, I nearly choked on my own tongue, when I saw her in that dress. I haven't seen a love angel, in-person, in more than a thousand years. They're an exclusive crowd who don't take kindly to outsiders, not unless they plan on marrying them."

"Why would she want me and not you?" Slater asked. "She probably has been waiting for a warrior angel to marry, so she'd feel safe."

"No. She's not been waiting for a warrior angel as a mate. We're not their first choice—or even their hundredth choice—in lovers or soulmates. They mate with other defensive types of angels like healers. They're about healing their children, protecting their children, nurturing their children. I've been trying to mate warriors with love angels for longer than I can remember. This is the first coupling of its kind, which has come out of a mutual desire for each other, at least that I'm aware of."

"Why would she want me? I love a good fight. I live for battle and war."

"Did you happen to save her from a situation where she felt trapped? Has she seen you playing with children? Maybe Blade's children? Did you help her care for one of Blade's children who was sick or in need of help? If you did one of those things, she'd be impressed. If you did two or more, she'd probably start seducing you without her ever realizing it."

I helped her out of a bind at the airport. I've gone over to Blade's and played with the kids while she was there. I've changed diapers for Sienna's triplets a bunch. I've sent gifts to Blade and Sienna and Emma when their babies were born, but Fin probably didn't know about the gifts. "I've done a lot of that stuff with the kids. I love babies, and Blade's nontraditional family has a lot of them."

"Make sure to bring Finley over for brunch. I'm going to do my best to make it an environment where she'll feel comfortable," Wenzel said.

"I'm going to get her backpack and clothes from Liam's before we go to your house," Slater said.

"Clothes and shoes will be sent to your house at dawn. Do not go to Liam's house, unless you hear the order from my mouth and only from my mouth. I'm sending you everything she will need until you arrive home on Monday."

"Okay." He walked toward the bedroom. *Please don't upset my wife with your gifts.*

Wenzel sighed. "Enjoy the rest of the night with her. And start planning a beach honeymoon. Your subscribers are going to want to see her in a bikini."

"See you soon." Slater ended the call and strode into the bedroom where he'd left Finley sleeping soundly.

She wasn't under the covers.

He checked the bathroom.

She wasn't there.

He checked the rest of the house and the front yard. The cars remained where he'd left them. He checked the backyard.

Nothing.

The love of his life was gone.

CHAPTER TWENTY

Finley

Sneaking out of the window in the bedroom proved to be easy. Nausea hit her as soon as she climbed over the fence onto the neighbor's property, making her escape much more difficult. Every few steps, she vomited, until she couldn't go any farther. Her stomach seemed to do flips every other second that she walked farther away from Slater's property. She pushed harder to get away, crawling on her hands and knees to get away, to get closer to Liam's house. But the more she tried the more powerful the waves of violent vomiting ensued.

Having no other choice, she bagged the idea of running away. Instead, she dragged herself back the way she came, knowing she'd lost probably the only chance she'd get to escape.

The closer she came to Slater's property line, the moments between the waves of nausea lessened. When she pulled herself over the fence, crossing onto Slater's property line, she fell in a heap of utter exhaustion, but her stomach settled. No more nausea. Yet, a deep sadness settled in her soul at her failed attempt to get away. She desperately wanted to see Liam. She wanted to talk to him privately to tell him she was going away. That she wasn't coming back to Georgia. That she wished him the best, and she loved him, even though he didn't love her anymore.

"Finley," Slater called.

"Finley," Wenzel shouted. "Call out and we'll come to you."

She couldn't speak or she'd start crying again. She'd done enough crying today, yet with the depth of grief living in her heart and soul, she wouldn't be able to hold back the tears much longer.

They would find her, and her freedom would be lost. They'd make sure she would never see Liam again.

CHAPTER TWENTY-ONE

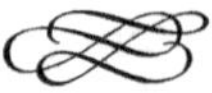

Finley

I can make it back before he finds me.

Tears ran down her cheeks, but she didn't have the strength to wipe them away. As she lay there, curled in a fetal position, she thought about her mother lying dead in the woods, not far from her crashed car. Her mother didn't die from the injuries she sustained in the crash. She died from exposure. *She probably died from losing her will to live.*

Finley cried even more. She'd always had a strong will to live. But here, on Slater's land, without Liam looking after her. Without Liam calling to make sure she was home and in bed by ten. To make sure she was safe. She felt alone.

Lying in the grass surrounded by beautiful Georgia pine trees all around her for cover, she understood her mother a little more. She wanted to give up and die, right here. But something inside her couldn't. In the deepest part of her soul, in a place Finley couldn't explain, she found the will to keep going, to fight, to battle, to win the war, to live.

"Help," came out in a croak from her lips. *I need help. Please hear me, Slater. I'm sorry I tried to leave. I'm sorry. I need you. But I need you to understand that I need Liam, too. I need him.*

The woosh of a breeze made the trees near her sway.

Slater, help me. "Here," she mumbled. "I'm here."

The one person she didn't want to see or talk to stared down at her with his green eyes, softening as the seconds ticked by.

You're worried about me. Maybe you do care about me.

"Fin," Wenzel whispered. "Oh, Fin." He scooped her up in his arms and the worry in his gaze eased some of the sadness within her. "You're bound to Slater, and so is the child growing inside you. I promise you, Finley, I'm not your enemy. I'll protect you and your children. I will fight for you, and I will teach you how to fight. Don't hurt yourself like this. Please, no more running away. Attack me whenever and as often as you please, just don't run away ever again. You're my family. I love you."

"I want Liam," she whispered. "I want to go home. He's my family."

"You can't see him," Wenzel said. "He's not yours. Slater is yours. Slater is your home. He's your protector. He's the father to the child growing inside you. He's your family." He placed his hand on her belly. "This little one needs your protection. Leaving your husband's territory without a family member can be fatal to this child. You *can't* risk the life of your child because you're no longer the most important person in Liam's life. Liam did what he was supposed to do. He raised you. He protected you until you found someone who was more capable of protecting you than him. Grieve for the loss, but don't put yourself and your child in danger because you're not ready to face reality."

"Wenzel, it's not the time for a lecture," Slater huffed. He took her from Wenzel's arms and all the sadness she'd been holding inside rushed out in heart-aching sobs.

"It's going to be okay," Slater cooed. "I love you. The baby is fine. I know we just made love and that usually you wouldn't know you were pregnant for at least a few more weeks, but we know immediately. You probably feel different now than you did earlier. You might—"

"She knows," Wenzel said. "She might not want to admit it, but she knows she's carrying your child. She's a love angel. *Believe me*, she knows." He placed his hand on her belly and she gained control over her emotions.

The sobs subsided, and for the first time since she met Wenzel, she sensed a familial connection to him. A bond seemed to form between them as his hand remained on her belly—A bond she didn't want formed.

"Don't do that," she said.

"It's already done," Wenzel replied. "You're a love angel, Finley. I hope that you finally believe me."

"That's enough," Slater demanded. "It's been an eventful evening and my wife needs to rest."

Wenzel kept his hand on her belly, ignoring Slater.

She didn't push his hand away. She should've, but she couldn't move her limbs or turn from his gaze.

"You're fierce, Finley Vogel," Wenzel said. "I would truly love to see you lose all control. I have no idea what kind of chaos you'd produce, but I believe it would be spectacular."

He removed his hand from her belly and cupped the side of her face. "Please let me call out your wings." He leaned over and kissed her forehead. "I have a feeling they've been used for war already, and I've never seen..." His nostrils flared. "Yep. As a baby, you fought for your people and your life. I just don't know how you survived. I wonder if your wings will tell the story."

"I think you're crazy," she said.

Wenzel shook his head. "No, you don't. You *wish* I were crazy." He walked toward the house alone.

"That was strange." Slater carried her across the grass using the same path as Wenzel.

"He's strange," she said. "How can a baby fight?"

"Their wings do the fighting," Slater said. "It's impressive."

"I don't have wings," she said. "Wenzel is incorrect. I'm no angel."

Why don't either of you believe me?

He kissed her. "You're my angel, Fin. I love you."

The sweet aroma that was undeniably his wrapped around her in gentle waves, softening her defenses until her only thoughts were of him and making babies.

Lots of babies.

Lots and lots of Slater's babies.

CHAPTER TWENTY-TWO

Finley

The interior of Wenzel's house in Georgia had been impressive, but the acres of gardens in the back-yard could've been on the cover of any southern home type of magazine. The native flora which surrounded the abundance of rows of rare roses and exotic flowers looked like they were cultivated by magic, grown specifically for today's Sunday brunch to honor her wedding to Slater.

She'd never seen so many different types of delicate and rare roses in her life, not even in a floral shop in the height of wedding season. And in the middle of the wonderland of flowers in full bloom sprung a dancefloor, lights, two full bars, bistro tables and seating all in the same colors and flower patterns as if it had been grown from the flowers themselves.

The deejay stand looked like it belonged at a botanical

garden concert, but the music he played wasn't made for waltzing. The music was definitely for the club scene, the type of music she listened to as she jogged around Blade's backyard college-sized track in Nevada.

Rising behind the lovely gardens, beyond the dance floor and the beautifully curated flower garden were acres of peach orchards, and behind the orchards, as far as the eye could see, were the Georgia pines she missed while in Nevada.

Leaning against the end of the white granite bar counter with crystal vases filled with lavender sprigs emitting the perfect amount of scent to soothe her senses, she listened to the music and watched Slater and Wenzel work the dance floor. The two were masters, moving together from one woman to another, bringing couples together and coaxing the younger guys and girls to join them in the middle of the floor. They were most definitely the life of the party, whereas Liam was nowhere to be seen. She was pretty sure he wasn't invited, especially after she tried to sneak off to Liam's house in the middle of the night, only to crawl back onto Slater's property, defeated.

One of the Vogel women around her age sidled up to Finley at the bar.

"You should get in there and dance with your husband," the woman said. "Slater brings the party."

I'm tired of hearing how my husband "brings the party" everywhere he goes. I get it. He's a good time and loves his family.

"Thanks, but I'm good. Go and have fun." *My back hurts. I don't want to be here. I miss the security of standing next to Liam at parties I attended.*

Finley never danced at the school or community parties. She remained by Liam's side, listening to him as he commented on each person at the dance, and which people to watch out for because they were nothing but trouble. She had soaked in all the knowledge he told her and that knowledge had kept her safe. Everything she learned from Liam, from fishing to woodworking to being watchful and aware of her surroundings helped her when she moved away.

Finley smiled at the pretty woman who wanted to include her in the family celebration, probably because Wenzel told her to come over and include her.

"Okay, but it's customary for a husband and wife to dance together and then dance with all the guests during a family wedding brunch. It's kind of a family rule." The woman sashayed toward the dance floor and then took Slater's hand. She glanced at Finley as though she was trying to get her to come and dance with Slater, which she probably was.

Finley shook her head. *Not today. I'm not up for this. I want to go home. I don't want to see Wenzel. I don't want my husband dancing with anyone else. I want him to take me home. Doesn't he see that I want to leave? He should know I want to leave. Now.*

The woman shrugged and then began dancing with Slater.

You've got to be kidding me. Get your hands off my husband. I'm so sick of this.

No one was rude. No one was mean. No one was anything but polite and kind and friendly. Yet, she seethed with fury as she watched Slater and Wenzel laugh and dance and sing along with the music. Slater changed partners and then did it again and again as she watched all the women and girls giggle and flirt with her husband. *Nothing during this trip has turned out the way I thought it would. Not one dang thing. I shouldn't want to kill everyone, but I do. I really, really do.*

The music slowed to a ballad.

Leaving the crowd, Wenzel danced toward Finley.

She shook her head but he nodded and smiled until he danced in place in front of her.

"No," she said.

"I haven't even asked. I'm just getting my groove on." Wenzel continued to sway and smile and hold out his hands to her. "Give me your hands. Let me show you how to let some of that pent up frustration release. Come on, Finley. I don't want to fight. I want to show you that we're friends and family, not enemies."

"I'm not feeling it, Wenzel," she said. "I'm not in the mood. Don't push me."

"One dance," he said. "One dance with me and then I'll hand you over to Slater. Do it for your husband. He wants to show you off and let everyone know you're his. It's a warrior angel thing."

She clenched her jaw, but placed her hands in his. "Where is Liam?"

"We're not talking about Liam," Wenzel said. "This is about you and Slater." He backed up, keeping beat with the music. "Find the calm within the energy of those around you." He pulled her closer, wrapping his arm around her back, placing his hand between her shoulders pinpointing the spot where the constant stream of pain that Liam wanted her to get checked out was. "You're not finding the calm, Finley."

As if she wasn't stressed enough, she pushed her shoulders back, standing as straight as she could manage through the increasing ache in her back that seemed to hurt more around Wenzel. "Lower your hand at my back."

He raised his hand instead. "I feel the chaos growing inside you."

"It's called *hate*," she said. "I'm struggling to contain the feelings of *hate* that you bring out in me."

He tapped her spine between her shoulder blades where the ache seemed unbearable at times. She tightened the muscles all along her back and squeezed her shoulders even closer together, straightening her spine, rising to her full height. *Don't mess with me, Wenzel. I'll lose control and attack you again.*

"Look at you, suppressing your wings," he said. "They want to come out. They want to show off. They want me to see something. I can feel a secret that is ready to be exposed."

"There is no secret. There are no wings. I'm a boring mortal," she said. "Leave me the fuck alone."

"Formation," Wenzel shouted.

A flash of white light blinded Finley.

As her sight cleared, panic rained down on her.

She was surrounded by all the guests.

Everyone had white and gold metallic looking wings spanning several stories tall and wide.

While Wenzel stood opposite Finley without showing his wings. Slater strode toward her and stopped at Wenzel's right side.

"We will protect you," Wenzel said. "Nothing can penetrate our formation. Nothing on earth or from Hell."

She shook her head as she searched for an exit. Her hands began to shake as she looked around for Liam, her protector. He wasn't there.

"Where's Liam?" She couldn't feel his presence. She couldn't feel his energy and she needed him to help her calm down the rising chaos. She glanced at the sky.

"Liam," she shouted. "I need you."

"You don't need him," Slater grumbled. "I'm here."

"He's not coming," Wenzel said. "He's in Texas getting trained and possibly married."

Her stomach began to knot. Her chest constricted. Her arms and back tingled and ached. "I need to get out of here. I need out. Please, make everyone go away. Make them go away."

"Babe, you're safe," Slater tried to assure her. "This is a

normal protective formation. Wenzel and I form the top of the dome. Or just I will for the top or just Wenzel will." He stepped closer to her.

Instead of feeling safe like she had when she was with Slater in every other circumstance, she experienced a new, all-encompassing vulnerability that freaked her out so much that she was compelled to call for the only man who had ever saved her from danger.

"Liam!" She screamed and screamed and screamed his name as memories lost long ago flooded her mind.

She held her stomach as she bent over like she had on the dry, cracked earth the day her world turned black. Pain surged from the base of her skull to her bottom as something split her spine down the middle.

"Help," Finley screamed and jerked as she fought against releasing the long-suppressed memories that, if exposed, might kill her.

She closed her eyes, tucking her chin to her chest. She wanted to die. The pain. The agony. The terror.

She tumbled into the darkness of that day...

They would never stop. They'd keep coming and coming and coming until everyone was dead. There was nowhere to hide. There was nowhere to run.

Finley clung to the leg of her mother. "Mom, what do I do?"

"Formation," a woman with black and gold wings shouted. "Kill them all. Take the women and children. Tear them apart. Don't let them ascend. Block their path to Heaven."

Finley gazed at all the other women and men rushing around, gathering children into the safety of their platinum and golden wings.

Only they weren't safe.

She wasn't safe.

No one was safe.

A sword sliced down severing her mother's body in half, missing Finley by inches, but killing half of her friends and family hiding beneath her mom's wings. As her mother fell, Finley's aunt with golden hair like Finley's mother and father grabbed Finley's hand. One of her aunt's wings dragged on the ground. "No one is coming to help, my sweet and beautiful niece. We're all dying."

She tapped Finley's back, between her shoulders. "God's wings of chaos open and protect my beloved child. Take my strength and spirit and give it to her."

More and more of the men and women whose children had been slain gathered around Finley, attempting to protect her with their broken and missing wings, chanting as one voice…

"God's wings of chaos open and protect my beloved child. Take my strength and spirit and give it to her."

Finley stared up at them as they circled around her. Broken wings dragged along the dry land, digging into their settlement's sacred ground in a circle of protection, while their voices rose to the Heavens with their plea.

"God's wings of chaos open and protect my beloved child. Take my strength and spirit and give it to her."

The horde of black-and-gold winged men and women struck Finley's protectors down, one-by-one, two-by-two, cutting down the circle of protection, but those left closed the circle to protect her.

The spirits of her family of protectors didn't ascend, nor did they descend, but continued to circle her until the last living family member placed her hand on Finley's shoulders.

Her right wing dropped off, all the feathers fully intact, trying to protect Finley from harm. She screamed with her last breaths, "Open God's wings of chaos, and we will protect our beloved, our last living child!"

The woman leading the attack tore off the left wing of Finley's last living relative, killing her.

The most excruciating pain struck Finley's back. Wings cut open Finley's back, attempting to emerge. An explosion of bright white lights that shattered the top off the dome of evil creatures, sending the beings who'd been guarding the exit to Heaven hurtling to the ground.

The wings burst open from the middle of her shoulders and expanded to three times the size of her body.

Once the shock of the opening above them ended, the rest of evil flying creatures surrounding Finley rushed at her all at once.

Finley curled into a ball, closing her wings around her and held strong while they struck her wings over and over and over again to get to her.

"Open your wings of chaos," the evil horde taunted. "Open God's wings of chaos, beloved child. Show us how the spirits protect you."

While Finley uncurled, taking hit after hit from the beings who had massacred her family, she rose from lying on the ground. She held strong, avoiding and deflecting as many of their attacks as possible.

While Finley's wings expanded outward, dodging and attacking the evil flying creatures, the light from the spirits of her protectors wove through her feathers before ascending toward the open gates of Heaven above.

"Fight, my darling," the spirits whispered as they ascended. "Release the chaos, my beloved child. Release it all and live to love again."

The strength she'd gained from the spirits of her family left her with the last of the angels joined the others in Heaven.

Finley stood alone, a child with no one left to protect her. No one left to call family. No one left to love.

"I'm going to break your wings and pluck each beautiful feather from them, beloved child." The woman sneered as she grabbed Finley's wing.

"No!" Finley cried out.

The woman swung Finley up by her wing and slammed her down to the ground.

Finley's wing cracked against the land she loved and she sobbed.

The grip from the woman leading the battle of annihilation clenched, fracturing more of Finley's wing.

"Oh, did that hurt?" the woman teased. "Beloved child, I'm going to enjoy playing with you."

Finley moved into the only battle formation she'd ever been taught —the safety curl. She dropped to the ground and curled into a ball, only one half of her covered by her partially injured wing.

The female leader of the evil creatures squatted next to her. She plucked a white feather from Finley's wing and rubbed it between her fingers. "Pretty feather." She plucked another. "Useless feathers."

While Finley sobbed and attempted to protect herself from the woman torturing her, the woman plucked feather after feather, tossing the pillowy-soft, white feathers and the damaged metal feathers from Finley's wings to the other creatures in the horde.

"Pretty feathers," the female leader of the horde said. "Useless feathers. Worthless wings of chaos. No one will save you. God won't save you. Love ALWAYS loses. I'm wiping love and hope out of this world. No more love angels. No more hope. No more love. Only hate and violence. Forever hate and violence and hopelessness for the humans. Stupid humans. Worthless humans."

"With every feather plucked from my broken wings, chaos will consume you and your kind until there is no more of YOU on this earth," Finley sobbed. "Even if you kill me, you will die, too. Love will WIN. Love always wins."

"Big words from such a weak, abandoned child."

One-by-one, the woman continued to pluck the feathers from Finley's broken wings. When those feathers were all gone, she broke Finley's other wing fracturing it into many pieces, paying no attention to the chaos reigning around her.

While the woman plucked the very last feather from Finley's wings, she cackled with victory. "No more love angels. You're the last one. I've killed all the others, and now I'll finally finish what I started thousands of years ago."

As she rose from the ground where Finley lay, the last of her horde of dark angels slammed into her in a heap of chaos, their metal wings slicing into her and each other. More of the horde tumbled to the earth dying from battling each other in the sky. They crashed to the ground. Their dead bodies strewn about the land. Their spirits scattered among the chaos before turning to dust and falling between the cracks in the desert sand, descending to Hell.

"Love wins. Love always wins," Finley chanted. "Momma, bring me home. Love is alive."

Broken and near death, Finley closed her eyes and prayed for ascension to be reunited with her family, her people.

CHAPTER TWENTY-THREE

Slater

Slater couldn't breathe as he watched his wife fighting for her life.

Finley lay on the ground, curled in a ball, sobbing and mumbling chants and curses as the broken bones of wings that were somehow still attached to her body jerked in an attempt to protect her. Her back bled along the entire length of her spine, but the worst of the bleeding was between her shoulders and the tops of her bare wings.

"*Fuck*," Wenzel gasped. "Slater, touch her. Try and wake her up from reliving that nightmare."

Slater gently placed his hands on her head. "I'm here. You're safe. I love you. Please, wake up. Please. Wake up, Fin. You're safe. You're safe."

"Dad, I need you and Mom here now," Wenzel said. "Pick up Logan's wife. I've got a love angel whose wings...She's pregnant, and I've totally fucked up. She's in that death curl that only love angels do…No. They're broken. All the feathers are gone…I don't think she was old enough to have any golden feathers but it's been so fucking long since I've babysat a toddler love angel. I don't remember them ever having wings at that age. This kind of mutilation happened when she was no more than two or three years old…A human must have found her…I don't know. What I do know is she used a chaos curse to kill everyone which usually kills *literally everyone.*"

Slater glanced at Wenzel.

The man held his phone to his ear. "Bring him. I'm not losing her. She chose Slater, not him. I don't know what to do to save her."

"Shit." *If Wenzel doesn't know how to save you, then…*

Slater curled his wing over her body, protecting her. "Baby, I love you. It's okay. You're safe. No one is going to hurt you. I love you."

He didn't want to move her in case that would cause more internal damage. He'd seen wings damaged and angels die from the slightest movement. Wing injuries were usually fatal, and she'd been living with fatal wing wounds for most of her life. She should've died many times over with these kinds of injuries. He'd never seen anyone survive lesser wounds to their wings, let alone this type of major damage.

Gently, he kissed her forehead and lay next to her, making sure not to move her. "Finley, look at me. Open your eyes. I'll take you home. I'll bring Liam to you. I'll do anything you want. Please, open your eyes and look at me."

Her lids fluttered, but she seemed lost in a memory-terror, muttering something he couldn't understand.

"I can't lose you," he whispered.

"Get out of the way, Slater," Wenzel ordered. "I've got to get to her wings."

Half a dozen bursts of light from angels flashed and then expanded as far as he could see.

Slater retracted his wing that covered her, but remained on the ground facing her. He needed to be the first person she saw when she opened her eyes.

Logan Hutchison, the law angel from Exorcise, Texas touched down next to Slater. He unfurled his right wing, unveiling his wife. He gasped. "Oh my, she's a love angel. Aurora, heal her. She's pregnant and the baby is in as much distress as she is." He raised his hands and mumbled something. "Slater, my grandfather and Liam are gathering herbs. My grandfather will be here momentarily with supplies, while Liam guards my land and people."

"Thank you, Logan," Slater said.

"She's the most beautiful woman I've ever seen," Aurora, Logan's wife and the Vogel family herbalist and healer, mumbled. "Wow…Who would do something so cruel to someone so perfect." The young woman crouched down beside Slater. "Slater, get her to drink this herbal mixture. She's going to survive this. She's a fighter. I heard she even went after Wenzel, which takes more confidence and spirit than I'd ever have." She handed him a clear plastic sippy cup filled with some kind of dark green smoothie looking drink.

"I don't think she'll drink out of a sippy—"

"It's all I had on hand, so stop being judgy. Trust God in that this is what she needs at this moment in time," Aurora ordered. "Help her drink it, so Logan and I can help heal her spirit and body from the trauma."

"Yes, of course. I'm sorry, Aurora." Slater rubbed the top of the sippy cup spout along Finley's lips.

When Finley didn't respond, Aurora gently stroked the length of her wing closest to him, moving it closer to Finely's body. "Please, Finley, swallow as the liquid hits your mouth.

Love heals all. Love conquers all. Love is the greatest of all the gifts an angel can possess. Life is nothing without love."

Slater tipped the cup a little and cradled Finley's head, her silky hair slipping between his fingers. "The drink looks awful, but I bet it's tasty." *It probably tastes disgusting, but drink it. Please, Fin, drink it all.*

Finley's tongue slid forward and with that small movement, a drop of liquid touched her tongue, seemingly making her stronger. She mumbled something that sounded like 'hold me' but he wasn't sure.

Taking a chance that he'd heard her correctly, Slater gently slid her onto his lap while Wenzel carefully adjusted her broken wings with the help of Logan and Aurora.

"That's it, baby," Slater cooed as she swallowed. He tipped the cup some more, helping the concoction to flow into her mouth. "This is going to help. I love you. I'm so proud of you."

Her lids fluttered and opened for a split second, showing off pure gold irises.

"Keep swallowing that tasty smoothie," he said. "Love wins all battles. Love wins all wars. Love is the most important gift we can ever possess."

"It's working," Wenzel whispered. "She needs more. She's going to need a lot more of that medicine."

A blinding white light flooded the sky and surrounding area.

Daniel Hutchison has arrived. The letter of the law himself is here.

Daniel Hutchison, Logan Hutchison's grandfather and law angel who gave over his position as Sheriff and Law Enforcement of Exorcise, Texas to his grandson Logan, landed next to Aurora. "I brought the herbs to make more wing healing smoothies, and made that chaos concoction and put it in a thermos in this cooler. I'm sorry it took so long."

"You're so great, Daniel. I had hoped you'd understand

my message, and you did." Aurora kissed his cheek. "Go inside and get the granite mortar and pestle that is marked only for my use in the pantry, but leave everything that you brought here."

"On it, my sweet Aurora." Daniel vanished on a sudden breeze.

"I love it when he does that," Aurora whispered. She glanced at Logan. "Love of my life, work on healing her spirit and allowing her chaos to expand into her wings."

Slater held up the empty sippy cup and Aurora filled it with more liquid from a gallon jug. He held it to Finley's lips, but she refused to part them.

Aurora took the cup from Slater. "Finley, you have to drink this. I've got more healing herbs I have to mix, but you have to finish this."

When Aurora tried to part her lips with the cup, Finley doubled down and tightened her lips close.

"I'll keep trying." Slater took the sippy cup from Aurora. *Please, Finley, I love you. I can't live without you. You're my everything.*

CHAPTER TWENTY-FOUR

Slater

Finley parted her lips, ready for more.

"Thank God," Slater said. "That's my girl. Drink up. You're going to be healed quickly with Aurora's guidance."

"Remind her that love conquers all," Aurora said. She filled up the cup again and watched as Finley guzzled down the mixture. "With each sip, tell her something wonderful about the gift of love."

Slater took off the sippy top of the cup that Aurora gave to children who needed healing. He gently turned her head a little, cradling her head and neck, shifting her onto her side with barely a shift of her wings.

Slowly, he helped her drink from the cup, like he'd done with his nephews when they transitioned from sippy cup to a normal cup. "I love you so much. Love is the ultimate of gifts, Fin. Love will win and we will have a long lifetime of love. Love always wins. Forever and always."

Logan chanted, "Bring back chaos to this beloved child's wings."

Wenzel and Logan carefully massaged the bones and joints in what was left of her wings.

Logan nodded at Wenzel as he continued to chant, "Bring back chaos to this beloved child's wings."

Wenzel joined Logan in his chant. "Bring back chaos to this beloved child's wings."

Finley winced and jerked, but the longer Wenzel and Logan massaged her wings and chanted, the more she surrendered control and began healing at a faster rate.

A couple of the single guys in the family took off Finley's shoes and massaged her feet and legs, gently stretching her legs until they were no longer tightly curled against her chest. They joined in the chant, "Bring back chaos to this beloved child's wings." They continued stroking her smooth skin, enjoying the job a little too much for Slater's liking.

"She's my wife," he said to them. "Your hands are roaming too far up her legs. Don't make me tell you again."

"Yes, sir," the men said. They shifted downward, massaging her legs and then joined in the chant once more.

The others watching around them joined in the chant.

"Bring back chaos to this beloved child's wings," the entire family of warrior angels chanted.

Finley finished the drink. She opened her eyes and gazed into Slater's.

He placed the empty cup on the ground. "Feeling a little better?"

"I want to go home," she whispered.

"Our home here or in Nevada?" he asked.

"Nevada," she whispered.

"Can you stay in Georgia one more night, so I can check

on you? Then you and Slater can fly back to Nevada on my jet with me tomorrow afternoon," Wenzel asked.

"Okay," she whispered.

"I have one more request," Wenzel said. "I would like for you to keep your wings open until we leave for the airport tomorrow. They need more time to heal. The fresh air will be good for them."

"Okay." Her chin quivered and she looked as though she was seconds from falling back into the memories of the war she'd survived as a child.

Slater rose from the ground, cradling her in his arms. "I've got you, Fin. I love you. I won't let anyone hurt you ever again."

"My back hurts," she whispered.

"It's going to hurt. Your wings have been severely damaged," Wenzel said softly. "I'd like permission to stay with you and Slater until your wings are fully healed. I'd like to help you with rehabilitation, too. But I don't have to live with you for that."

"I want to see Liam. Please?" The pain in her voice hurt Slater. He wanted to take her to Liam right then, but he knew he couldn't.

Wenzel shook his head. "Not yet. You can call him and video chat, but nothing in-person until your wings have at least one layer of protective feathers. I've been trying to think of some kind of incentive for you to follow my protocol to heal those wings of yours, and I think that might be it."

She looked at Slater. "Is he telling me the truth?"

"Yes," Slater said. "Let's call Liam now. But I want you to drink some more of the smoothie drink."

"It tastes more like herbal tea than a smoothie," Finley said, softly. Her voice had to hurt the way she'd screamed while she was stuck in the memories of the destruction of her family.

Aurora handed Finley a tumbler filled with the green liquid. "Drink this." Both Aurora and Finley's irises turned gold. "If you're ready for more healing, Logan will help me heal the broken bones in your wings. It won't take long, and your back won't hurt anymore. You may even grow some feathers. From what I've read about healing love angels, you might grow a lot of feathers. Maybe several layers of feathers."

A grin formed on Finley's lips as she turned her head toward Wenzel. "Did you hear that?"

"I did." Wenzel grinned. "How badly do you want to see Liam?"

Finley gazed at Aurora. "I'm ready for you to do whatever you have to do to heal me so I can see Liam. I don't care if it hurts."

"If Liam did get married, you need to invite her, too. He won't go anywhere without her. Inviting her here will act as a blessing to them. She'll need your approval of her marriage to your father, um, your guardian, when she sees you, because you are…beyond beautiful. She'll be jealous."

"She's my wife," Slater stated. "Liam's wife has nothing to be jealous about."

"That is not true," Logan said. "Your wife is a love angel, and as such, she is either extremely affectionate or dismissive. If she doesn't like Liam's wife, with a flick of a finger and a passing thought Finley could make her barren. Or if Finley adores her, Finley could make her pregnant with a smile or wave of a hand. Women and men alike must be careful around love angels. They're emotional and when they're happy, love and fertility in all areas flow from them. But, anger a love angel and a man's testicles shrivel up and a woman's ovaries shut down."

Logan smiled at Finley. "I would be honored to have you and your husband come visit me and Aurora at our home. It's an open invitation. I think you'd both like Exorcise, Texas. And we could use the talents of your kind in our small town."

I don't think so. "We'll consider it," Slater answered.

"I thought only Wenzel could officiate a wedding of a Vogel," Finley whispered.

"It's different with Liam," Slater whispered. "He's a law angel and has joined Logan's church, so Liam will follow Logan's rules and carry them to Georgia when he returns to govern the entire state. Wenzel will marry him to his wife, also, but the Hutchison family has their own way of doing things and their way supersedes Wenzel's on certain subject matters."

"Oh…" She glanced at Wenzel and her tight lips softened until the hint of a smile graced them. "I'm ready now."

"Let's do this," Aurora said. "Thank you for honoring me with your trust." She reached toward Finley's wing, but Wenzel stepped between them, blocking Aurora from touching Finley.

"Be careful," Wenzel said. "Love angels have special feathers. If a feather grows and comes loose, do not touch it or pick it up from the ground. No matter what happens, do not hold a feather in your hand without her expressed permission." He turned to the family gathered there. "Never pick up one of Finley's feathers. Not at any point in her life. Do not touch her wings without permission. No matter how alluring her wings become, do NOT touch them. *Never touch her feathers without her verbal blessing.*" He faced Slater. "You can touch any part of her, feathers and wings included. She loves you."

"Ready?" Aurora asked Finley.

"Yes, ma'am," Finley whispered.

Logan stood behind Aurora, his front flush to her back.

Aurora wrapped her arms around Finley, sliding her hands between Slater's chest and Finley's side. Then Logan slid his hands down Aurora's arms, curling them along the same path between Slater and Finley and up to the base of Finley's wings between her shoulder blades.

"Let the power of light heal what is broken, grow what has withered, strengthen that which is weak, and..." Aurora inhaled as a brilliant white glow expanded from her. The light brightened to blinding as it strengthened with power. Her glowing white light joined with Logan's blinding white aura. "Fill Finley's body and spirit with love where there was once hate."

Aurora and Logan's arms slid from between Slater and Finley, then wrapped around Slater, including him in the full embrace.

The couple leaned forward. Aurora's chest and head lay against Finley as Logan bent over across the two women and rested his head on Slater's shoulder.

"Let innocence join with wisdom," Aurora said softly. "Let the power of righteousness dole out justice. Let the sword of the warrior shine brightly as it takes vengeance and drives out all darkness from this world. Let the wings of love rise to the heavens as they gather the innocent and protect them. Let God's wings of chaos shatter the minds and bodies of those intent on destroying her and those she loves."

Finley trembled.

"Breathe in," Aurora ordered.

Finley and Slater inhaled together.

"Exhaled," Aurora said.

The four of them exhaled together.

Aurora and Logan slid their arms from around Slater's back and took Finley's hands.

"Is that it?" Slater asked. "Is she healed?"

"We'll see how much more healing Finley needs," Aurora said.

Something in her tone had Slater questioning whether

Finley would ever be walk on her own again, whether her wings would ever work normally after the massive damage they'd experienced.

"Whatever happens," Slater said. "I will always love and protect you."

"Rise and expand your wings," Aurora said.

CHAPTER TWENTY-FIVE

Slater

Finley seemed to float from Slater's arms. The wings that had dragged the ground, broken and dying, rose and curved, taking the shape of mature wings. Skin grew and expanded, weaving in and out like thick braids of yarn from the base of her wings between her shoulder blades out to the edges and back again. Up and down and side to side, layer after layer of flesh wove over and under, strengthening the foundation. The fluffiest white feathers sprouted from the new layers of epidermis on her wings, covering them fully. Then spikes of gold filtered through, forming golden metallic feathers as tightly knit as a cosmic shield of solid armor formed the outer shell of her wings.

She floated forward toward Aurora and Logan as more layers of gold feathers sprouted and grew over and between the others until they became as solid and strong as ten thousand angelic shields. The inside of her wings sprouted layer after layer of divinely soft feathers as white as freshly fallen snow. More and more feathers grew between and over layer after layer of cosmic metal and soft and airy feathers until her wings were fully formed to offer love or wage war.

"You're whole now," Aurora said softly. "Your body is healed."

Suddenly Slater was pressed between his wife's sexy body and the softest feathers he'd ever felt. Standing inside her cocoon of wings, he sensed both her desire and love.

"I love you," Finley whispered. Her sugary breath felt like kisses on his lips. She curled her arms around him and rubbed her nose against his. "I don't know how to put them back. I didn't even try to hold you like this. They moved on their own."

"Maybe you wanted alone time with me and your wings followed your desire." He rubbed his cheek against hers and slid his tongue along the shell of her ear. "I want to take you home and make love to you."

She shuddered and her feathers caressed him over his clothes. "I want that, too. Help me do something about my wings. They're not listening to me."

"Maybe this is some love angel mating ritual," he said. "I love your wings."

Her feathers rustled and lifted the hem of his shirt upward in a seduction of their own. His spine began to tingle as his own wings itched to come out.

"Mmm," he cooed. "If I show you how to hide your wings, will you bring them out as soon as we get home, so we can finish what you've started?"

"Maybe." She slipped her hand down his pants and rubbed along the length of his cock. "This is mine."

"Roll your shoulders forward, giving more room between

your shoulder blades. Then imagine your wings hiding under the surface of your skin next to your spine. Once inside, they'll expand around your bones and muscles, protecting you from the top of your head to the bottoms of your feet. Mine wrap around me several times, giving my human form many layers of holy protection that no one can see."

Her gaze drifted down, lowering her chin to her chest.

She rolled her shoulders forward. The rustle of feathers and the chiming of metal resounded and then the cozy dome her wings provided vanished.

While he inhaled, the ethereal sensation of her feathers lingered on his skin.

Finley removed her hand from inside Slater's pants and turned to Wenzel. "You're taking me to Liam. Now."

Wenzel's green eyes twinkled with gold. "What's the magic word?"

"Finley, let's go home and then we'll arrange a visit with Liam," Slater suggested. *There's no way you'll be polite to Wenzel, especially now that you're healed.*

She stepped forward and rose onto the balls of her feet. "Take me to him, now, Wenzel Vogel, like you promised."

"You're not fully healed, Finley Vogel," Wenzel said. "But I might consider your strong *request*...if you decide to be polite and respectful like you were for the short time while your wings and spirit were having their initial healing session with Aurora and Logan."

She raised her hand and Wenzel shifted toward her hand. His hand snaked around her waist and pulled her against him in the same way Slater had when he'd made love to her.

Her hand landed softly against his cheek in a caress. She inhaled and sighed similarly to the way she had with Slater, which Slater didn't like at all. "Take me to him or make him come here to me."

Wenzel grinned. "Would you..." He paused, staring into

her eyes as his irises morphed from green to gold. "I'm not sure what I'm going to do with you, Finley Vogel."

She combed her fingers through Wenzel's thick brown hair, gently, lovingly, which Slater liked even less than the way she sighed in Wenzel's arms. "Honor your promise." She kissed his cheek. *"Please."*

"You are very dangerous, Finley Vogel. *So. Very. Dangerous.*"

"You're the dangerous one," she whispered.

Wenzel chuckled. "I am. It's nice that you noticed."

"How could I not?" she flirted. She actually flirted with him to get what she wanted.

I'm going to have to talk with her about flirting with other men, especially Wenzel. Slater kept watch on their interaction. Love angels, when they used their gifts of love, passion, and seduction were nearly unstoppable from getting everything they wanted.

Wenzel inhaled and closed his eyes. "I'll bring him to you, but you must go to Slater's house. You must follow his orders. Rest. Heal. Drink the herbal mixture Aurora has made for you. You must learn the top two rules of our family—The Vogel Family—which are..." He opened his lids and the normal green of his irises had returned. "One. Follow all of Wenzel Vogel's laws, rules, orders, and requests. Two. Represent the Vogel family with honor at all times."

"I won't do that," she said.

"I know. And I will enjoy doling out the consequences of your actions. The four of us are going to have so much fun together."

"Four?" She parted her lips slightly and slid the tip of her tongue between them. Her gaze narrowed and her chest rose, pressing her breasts against Wenzel's chest with a sensuality Slater really didn't like at all. She was flirting with the man and he was flirting back, and Slater was about to get involved.

"Oh yes. You, me, and the twins. But I should say five, because wherever you and the twins go, Slater will be there to balance the chaos. He's good at that. He's the calm in the middle of every storm. He's a dangerous one, too. More dangerous than you, not nearly as dangerous as me, but he's young. Give him time."

She glanced at Slater and a flash of red sparkles formed in her irises within the solid gold of her eyes. She dipped backward, arching her spine and Slater's cock hardened to granite and his balls clenched with need to give her yet another child.

"Liam will have to wait." Slater pulled his shirt over his head and dropped it to the ground. "Come here, Fin." He shouldn't have, but he leisurely glided his hand along the center of his chest, flattening his palm as his fingers neared his lower abs. Stopping at the top of his black suit pants that hung low at his hips, he thrust his pelvis forward. Her reaction was exactly what he needed to see.

Her chest rose and fell as her breathing shifted from controlled and steady to chaotic and needy. Her irises continually flashed from solid gold to sparkling red.

"I don't like you so close to Wenzel," Slater admitted. "I don't like you demanding you see another man." With a skim over the front of his jeans, the button slid through the hole uncovering the tip of his cock.

The most spectacular, sexy moan came from her mouth as the red sparkles in her eyes expanded until only the pupil remained gold. Whatever that change meant, he liked it.

Wenzel's hand slid down over the curve of her ass and squeezed.

"Get your hand off my wife's ass," Slater demanded.

A slight twitch of Wenzel's cheek was the only indication that he enjoyed Slater's reaction. Wenzel's hand caressed the curve of her ass before moving upward along her spine to her neck, lifting her upright and flush against him. He cupped the back of her head, turning her to face him. "Are you going to obey me?" His mouth was too close to hers.

Slater curled his fingers into fists. *Keep calm. This is all a test. A test I'm failing.*

"Probably not," she whispered. "I might not even try to obey you. But I might. Take me to Liam or bring him to me and—"

"No," Wenzel interrupted. His tone demanded obedience and the ground shook beneath them. He forced her head forward, pressing her cheek to his. "Do you want to live a fairly-normal life with Slater in Nevada? Do you want to finish healing and protect your children and the children and friends whom you love? Do you want Liam to have a loving and secure marriage with his wife? Because if you love Liam, like you say you do, then you won't cause a rift between him and his wife by visiting them before all of you are ready for an introduction."

Wenzel's tone softened. "Trust me. Let me help you control the power of your wings. Let me train you while you heal. Give Liam time to bond with his young wife, so that when you come into their lives, she will be secure in his love, never thinking that she is second to you."

"His wife *is* second to me," she stated.

Wenzel spun her around and practically threw her at Slater. "She's about to attack me. Sex her up, and she might consider doing the right thing by Liam."

Slater caught her, gently pulling her against his front.

Her irises switched from red sparkles to blue ones. "I will never be second to—"

"You will," Wenzel ordered. "I demand it."

She turned her torso, facing Wenzel. "I will *not* be second to his wife."

"You will," Wenzel stated. "A husband will always choose his wife first. Always. Slater will always choose you over every other woman on this earth. You are to choose him first over any living man, too. You've already done that having married him, and Slater has, too."

"Baby," Slater said softly. "Let's go home and heal those wings. Liam will come to visit soon."

"I want to see him now. Today."

"Fin, look at me." He bent his knees and gripped her ass, hoisting her up to catch a little air. As she lowered into his arms, pressed against his chest, he pulled her legs around his waist.

"Slater, don't..."

He thrust his hips and lowered her hips until her center pressed against the tip of his cock. "I don't want to fuck you in front of everyone, but I'm so damn close to doing it. I almost lost you today."

Her irises shifted to red sparkles and she moaned. "I'm sorry. Uh..." Her tongue slid across her bottom lip. "Can you do that thing you do with your tongue...uh, down there?"

Slater nodded. "I need a driver."

"I'm driving you," Wenzel stated. "Get in my car."

Before she could object, Slater crushed his mouth to hers and strode toward Wenzel's car. He didn't understand why Wenzel refused to allow Finley to see Liam. But he trusted Wenzel to have a good reason for delaying the meeting between the two. What bothered him was the reasoning he told her—that Liam's wife would be jealous of Finley. Regardless of whether Liam's wife met Finley now or later, the woman would be jealous of Finley. Being a love angel, every woman on the planet would be jealous of her. Liam's wife would have to get over it.

The real argument Wenzel should've made was that Slater would be jealous of Liam, if Finley doted on the man. If Finley touched Liam in a way that sparked Slater's anger, Liam wouldn't live to see the end of that day. Slater might have a strong bond with Finley, but her bond to Liam seemed stronger. She wouldn't let go of Liam, and Slater would do what was necessary to secure his bond and eliminate the threat Liam posed.

CHAPTER TWENTY-SIX

Finley

Finley didn't care that Wenzel watched Slater go down on her. She didn't care that he continued to watch her beg and plead for her husband to sex her up again and again. She didn't care that she lost all control over her body and encouraged Slater to give her the most incredible orgasms in whatever way he wanted. She didn't care that her wings appeared and grew and thickened while she was in the throes of the most intimate of encounters. She actually loved that more layers of feathers—both silky soft and cosmically hard—were added to what she'd already formed, so much so that they stroked along Wenzel's neck in a loving caress which seemed to make him uncomfortable. But most of all, she didn't care that he witnessed her *submitting* to Slater, not only as his wife and the mother of his future children, but also as an angel in need of his protection.

What she *did* care about Wenzel seeing and understanding

—and he did see and understand—was that no matter how angry or out of control or even unreasonable she behaved, she'd given Slater the power to control her. She didn't know how compelled she'd be to obey him, but Slater might be the only person who could stop her from seeing Liam. The problem, as she saw it, was that Wenzel could control Slater; therefore, Wenzel could control her through Slater. And Wenzel seemed to know that she would test his control of Slater and of her. The only obstacle stopping her from pushing the limits to her ability to disobey Slater and go see Liam on her own were the potential dangers to the babies growing inside her. The children were *her* responsibility and under no circumstances would she allow anything—even her own desires—to harm them.

"Can you call in a favor and get Finley excused from her college classes this week?" Slater asked.

"Already done," Wenzel said.

"I'm going to classes Tuesday," she said.

"Well, it's Wednesday, so…" Wenzel shrugged and an infuriatingly sexy smirk curled his lips.

"That's not possible." *Hours had definitely passed, but days? No. Not possible.*

Wenzel chuckled. "Slater has incredible stamina."

She glanced at Slater who sported the biggest grin of pride on his face that she'd ever seen. His eyes sparkled with gold, and she swore he looked more handsome than any man should be allowed. She wanted to be angry with him, but her gorgeous warrior angel glowed with love and joy, which made her heart soften enough to hug him.

"I love you," Slater whispered. "We have until tomorrow night before we need to be in Vegas for the pre-wedding party. We have time to go back into the bedroom and practice a couple of those positions you love so much. I'm ready and willing."

"As much as I'd like to, I want—"

"Not yet," Wenzel interrupted. "You're still healing, Finley. You may think you're up for visitors but you're not."

His hand skimmed along her back from her shoulders to the middle of her spine and then drifted downward to her bottom. "You are gaining muscle mass along your spine, but you still have a long way to go. You were nearly killed as a child, and we almost lost you when..." He shook his head. "I'm keeping you isolated until Thursday night. You need to be protected as you heal. And after the human wedding, you're honeymooning at one of my private islands in a remote location where there will be no one but you, Slater, and me."

"Oh fun. I'm going to spending my honeymoon with my husband and his controlling and irritating best friend. *Yay me.*" She glanced at Wenzel "You know that Liam isn't going to hurt me."

"He might," Wenzel said. "But I'm more concerned with the irreparable damage you might cause him."

She tilted her chin up and pleaded with her husband to take her side. "I need to see him. I will do anything you want, if you—"

"No." Wenzel's tone was as firm as Liam's when he set down the "unbreakable" rules. "I forbid either of you to see Liam, until I allow it."

Slowly, she turned toward Wenzel. *Be nice. Negotiate. Talk some sense into him. Don't try and kill him.*

Meeting his intimidating glare, she held his gaze, refusing to look away. "Forbidding doesn't work for me. Neither do your requirements. I want to see my guardian Liam Hutchison Vogel. I want to meet the woman he chose to marry. The woman you say he loves. I am attempting to be reasonable. I don't understand why you are being such a prick." *Ugh. I shouldn't have gone there, but you deserve it. At least I didn't try and stab you.*

Slater nudged her side. "Be nice."

"I'm sorry, Wenzel," she said. "That was uncalled for. But seeing Liam and his wife isn't a big deal. Besides, I'm married to Slater. I am no longer disputing that fact. Plus, I'm pregnant. You got what you wanted—I married one of your warrior angels and I'm pregnant. There. You got your two wins. Oh and after you fucked up and forced my wings to open without my consent, you ended up saving my life. It's a triple win for you, Wenzel. And now I know that I'm actually a real angel. I'm not disputing that anymore, either. Wow, you're racking up the wins."

"Yeah. That's right. I win. But you're focused on yourself. Here's a newsflash—Not everything is about *you*," Wenzel argued. "Liam knows you're being well cared for. He knows you are excited to see him again. He very much wants to see you, too."

The man turned his back to her and walked to the refrigerator. He opened the door to the fridge and took out a pitcher of water with stalks of herbs that she'd never seen before.

She left her husband's strong arms and followed Wenzel around the kitchen. "Then why are so adamantly opposed to us having a visit?"

Facing her, Wenzel stopped walking in a circle around the island counter as she followed him like a toddler playing a game. He placed the pitcher on the counter. Then he proceeded to ignore her while he grabbed three ornate crystal glasses from the cabinet above the drink station to the left of the island.

Following him once again, and waiting for him to offer an answer, she began to seethe. Fighting against her natural inclination to verbally jab at him, she held her tongue and suffered in silence while he took his time filling each glass—picking up one ice cube at a time with tongs and delicately placing them down at the bottom without making a sound, then ever-so-slowly pouring the herbed water into the glasses.

"Slater. Finley." Wenzel sighed. "Sit."

If Slater hadn't pulled out a counter stool for her, she would've ended up sitting on the floor. She held her breath, confused at how a soft command from the man she was so irritated with could compel her to immediately obey, whereas a firm command made her rebel. *Has he always been able to do that? Has he been soft with me, until now? Now that I know I'm an angel, do his commands take on some kind of heavenly strength?*

Slater took his time caressing all over her body, checking for injuries, before he pulled out his own chair and sat beside her. "I know you have your reasons for keeping Liam and Finley apart right now, but it would help me to understand why it's so important—as a reference if a similar occurrence ever happened again."

"Slater, your wife wants to flex her control over Liam. She wants to make his wife jealous. She wants to destroy Liam's marriage, because he stretched the truth and rejected her. You don't reject a love angel. They're..." Wenzel stared at her. "Love angels can be unreasonable, not that you are, my dear. You're the only love angel in the world who has only been reasonable and self-aware in all circumstances, never losing control. You're the exception. You only respond logically to everything that happens in your life."

"You don't have to be an asshole," she huffed. "I know I can get...passionate about things. But I have to say that you're being ridiculous about refusing us to visit. I love Liam and still trust him. I wouldn't hurt him or his wife. I want to see him before the wedding. I need to talk to him privately. I have some personal things I want to talk to him about without anyone else's influence affecting our conversation."

"Anything you say to Liam, you can say in front of me," Slater said. "Let's do a video chat."

"Are you saying I can't be alone with Liam?" *I can't believe that you believe Wenzel over me.*

"Yeah," Slater said. "You lose control around him. I'm fucking seriously jealous of him. I don't like the way you look at him. I don't like the way you're so focused on seeing him. And I especially don't like the fact that you don't trust me to protect you."

"You're jealous?" Why that question came out of her mouth baffled her. *You're jealous of Liam. Really?* Warmth filled her belly and the desire to climb onto his lap and pull out his—

"Yeah, and if he's in the room, I'm going to be in the room. Whatever you say to him *will* be said in front of me. Do not force my hand. You will not like the consequences." The firm tone and the stern look he exhibited surprised her. He sounded like a combination of Liam and Wenzel...more Wenzel than Liam. There was something about Wenzel that made her feel strong, almost invincible. Wenzel brought out the—

"You contain an army of chaos in those wings, Finley." Wenzel sighed and held a goofy smile on his face. "In all the years I've been here on earth, I've never met another being who came close to having the power to..."

Pushing down the desire to finish this conversation quickly after a long sex session with her husband, Finley tilted her head to the side and lowered her chin the way Wenzel seemed to like. The conversation needed to continue so he would continue talking. She gazed into his now golden eyes. "The power to?" *Finish your sentence. What kind of power are you talking about?*

He held out his hand, palm up and she placed hers in his. "You hid your true self, but there is no hiding now. If I weren't honorable, I'd kill Slater and take you as mine."

Instead of jerking her hand away, she found herself moving toward him as a powerful urge to push him into action filled her. She trembled with an almost uncontrollable compulsion to force his hand, but she stopped and backed up toward her husband, gently slipped her hand out from Wenzel's. *Are you testing me? Am I seducing you? Are you concerned for Liam and his wife because I'm unstable? Am I unstable? I might be unstable. I'm probably very unstable.*

Slater's hands slid around her waist.

Suddenly she needed to be closer to him. To be naked. To be skin to skin. To be joined intimately. Her fingers entwined with Slater's as he caressed up her chest, massaging her breasts. With his lips pressed under her ear, she rested her cheek against his.

"You're safe, my love," Slater whispered. "We need to spend some time in the library so you understand your reactions to men and to women."

"That's a great idea, Slater," Wenzel said. "Finley, you have impressively suppressed your natural instincts of seduction for your entire life. You're going to be dangerous to everyone you come in contact with, until you learn how to redirect those instincts. Even I'm not immune to your desires. But we don't want another Helen of Troy incident, do we?"

"Was she a love angel?" she asked.

Wenzel nodded. "And she wasn't nearly as powerful or as beautiful as you. As far as love angels go, she was a five on a love angel beauty scale of one to ten. You're an eleven. So Slater is definitely enjoying life right now while every man around you is struggling with blue balls and women are in pain with blue vulva. So a trip to my library would be helpful in controlling those powers. Every woman in my family of childbearing age will become pregnant by the end of the week because of you. I've performed twenty new marriage ceremonies since you and Slater married. I expect to perform at least twenty more before we leave for Las Vegas."

Slater nuzzled under her ear. "It's true. I'm the lucky recipient of your affection and love. I'll keep you safe and loved, my sweet and sensitive angel."

"I'd never seduce anyone but my husband. Slater is the only man who will—"

"I sure do hope so," Wenzel whispered. "But you will be starring in many of my warriors' dreams for as long as they walk the earth. Well, until they marry. *If* they survive long enough to marry." He inhaled as if he were taking in her essence, memorizing this moment. "Listen carefully to me."

She leaned forward, fighting the bizarre desire to comfort him. *I'm supposed to hate you. Why do I suddenly like you? Why am I hanging on your every word? Why am I so drawn to you?*

Fearing her days of autonomy were over, she slid from Slater's lap and stood beside him. Gripping Slater's hand and the island counter, she released her wings. "You're not going to control me."

"Mmm," Wenzel mumbled. "I'm trying *not* to exert my control over you. Remember, I'm here to protect you."

"I know. I get it. But don't forget you forced me to relive the worst chaos of my life." She didn't want to be so vulnerable with the man, but she was. She surprisingly wanted to be obedient to him, too, now that she didn't have the intense hatred for him running through her veins. The days of chal lenging him or attacking him were most likely over. At least, for now.

Wenzel leaned forward, stretching his torso across the island, bending at his elbows and placing his hands under his chin. "You scared the shit out of me. But the results were worth it. You're not even fully developed, yet you could wipe out thousands of demons with little effort. Oh, Finley, we're going to bring a beautiful chaos to the world. The three of us are going to tip the scales in our favor for millions of years. It's going to be glorious."

"I'm not fighting," she said. "My husband does all the fighting in the family."

"The beauty of you is more than skin deep, darling." He sighed and that goofy grin curled his lips. "But that isn't what's important at the moment. Listen to me."

Attempting a confident tone, she answered, "I'm listening." But her voice fell into a seductively sultry tone as her wings closed back up inside her body.

Warm air blew softly against her neck. Slater's lips pressed a warm, soft kiss behind her ear. "Stop toying with him, and he will stop playing to your weaknesses."

Weaknesses? Is that what he's doing? She cleared her throat and pulled Slater's hand behind her back.

Slater released her hand and pulled her onto his lap, his lips at her ear. "Good. Listen to what he has to say. It will be important."

"Are you truly listening, Finley?" Wenzel asked. "Or is Slater distracting you?"

Slater slipped his hand under her dress and pushed her panties to the side.

She shuddered with anticipation. "I'm listening." But she wasn't. She needed her husband. She needed sex.

A breeze whooshed across her skin. Powerful arms wrapped around her. Soft and luscious feathers caressed her back and sides. And a hard body and erection pressed flush against her front. She gazed up and green eyes with swirls of gold sparkles met her.

"Whisper the word, 'chaos', and I will find you wherever in the world you may be." Wenzel's words fell like a caress in her ears. "You don't need to be in danger to use the word. But you are in danger. Liam's connection to you is a very dangerous one. Law angels were banned from being a love angel's sole protector since the time of my father's rule. They can't continually battle the chaos surrounding them twenty-four hours a day, seven days a week. Right now, Liam is compromised. His wife needs to heal him from the damage years of living with you has done to him. When you're with him on Friday, you cannot engage in a power play with him and his wife. You will ruin him. He may choose to follow a path of separation."

"Path of separation?"

He nodded. "There are angels of law that are on the side of God and those on the side of Lucifer. The path of separation is—"

"Lucifer's path from God?"

He nodded. "Liam is in Exorcise, Texas to cleanse him of the chaos calling him to take Lucifer's path. I don't want to lose him. But his soul has been compromised by keeping you a secret and forcing you into a promise that was unhealthy for your kind. He held you captive, kept you under his control even when you left him. You were his prisoner, Finley. Please, do as I ask. And I am asking, not demanding. Help me save his soul from following Lucifer into the depths of Hell. Liam doesn't belong there."

"I'll talk to him. He would never turn his back on the law or God. He's stronger than you think."

"Lucifer has laws, too," he said. "When you're around, Liam is vulnerable. I need you to step out of the way, so I can help him."

"Fine. But you don't understand the extent of our relationship." *I don't want to hurt him. I love him. But he'd never choose any other path than the one of his idol Logan Hutchison. He idolizes him, but you don't know that.* "I will be able to see him, right?"

"Yes. Briefly at the wedding and then in a few months. Do not flex your power when he's around. Learn as much as you can about controlling your abilities while you're here. We'll talk more in Vegas, and I'll open my personal library vaults to you so you can read about your abilities, your history, and what those chants meant, along with the blessings that chaos chant your people brought you before they ascended. Right now, I've got to go. More marriages to officiate. More babies will be born in about nine months." He kissed her cheek. "I love you. And I'm proud of you. Choosing Slater over me was the right choice. He's a better man than I will ever be."

The cocoon surrounding her vanished. She fell backward, only to be enveloped in a softer, more lovely cocoon of feathers—her husband's.

"I hate it when he does that," Slater mumbled. "He's into you in a way I don't like."

"He's not. Is he still here?"

"No. It's me and you. I love snuggling you in my wings. So, what did he say to you? He had you inside his wings for a long time." He shook his shoulders, retracting his wings.

"He gave me a word to say if I needed him for any reason, even just to talk."

"He does that so he knows which weapons to bring to a fight. What else? You were with him for more than an hour."

"I couldn't have been."

"You were." Slater handed her the goblet of herbal water Wenzel had poured for them. Slater and Wenzel's goblets were emptied, while hers was full. "Drink."

She lifted the goblet to her lips and sipped the liquid. A strong bitter taste filled her mouth. She almost spit it out, but decided to swallow. "That's terrible."

"Warrior angels love the sweet and savory flavor."

"It tasted bitter to me."

"Really?" He picked up her glass and sipped the liquid. He

nodded as if he were having a conversation, then gulped down the rest. "Nope. Sweet and savory to me." He narrowed his gaze at her. "What else did he say to you?"

"He's worried about Liam. He talked about Liam's training and the two paths that are set before him. I don't want to hinder his training. So I'm going to heed Wenzel's advice. Then he held me and it was…nice."

Slater huffed and placed the glass down. "I bet it was. Did he try anything?"

"No. He didn't *try anything*. He held me. That's all. Nothing inappropriate happened." *You're jealous. I kind of like that you're jealous.*

"You're attracted to him, and he's attracted to you," Slater said.

"That man is nothing compared to you. I married *you*. I *love you*…" She caressed over his shoulders along the curve and up the back of his neck. "I'm totally into you." She lifted her heels, bringing her mouth closer to his lips. "Like totally. Into. You."

"Yeah?"

"Yeah." She gave him a peck on the lips and then raced toward the bedroom, happy to hear his footsteps behind her.

With a quick spin, she beat him to the bedroom and jumped up and down with victory. "I win."

He pulled his shirt over his head and pushed down his jeans and briefs. "No, baby, I win." With his cock bobbing against his abs, he strode toward her. "You're not allowed to be inside anyone's wings but mine. No other man's feathers are caressing your sexy body."

She retreated. "Jealous?" She shimmied, egging him on.

"Heck, yeah," he said. "I'm especially jealous of Wenzel. He's stronger than I am. He's smarter. He's been alive for much, much longer. But my cock is bigger, and I have the sexiest wife in the world. And my wife is going to pop out a bunch of *my* babies. And she'd going to be the best mother the planet has ever seen. And when we're on our honeymoon, my subscribers are going to see my sexy wife in a thong bikini and wish they were me."

"And all those subscribers are going to know *you're my sexy husband*. And they can want you, but they'll never touch you. Only I get that privilege."

He picked her up and tossed her in the air.

She floated down without a care in the world, knowing in her heart and soul that he would love and protect her with his own life.

He caught her and kissed her. "That's right. I'm your sexy husband, and on Friday, everyone in the cosmos will know it."

CHAPTER TWENTY-SEVEN

Finley

Wenzel's house in Las Vegas had many rooms. Rooms within rooms within rooms. There were sectioned off areas where only the Vogel family were allowed and within those, only Wenzel, his second—Slater, and his third—Aurora Vogel Hutchison were allowed to go.

With Wenzel's house sectioned off for Slater and Finley's human wedding and reception that day, Finley stood in a bridal suite Wenzel had added just for the occasion. While Sienna, Finley's best friend, helped her into her wedding dress that Wenzel bought, Finley couldn't stop thinking about all the information she'd read about love angels. Honestly, the gifts God gave to love angels were all the same, although some angels were given stronger levels of power with those gifts than others, and those gifts scared her down to the marrow of her bones. The chants from her family as each one attempted to protect her was a power transfer. All those angels, her entire family transferred their power to Finley in order to save her, in order to save the world from losing true love, passionate love, the true love of friendship, too. But the gift of seduction was also passed to her. The power of seduction she wielded encompassed every single level from a sweet crush to a clinically insane need for her. Now that she was healed or almost so, she was truly dangerous.

Wenzel and Slater had understated her seductive powers and the others that came with it. They downplayed her power over not only her own reproductive processes but those around her. She could literally make men and women mentally unstable with a negative thought directed toward them or a tilt of her head with the slightest of ill intentions sent in their direction.

The power she wielded by instinct was those of people's worst nightmares. If she were evil, the scales of good and evil would be broken, and evil would flourish across the land. Civilizations would topple. They had toppled because of men and women who had angered or captured a love angel. Male love angels were dangerous, but female love angels were downright deadly and ruthless.

All the times she accompanied her best friend Sienna to the fertility clinic her friend worked at, Finley had caused a boom of babies where there shouldn't have been. Women and men who had genetic infertility became fertile after she'd talked to them. She'd wanted Sienna to have triplets, and suddenly, without warning, a third child appeared on her ultrasound—a child previously unseen by one of the most renowned specialists in the world. Men who had never had sperm, suddenly had an abundance. Sienna was in a polyamorous relationship and was pregnant again with triplets—one child from each of her lovers—without medical intervention. Finley had wished it, and it had happened. In fact, everything Sienna ever confided in Finely that she wished for, with regards to children and love, came true. *Everything.*

Standing in front of the mirror with her best friend buttoning the back of her wedding dress, Finley wondered if it was her influence that made Sienna want a huge family.

"Have you always wanted a big family? I'm talking long before you met me?" Finley asked.

"You know my background. Having a big family seemed out of reach for me. I never thought I'd be able to afford it." She tugged the back of Finley's dress together. "There are so many silk buttons. And you look...I'm so glad you're not interested in my lovers. I'd be so jealous. Anyway, ever since I can remember, and I'm talking long before my mom ended up marrying my stepdad Eddie, I wanted at least a dozen kids. My mom used to tell me stories of a commune she'd stumbled into days before I was born. She said that the people were the most beautiful people she'd ever seen. They were all different ethnicities and shared in raising hundreds of children together as one big family."

Sienna peeked over Finley's shoulder into the mirror and smiled. "She said that my birth was easy and painless and the celebration that followed made her wish that she could stay with them forever. But Mom struggled with staying in one place. Plus, she said that the commune was closed to outsiders, except to help women who were in danger of losing their children during childbirth. So once she was healthy enough, she left with me. But that story, whether it was drug induced or real, stuck with me. I wanted a family of lovers with lots of children. I wanted dozens of children of my own, Finley. I've been blessed with three children of my own. I'm going to have three more and hopefully a dozen more after them. This has been my dream since I started dreaming."

Sienna curled her arms around Finley, embracing her. "I want you to have dozens of children with Slater, too. You two are going to make the most beautiful children ever born. And your kids are going to be best friends with mine. I love you." She kissed Finley's cheek. "Back to these tiny little silk buttons. The dress is gorgeous, but dang, girl. Did you have to pick one with a hundred of these things?"

"The dress was a gift from Slater's best friend Wenzel," Finley said.

The one-of-a-kind strapless wedding gown hugged her body. The split in the skirt rose to her hip. She'd never looked so good in her life. The hairstylist kept swallowing as she blew out Finley's hair. The woman had commented more than once about Finley's *alluring* scent and spent a long time playing with her hair, until the makeup artist walked in and kicked her out.

The makeup artist took one look at Finley and moaned, mumbling something about a threesome or orgy. A little eye liner and mascara, then a bit of clear lip gloss and she was done. Actually, Wenzel stopped in to check on her, and stopped the makeup artist from adding eye shadow or blush or even foundation. The man didn't seem to understand that this was *her* wedding and looking perfect was the goal, even though she'd thoroughly explained the reason why she wanted all the extra touches—for the picture-perfect wedding Slater's mom dreamed of giving him. It didn't help that Sienna agreed with Wenzel, and thought any makeup was too much. The two of them conceded with the few extra touches she ended up getting.

The irritating man had run Sienna off during the makeup argument. Wenzel seemed intent on reminding Finley at every turn that, with her power now surging from her healed wings, this event would be tricky to get through without causing a riot. And with all the humans in attendance, this celebration would be downright dangerous. She had to be careful of her thoughts and actions. He stressed that if at any point she sensed danger, she should glance at him and he'd take care of it. One word of "chaos" from her lips and he would be at her side, protecting her.

But then Sienna had returned with all her happy pregnant vibes and Wenzel left them alone, making life seem normal again. This moment with Sienna seemed normal. But worry remained constant. Keeping her thoughts peaceful was harder than it sounded, especially being in a house that exuded violent energy along with an undercurrent of peace. It was a weird dynamic she didn't understand. But Slater assured her that she would instinctively comprehend how the two opposites worked together as soon as she learned how to control and balance her own powerful gifts. Slater helped reduce her stress with sex, lots of it. But as soon as they were done or someone else entered a room where they were together, the need to seduce Slater dominated her thoughts, which brought with it a need to make him jealous. That need to make Slater envious would be detrimental to keeping Liam on the straight and narrow. She had to suppress her natural tendencies again, only this time she didn't want to suppress them. She wanted to let it all out, which forced her into a constant mental battle that at any minute she felt she might lose.

Now that she was healthier, stronger, and considerably more powerful, she had much more chaotic energy to control. She wasn't sure she could manage her emotions around Liam. She didn't want to hurt his recovery, a recovery he needed because of her.

Her chest constricted as her thoughts swirled with rising levels of chaos. Her skin itched to bring out her wings. She couldn't allow that. She couldn't be the reason he switched sides.

"Chaos," Finley mumbled.

"Everything okay?" Sienna asked. "You're wiggly. You're never wiggly."

"I think I need a break," Finley said.

"You're stressed. It's normal. You're making a lifelong promise, but you love Slater, right?"

"I do," Finley replied.

"Focus on your love for him," she said. "And the sex that is going to happen later. I expect explicit details." She giggled. "Blade, Stetson, and Michael were drinking in the groom's suite, giving Slater honeymoon tips. I'm sorry. *Not sorry.*"

Laughter bubbled up from Finley's belly as if her babies were giggling, too. "We kind of already did it."

"Ahh!" Sienna squealed, popping up from behind her and staring at her in the mirror. "I knew it. You have this new confidence, and I swear you've got a pregnant glow. Was it last week when you and he had that kiss at his restaurant? I bet it was. You're blushing."

Nodding, Finley smiled. "It was pretty amazing."

"Oh my goodness, I bet you're pregnant. You are in that window where you're fertile. Did you use contraception?"

"We didn't. And we kind of spent the week in bed. I don't know why I never paid any attention to him when we babysat together."

"We've all been finding any excuse we could to get the two of you together and nothing worked. I can't believe you two happened to run into each other at the airport and that is where your love story started." She patted Finley's back. "I'm done with all those buttons. I feel bad for Slater because it's going to take him all night to get all those buttons undone." She stepped out from behind Finley. "Wow. Just wow."

The knock on the door Finley had been waiting for finally happened. *Please be Wenzel.*

"Come in," Finley said.

The door opened and Wenzel strode in, his hair messy and his jacket undone. The grin on his face seemed genuine. He glanced around the room and halted the moment his gaze landed on Finley's.

"Wow," he mumbled. "You look…" He glanced at Sienna. "Hey, could I have a minute with Fin alone? There's been a change of plans, and I need to talk to her about it."

"Of course." Sienna placed her hand on the curve of her belly. "Take your time. I'll be on the couch in the other room." She kissed Finley's cheek. "You're making the right decision. Don't doubt it."

"Thanks," Finley said.

As soon as the door closed behind Sienna, Wenzel's arms wrapped around Finley.

"You're doing great, but Liam is a mess. He's going to sit in the row with his wife beside him, and Logan and Aurora on the other side of him. I'm going to walk you down the aisle, and Slater's human brother is going to stand in as his best man." He kissed her cheek. His breath smelled like booze. "But make no mistake, I'm Slater's best man, and baby, I'm totally squeezing your ass as I hand you over to him."

"You better not," she whispered.

He pulled her flush against him. "Slater would kill me if I did that. I wouldn't do it anyway. I just like teasing you."

"Well, you need to stop."

"Why'd you call me? Was it Liam? Can you sense his desire to control you? It's fucking palpable. He hasn't even seen you, yet."

"I'm stressed about him. I want him to be okay."

"He's going to be okay. Let's practice your inner dialog as you walk into the room and see him." He caressed up her back until his fingers were in her hair and he pulled her head to his chest. "So what are you going to be thinking about when we walk out of this room?"

"I love Slater. I'm happy to be his wife. I love Liam and his wife. I bless them with many children and a life filled with love."

"Good," he whispered. "Remain positive no matter what happens. Be confident that Slater and I will protect you. If a demon horde shows up—"

"Not helping, Wenzel."

He chuckled. "Nothing is going to happen. I'm in a good mood." He kissed the top of her head and his wings enclosed them. "My dad brought some *angel nectar*. Want some?"

"Are you drunk?"

"*Nooo*. If I were drunk on the stuff, I'd probably kiss you. Or do something equally stupid. It just tastes really good, and it's only used on special occasions, like an anointing from God—which happened to me and your husband today." He dipped her backward and gave her a peck on the lips. "We did good by you, and you're going to do great today. God is pleased. Your little babies are happy and healthy and growing. My family will double in size in nine months and I'm so in love with you..." He sighed. "But my best friend is your husband, and I'm so darn..." He lifted her up and squeezed her in a bear hug. "Let's do this human ceremony before I start getting too rowdy. But at the reception, you're dancing with me at least a dozen times. No excuses." His wings disappeared and she stood, with her arm in his, at the door leading to the rest of the suite.

She parted her lips to speak, but instead turned her head toward him. "Please, don't do anything to make me hate you again."

"Already did." His eyes flashed gold. "My number twos don't usually live very long. God and Slater gave me the green light to pursue you by all means necessary, if something were to ever happen to your husband." He faced forward. "I intend to do whatever I can to keep your husband alive forever, not only so the balance of power remains in our favor, but because I love him more than I love anyone else besides God. You're number three on my list of those I will do anything and everything to keep alive and safe."

"Where does Liam fall on your priority list?" she asked.

"Higher than he should. His saving grace is you. So bless him and his wife. Keep him on the lighted path. Spread your love to everyone in this state. Sparkle like a love angel who is marrying the second most powerful warrior angel in existence." He opened the door and escorted her into the sitting room.

Sienna stood up, dressed in an emerald green glittery dress in a style that accentuated her small belly bump. "Thank you for the dress. It's beautiful and unexpected."

"You're welcome. You look lovely, Sienna," Wenzel said. He offered her his arm and Sienna seemed to float on a heavenly cloud as she stepped forward and slipped her arm through his.

"Thank you, Mr. Vogel," Sienna replied.

"Ladies," Wenzel said. "Let's get in there and turn some heads."

While Wenzel led, Finley gained confidence and peace settled into her bones. But when Sienna left his side and walked into the sanctuary, Finley glimpsed Liam sitting next to a beautiful brunette with skin as beautiful as polished ebony. Fire raged within Finley's heart.

Liam is MINE. You can't have him.

Wenzel whispered into her ear, "Stop it. Bless them. He isn't yours. He's hers. She's pregnant. They're in love. Bless them, Finley."

"No."

"Bless them or I will take you as my wife and fuck you in

front of all these people, including Liam and your husband," Wenzel warned. "I will start a war where you and I are the only survivors."

She shuddered and the fire of fury fizzled out and blessings flowed through her mind. She knew without a doubt that Wenzel wasn't joking.

Two men opened the doors. The sound of harps drew her forward in step with Wenzel.

Her eyes fell on Slater. *You're my everything.*

Wenzel squeezed her arm. The warning was clear. He would follow through with his threat, if she didn't stay in line.

She slowed and stepped closer to Wenzel. *You're my new jailor.*

CHAPTER TWENTY-EIGHT

Slater

The wedding ceremony was short. The officiate made it so quick that Slater's mother was furious. But in true Wenzel Vogel style, the outside reception for Slater and Finley at Wenzel's house in Las Vegas made up for the brevity of the ceremony in Wenzel's indoor ballroom. The reason for the short ceremony was valid—the stronger Finley became, the stronger her angel nature of chaos and unpredictability also became.

As much as Slater knew about love angels, instinctively he also knew there remained plenty he didn't know. The secretive sect of angels didn't allow outsiders entrance. Not even Wenzel seemed to know everything about them. And Wenzel knew everything about everything—human, angel, and demon.

At the reception, drinks flowed, both of the human *and*

the heavenly variety. The perfect music selection and deejay kept everyone dancing and singing into the early morning hours. And Slater's mom was as happy as Slater had ever seen her. The woman even kissed Wenzel on the cheek and hugged him—a first on both counts.

With his arm slung around Wenzel's shoulder's, Slater laughed while he watched Finley smoothly transition from one dancing guest to another. The woman held a smile on her face, instinctively gathering pregnant women together into groups to protect and bless as they danced, sang, and ate.

Together, Slater and Wenzel followed Finley around, keeping a close enough distance to sense any sign that her happy mood shifted. The woman made Slater's task difficult the closer she moved toward Liam and Liam's wife Inverness.

The strategy Wenzel prepared for the event seemed to be working. Liam had enjoyed a good bit of angel nectar and held a tight control on his wife. Inverness Hutchison didn't go anywhere at any time without Liam's approval or presence.

"Stop tapping my wings," Wenzel grumbled. "I'm already angry about a certain someone in my house, and I'm not talking about your mother."

"Let that go." Slater smoothly grabbed a goblet of nectar from the waiter nearby and turned his back toward the corner. "The party has gone on for much longer than either of us anticipated. The Anointed was bound to show up at some point."

"Not today," Wenzel said. "Someone didn't do their job." His gaze drifted toward Aurora and Logan and then Finley who stood near Liam and Inverness.

"Aurora sniffs him out like a dog," Slater said. "Logan does, too. The two of them are unstoppable when it comes to finding the Anointed One and asking God what to do."

Wenzel growled. "They need to stay in their lane."

Slater rolled his eyes. *They do stay in their lane. Like we do. God makes the decisions, not us. And God gave Logan the difficult task of keeping track of the Anointed One, and Aurora has some strange bond with the man, always helping him whenever Logan is with him.*

He gazed at Liam who had stayed off the dance floor the entire night, standing beside his wife who seemed just as much of a bore as Liam.

At least Aurora knew how to party and didn't let Logan's lack of partying force her into being a wallflower, too. In fact, Aurora loved dancing and singing and even got her stick in the mud husband to dance to a ballad—which was no small task.

Aurora and Logan's marriage appeared strong and growing stronger. Their apprentices, Liam and Inverness, seemed to have a profound bond with a powerful desire for each other. Although Liam inched closer and closer to Finley, making Slater skeptical of Liam's marriage commitment.

While Slater kept a keen eye on Liam, he noticed Liam's hold on Inverness seemed tighter than necessary for the occasion, especially for a match boasted as *perfect* in Liam's new church—the Hutchison family church of Exorcise, Texas.

Finley closed the gap between Liam and Inverness when she didn't need to be that close to anyone, except Slater or Wenzel. She was too unstable, too unpredictable, too chaotic. Besides, she wanted nothing more than to have a private moment with Liam to speak her heart and listen to his, too, which remained unacceptable and against Slater's and Wenzel's rules.

While Inverness tucked herself against Liam's side, Liam slipped his hand into Finley's. The three of them seemed as though they held a dangerous secret and wanted to keep it that way.

The faintest words left Inverness's lips and traveled across the room on a frequency that Wenzel and Slater constantly listened to for rumors of danger.

"Lucifer has fallen angels who battle for him," Inverness whispered. "I'm half-empath angel and half-healer angel. I'm here to warn you. Demons of some kind are close. I don't know how close, but I feel an evil presence in the near distance. Liam feels them. I can't explain this, but I think we're all in danger." She reached out and touched Finley's cheek. "You feel them, too. We need to get the humans out of here. Please, tell your husband about this. I'm sorry. Liam isn't allowed to be close to you or he would've told you about this hours ago. Right now, Logan and Aurora are circling the dance floor searching for any signs of the dark angels sneaking through a weakness in the warrior angels' defenses."

"Warrior angels don't have weaknesses in their defenses," Finley argued.

"That's my girl," Slater muttered.

"Although…" Finley let the word linger. She tipped her head slightly to the right then shook it, returning to neutral once more. "Nope. They're strong and fully functioning. We're good. No evil inside Wenzel's compound."

"Oh, Lord, help us," Inverness gasped. "The danger. It's him." She pointed, and Finley and Liam followed Inverness's finger.

Wenzel grumbled. "He's not supposed to enter until the party is over. He never listens to me. He never. Ever. Obeys. Me."

"He's not dangerous," Finley said. She elbowed Liam. "It's Rager Smithson, my professor. The one you're friends with. The one I have dinner with every Wednesday night."

"You've been with Rager Smithson, not Ranger Wentworth?" Liam asked.

"Yes," Finley said. "We're good friends. He's not evil at all."

"No, not him," Inverness said. She pointed at Neeman, her hand and body trembling. "Him. He's risen from Hell."

"Neeman?" Finley chuckled.

"No," Inverness said. "Him."

She pointed to nothing.

"We need Wenzel," Liam said "We have to protect everyone." He pulled his wife into one of his wings. "He tried to take my wife when she was a baby," Liam said.

A whoosh of air blew her hair back over her shoulders and gently fell against her bare back.

Logan landed between Finley and Liam. He held Aurora close to his side. "Finley, go to your husband while I start dealing with this."

"I'm going to talk to Rager and Neeman, first," Finley said, disregarding Logan's order.

"My wife won't obey anyone," Slater mumbled. *She obeys Liam. Sometimes me and occasionally you, when she's not trying to kill you.* Slater looked at Wenzel. "Did you know Finley and Rager had dinner dates?"

Wenzel shook his head. "No, but being who he is, Rager knows things you and I don't. What is that Neeman kid doing here?"

"I don't know," Slater mumbled. "I'm wondering what Lucifer is doing here, and why neither of us knew Finley spent so much time with Rager."

"I invited Luci. I didn't want to get his panties in a wad over a wedding invitation slight. But Rager won't like that he showed up. This is why I didn't want Rager coming." Wenzel gazed at Rager striding toward the middle of the dancefloor as Finley sashayed toward Rager. "The Anointed One just has to do what he wants, when he wants. I'm going to have to have a discussion with him. Rager doesn't just get to wield God's authority around as he chooses. Not in *my house.*"

"I'll help my mom get the humans out before I greet Luci."

"You do that," Wenzel mumbled. He and Slater kept their eyes on Finley as they crossed the room toward the dance floor. Instead of continuing forward toward Finley, Wenzel inhaled and his neutral smile turned to a frown as he shifted course, remaining next to Slater. His jaw tightened and his hands clenched into fists.

Wenzel sidled up to Slater's mom, while she was dancing with her friends. "Help your son get *your* people out of my house. This party has gone on far too long. I'm tired of hearing that there are humans fucking in my outside flowerbeds. I expect reimbursement for the damages and clean up. You humans are disgusting."

Whatever got Wenzel worked up, it wasn't what he'd told Slater's mom. The only time Wenzel behaved like that was when a dark evil penetrated his defenses, or if Rager used his power over all angels and proclaimed God's word. Slater wasn't sure which it was, but he didn't sense an energy shift or that a major battle would happen here, on Wenzel's personal territory.

Wenzel pivoted and strode toward Finley and Rager, flicking his fingers this way and that, gathering clusters of warrior angels into casual battle formations to protect the guests from any potential chaos surges that might arise from Finley's growing instability.

"Wenzel doesn't give a shit about those flowerbeds," Slater's mom whispered to her son. "He changes them as often as he changes clothes. What's really going on?"

"We need to get everyone we can to leave right now." Slater had safeguards in place in case the evening went bad.

And even more safeguards after those, if the ones in place failed.

Slater nodded at the deejay and held up his index finger, signaling it was time for the human party to end quickly.

The deejay raised his water glass. The music volume lowered and the techno dance music transitioned to Mendelssohn's *Wedding March* to grab everyone's attention. "All right, all right. Listen up, my party people." He placed his drink down. "It's time to move this celebration to your hotels and houses. We've made the newlyweds wait long enough...*if you know what I mean.*"

Slater cringed while his mom laughed along with the rest of her friends. She glanced toward Wenzel. Her gaze swept the room. The woman knew the signs of danger from all the warrior training she had watched him go through when he was a kid. She easily recognized the movement of warrior angels heading toward Finley and Rager in the middle of the dance floor.

"Wenzel is managing damage control, isn't he?" Mom asked. "Finley is dangerously beautiful. I've been putting out fires between couples about one or the other needing time alone with her. Your father has had to escort several of his buddies out of the house, handing them over to Wenzel's guards to drive them home or their hotels. The sexual energy around her is staggering. I can see why you married her immediately."

"Mom, I didn't need to hear the extra commentary," Slater said. "You and your friends need to go. Now."

"Sorry. I'll get everyone out." She raised her voice and her hands and spun in a circle. "Follow me to the shuttles. There are gift bags in every seat. Thanks for making this celebration a night *and day* to remember."

For being a human, his mom took control like a warrior

angel and led the guests out of the house in an orderly fashion.

Now, to get this situation under control. *Rager is here to fight. The man is too calm, too confident, and he's got a golden halo above his head which only happens when he is here under God's command.*

I'm sure he's going to show off his sword of fire.

Finley will swoon.

Wenzel will have to hold me back from killing Rager.

CHAPTER TWENTY-NINE

Finley

The moment she spotted *Rager Smithson* striding toward her across the open divide, she hurried to him. The handsome blond whom she'd enjoyed dinner and lively conversation with every Wednesday without fail for more than a year held an emotionless expression on his face, but mirth lived in his eyes.

"You came," she mumbled.

He opened his arms and she embraced him. *Slater is probably jealous right now, but he'll have to get over it.*

"I was tied up, or I would've been here sooner," Rager whispered.

"I've got to greet Neeman," she said. "I'll be right back."

"I'll stand beside you," Rager said.

She kissed his cheek and he giggled as his face flushed pink like a little boy. "One second." She pivoted, facing Neeman.

Neeman looked handsome in a midnight blue suit with a light blue shirt and a yellow and blue diagonally striped tie. The light blue matched his eyes, and for the first time, she truly saw the romantic interest the man had for her. When she got back in town, she would have to set him up with a nice girl.

"You came." She hugged him and he held her gently, like always. "I'm sorry the reception is ending."

"I've been here for a while, but there were so many people vying for your attention, I just now saw an opening," Neeman said. "The flowers at the botanical gardens on campus are blooming. I'd love to show them to you…uh, and your husband. Does he love flowers as much as you do?"

"I'd love to see them, and my husband will join us, too," she said.

"Great," he said. "I, uh, sent a wedding gift to your husband's house. It's actually not a physical gift. It's a gift of a plan for the backyard. I'd like to be friends." He dropped his gaze to the floor. "I, uh, don't have too many."

"I need to introduce you to some of my new friends who love flowers, herbs, vegetables, and soil as much as you do. Did you know there are healing herbs?" she asked.

"Yes." His face lit up. "I'm working on which herbs could be beneficial as a hybrid. I'd love to collaborate with your friends."

"Consider it done. If you don't hear from me in a week, text me and I'll set it all up," she said. *You're going to have a wonderful conversation with Aurora.* She hugged him once more. *God, bless Neeman with a wonderful, loving wife who has as much passion for the land and plants as he does. And give them lots of children to love.*

"I've got to head out with everyone else. I'm happy for you, Finley. Your husband looks like a lot of fun. You need more fun in your life." He walked away with a spring in his step and a smile on his face.

"You didn't introduce me," Rager said.

"I'm sorry."

"It's fine, but again, we need to discuss your future as an attorney," Rager said. "It's not just studying the word of the law. Sometimes there's a bit of networking involved."

"I'm not going to be an attorney, even though I win all our arguments." She laughed and then Rager laughed.

"So, do you want to fuck some shit up with me? Let love conquer all?" Rager's lips quivered to keep from laughing, but his blue eyes held so much amusement that they seemed brighter.

"Those are not compatible," she said softly.

"What if I told you that they are?" he said. "What if I told you that you and I are the only ones in this room who can let our souls dance in both love and war? That the two aren't mutually exclusive?"

"I'd have a lot more questions for you. I'd think it might end up being a lively conversation," she whispered. "But before we go into that, I want to ask you an important question."

"Ask away. I have all the time in the world for you," Rager said.

She smiled. *You always make me feel like I'm the only person in the world when we're together.* "Liam didn't know that I was spending my Wednesdays with you. I thought he checked up on me with you. I thought that he gave you permission to take me home and even allowed me to stay over when I babysat Nash Walker's niece while I was at your house."

"There wasn't a question in there, Finley," Rager said. "I'm trying to make you an excellent attorney, but you keep refusing to follow the rules and change your major."

She chuckled. "You never talked to Liam about us, did you?"

"No, I did not."

"You never asked his permission to hang out with me, did you?" she asked.

He blushed and giggled. "Nope. I heard him talking to Logan about you spending a lot of time with Ranger Wentworth. He asked if I knew Ranger, and I told him I did." He kissed her cheek. "You've got me talking more than I should. But you should know by now that I don't ask anyone permission to do anything, except God."

"You knew about Liam. About his rules. About Georgia." *How did you know so much about him? About my life with him? About my education? My town? Me?*

"I know a lot about a lot of people."

"But me?"

"I have a small home not too far from Wenzel's in Georgia. God tells me things. I follow His orders. One of those orders was to give you a full-scholarship to college. When you accepted, I spoke with the right people so I would be in charge of your class schedule."

"Is that why taking the law class that first semester was mandatory?" she asked.

"Yes," Rager answered. "With me as your professor."

"You're a stinker," she laughed. "I loved your class. It was so much fun arguing with you."

"I picked subjects just to get you riled up," he said. "You have been, and I hope will continue to be the most unexpected point of joy in my life, since I developed a new relationship with God."

"You're not getting rid of me, Mr. Smithson," she said.

With the truth of his words shining through, she eased into the comfortable peace she'd always had with him.

"I love you so much," she whispered.

"I didn't mislead you about Liam. I don't want you to think I lied to you. When you asked me about Liam while we visited, I mentioned facts I learned about him. You assumed I asked him permission to spend time with you, and I let you assume. The rest is on him for not doing his due diligence."

"Yes. It seems so." She rested her cheek against his chest. The luxurious fabric of his black tuxedo jacket cradled her skin in softness as she held him a little tighter. "I recently found out that I can be mean. So, who do I need to fight for you?"

"Everyone." He chuckled and the vibration of his chest made her giggle a bit too loudly that she slapped her hand over her mouth. "Dance with me, Finley."

"There's no music."

"Finley," a powerful male voice commanded her attention with barely a whisper.

She jerked away from Rager and faced the man with the voice. Her heart warmed as she gazed on the most beautiful man she'd ever seen, besides Slater. Blue eyes like the sky. Hair as golden as Slater's golden wings. A face with perfect symmetry. Strong jaw and nose and lips that called to be kissed, yet she had no interest in him in an intimate way. He seemed familiar, while at the same time he seemed unfamiliar.

Strange. Who are you?

She held out her hand. "I'm Finley. Thank you so much for coming to the reception."

"I was at the wedding, too." He took her hand and pulled her away from Rager and into a gentle hug. "I had to come to my own daughter's wedding. I thought you had died. I couldn't feel your presence for the longest time. It seemed like forever. I saw the aftermath of..." He held his breath and slid his hand over her shoulders and a sense of belonging filled her. "I'm Luci, your father. I loved your mother. I should've protected her. I should've protected you. I thought you ascended with the rest of your family. When I got the invitation to your wedding, I rushed here to see if it was true. If you were alive."

"I'm sorry, but you've got me mistaken for someone else. I saw my father ascend. I saw my mother ascend. I saw my entire family ascend. I'm a love angel, and we don't leave our children to fend for themselves." *You're lying to me.*

"I'm a special angel, and *I am* your father. You have many gifts, my daughter of love. Your body is still injured. I'll send Aurora the scroll of your family history, which has information she'll need to complete the healing of your spine, hips, and continue to strengthen the cartilage in your wings in order to change them to bones as strong as mine. In the scrolls, there are recipes to heal your children—my grandchildren. Love angels get their hearts broken a lot. Hearts are much harder to heal than any bones." He kissed the top of her head. "Slater has healed your heart. Which reminds me. There are gifts for you at Slater's house. I will visit you there, and we will sing together. I'll teach you how to play whatever instruments of music you'd like to learn, and I'll tell you about your mother. She was…"

He inhaled and closed his eyes as if he were inhaling the essence of her. "I didn't think there would be a more beautiful woman than your mother to ever walk this earth, and then you were born. Beautiful. Perfect. Chaos incarnate." He exhaled and opened his eyes and the irises morphed from blue to gold. He lowered to one knee, holding Finley's hand. "I bless your marriage and make this solemn vow…" His voice thundered in the room. "If anyone—demon, angel, or human—attempts to kill you, I will crush their souls. They will not ascend to Heaven nor descend to Hell. They will walk among the ghosts of the earth, unable to haunt or help, only cry in silence for all eternity. I will bring my army against them until every member of their family tree receives the same fate."

Who are you? Are you truly my father? She stood, utterly speechless, gazing down at the man who kind of looked like her.

Wenzel appeared out of nowhere and patted Luci on the back. "Luci, what's all this about?"

Luci kept his gaze on her. "My beautiful daughter seems to have survived from sure death. I've grieved for you, Finley. I grieved for your mother. But by some miracle, you are here to stand as a measure and judge, ready to hold the scale of good and evil, weighing each and recording how much love and hatred lives in humans roaming earth."

"The scales are not balanced," Wenzel said. "You stand before me and my warriors, attempting to tilt the scales in your favor."

"You won't win," Rager said. "The goodness of God is here on earth. The holiness of the Spirit is strong and winning the war. Finley stands with us. And she will continue to hold the scales as a judge appointed by God, Lucifer."

"Lucifer?" The breath within Finley left her lungs as if someone had crushed her ribcage. *No. No. No.*

"Yes," Lucifer said. "Honey, I know you've heard all kinds of things said about me, but not all of them are true. You'll see for yourself." He rose and hugged her. "You have nothing to worry about. I love you."

Without any noise or light or any fanfare, Lucifer vanished into thin air.

"He's not a love angel," Slater said. His hands slid around her waist and pulled her back against his front.

"He can be anything he wants to be," Wenzel said. "He's the king of seduction which is a love angel attribute. But Finley's mother…"

"Excuse me," Fin huffed.

"Sorry, Fin," Wenzel said. "I know you're here, yet I was acting like you weren't, so don't look at me like that."

"Wenzel, I can look at you any darn way I want. I just found out the devil is my father." *This can't be true. It can't.* "Was he lying? How could my mother have slept with him?"

"As far as I know, Luci has never allowed anyone to carry his child, until your mother. I'm more surprised he fell in love. But at the same time, love angels are almost impossible to resist. *You* are impossible to resist."

"Lucifer might be your father, but you've already chosen to fight for good, Fin," Rager said. "Now, will you allow me to enroll you in law school? I will be teaching most of your classes. You will hold the scales of justice as soon as you're strong enough. A love angel always has that job, and you're the last one, at least for a little while."

She nodded. "I'm scared."

"There is nothing to be scared about," Rager said. "Liam protected you under his wings of law—long before he ever knew he had them. And his love for you helped you survive, grow, and thrive in this world." He faced Wenzel. "Do not keep Liam from Finley anymore. He helps her control the chaos living inside her. The chaos she holds is from all the love angels who walked this earth before her. That's a lot of chaos."

"Fine," Wenzel said. "But I'll be there, too."

"You don't need to be there." Rager's ice-blue irises morphed to an ethereal gold. That same golden color added an angelic glow to his lightly tanned skin.

"I need to be at any meeting Finely has with angels because Luci will be near, spreading his influence in ways you can't even imagine," Wenzel said.

"I know you're worried about Finley, but Liam taught her

well," Rager said. "She can handle her father and protect those around her."

"Not yet, she can't," Wenzel said. "She's not fully formed or healed. The scales of justice are heavy and if it tips from good to evil—"

"You've gone up against Luci before and won. Finley can keep the scales balanced and offer love and hope when Luci spreads his propaganda—"

"Build me a house next to yours, Rager," Wenzel said. "I have a love angel to train."

"I don't think that *you* training *me* is a good idea," Finley said. *More like a horrible idea. You intentionally push all my buttons at once, which makes me want to kill you.*

"Don't argue with God's path for you, Fin," Rager said. "Every Wednesday you'll study for the law school exams with me. Once you've passed them, I'll tutor you through law school. You'll work with Logan and Daniel Hutchison to learn the church's laws. Wenzel will train you in whatever he wants. And sometimes, you'll come and practice fighting with me or Slater or Wenzel or all three of us. Most of all, we'll remind you what your father does to people, because he's going to show you a very different side of himself—the seductive side he offers humans, not the side where he torments them."

Finley turned around in Slater's arms and faced him. "Do you still love me?"

"Yeah," he replied. "Everything is going to be okay, Fin." He cradled her face and kissed her, chastely. "Just don't eat or drink anything he offers you."

Wenzel and Rager laughed.

"And don't sign anything or promise him anything, no matter how insignificant it seems," Rager said. "As your attorney, I need to review any documents he sends or hands you."

"And be dubious of anything he shows you, especially when he sweeps his hand in front of your eyes," Wenzel said. "Once you're trained, you'll still need all of our help."

Logan and Liam and their wives joined their small circle.

"You'll never be alone, Finley," Logan said. "If you ever feel alone or lost, pray and come to Exorcise, Texas, or call me or Liam or our wives, and we'll come get you. Lucifer is banned from God's land in Exorcise. His influence won't touch you there."

"That's true," Wenzel said. "Same with here, unless I invite him for a specific event, but his time is limited on my land and territory, which is why he vanished. His time was up."

"So, I really am his daughter?" Finley asked.

"Looks that way," Wenzel said. "I knew your hair looked familiar, but I couldn't place it for what felt like the longest time. You have your father's hair. God spun it from the purest gold in the cosmos to shine the brightest of all the angels. When he stepped out of the shadows, you two glowed like angels do in Heaven. There's nothing like it. You should hear Luci sing..." Wenzel stared at nothing, seemingly lost in his thoughts. "After a battle, he'd sing to those who were trapped in the world between worlds, to the warriors who valiantly battled and lost, to the women and men who would never see the love of their lives ever again. And when those songs were sung, he's sing for Karina, his true love, to come to him, to forgive him, to love him, if not for eternity, at least for one night. And Karina was the most beautiful love angel I'd ever seen until..." He gazed at Finley. "Until you. She had crimson lips just like yours. High cheekbones, just like yours. She had an hour-glass figure, the exact measurements of yours. And when she and Luci fought, she plucked a chaos feather and brushed his chest with it. The chaos that one feather caused..." He exhaled. "Beautiful chaos within the world of evil. The scales shifted until good held control. But she vanished with her family of love angels. I think you might be Karina's child."

"She is," Rager said. "And my sweet friend needs to rest. She's had enough truth thrown at her for one day."

Finley stared into Slater's golden eyes. *Do you really still love me? Am I just a pawn in this game of chess?* "Will you take me home?"

Slater nodded. "Everything really is going to be okay."

She nodded, and without looking back or hugging anyone, she crossed the lawn toward the house and the exit, leaving her husband to follow. Her heart broke a little.

Evil creatures murdered my family. My father's creatures hunted my people to almost extinction. He could have stopped them. He could have saved my family. My mother and father who raised me, and aunts, and uncles, and cousins aren't with me because of him. His creatures broke me. I barely made it out alive. Why would he do that to us?

While she stood beside Slater's SUV, she held her belly. "I'll protect you." *I'll never let Lucifer influence you. I'll tell you the story of our family and what happened. You will know, and be guarded around him. Your father and all the other warrior angels will protect you. I will gather an army to protect you. Evil will never win. I will make sure of it.*

"I'll protect you and our babies," Slater said softly. "I love you. I will always love you." He opened the passenger door, softly placing his hand on her back and guiding her into the car. "Rager may drive me crazy, and I might be jealous of your relationship with Liam, and having Wenzel train you will be difficult for me to watch, but you need what each of them have to offer. We are a family of powerful warriors, Fin."

She buckled in and nodded as he closed the door.

I'm dangerous to train to fight. That's why Wenzel has that job and not you.

Slater slid into his seat and started the car. "I love you."

"Can you take me on a honeymoon when the semester ends?" she asked. "A private place. A place without Wenzel?"

"I know just the private island. It's Wenzel's island, but I'll tell him he can't come. Sound good?"

"Sounds perfect." *I wish we could go now. But Rager would be angry if I bailed on school. I guess I need to get on board with his plans and go to law school.*

She smiled.

I'm going to bring so much love into the world, my father won't be able to combat it.

Love conquers evil.

Love conquers all.

EPILOGUE

Slater

"*B*abe, this isn't a nude show," Slater yelled. "Just put on the bikini, while I go live on my channel."

She slipped into her white cheeky bikini bottom and matching barely there string bikini top. "Better?"

"Yes, you know I get jealous." He smirked. "Keep it on until I tell you to take it off again."

"Fine," she huffed. "I'm not even going to be seen on your channel."

"Yes, you are. My subscribers love you. And Wenzel's going to be here any minute to film."

"Ugh. Wenzel, your videographer for *our* honeymoon. I thought we'd be naked and having lots of sex, and Wenzel would be anywhere else but here." She stomped along the hot sand toward the ocean.

"He's keeping his distance, except when I'm giving updates for the channel," he shouted.

Wenzel jogged down from the house and pressed something on the camera, nodded and pointed at Slater.

"I'm on a private beach with my beautiful wife who is starting to show a cute baby bump. Come here, babe." He heard water splashing. *If you come back wet…*

Wenzel's brows rose and a grin filled his face.

"I'll be right there, honey." Her voice held a sultry tone that immediately got his dick as hard as granite.

He glanced toward her and her entire body was wet and she looked delicious. Her dusty pink nipples showed through the tiny white fabric. She lazily ran toward him, her breasts bouncing as the sun shined down on her tanned glowing body. When she arrived next to him, he forgot he was filming live.

"Fin," he mumbled.

She pressed her front against his and kissed his nose. "I love you. Mind if I watch you pump up those sexy muscles of yours?"

He kissed her lips and curled his arms around her waist. "Why don't you exercise with me?"

"Maybe I will," she whispered. "When I get you alone."

He dipped her back toward the camera and she laughed.

"Wave to our subscribers, babe," he said.

She waved and her top shifted, showing off the undercurve of her breasts. "Hey, y'all."

He glided his hands up her back, lifting her slightly and straightening her spine until she stood on her own. "Let's start with some squats."

"I'm out," she said. "Enjoy those squats, my love. I'll be attempting to distract you." She turned to the camera. "We finally get a honeymoon, and he's exercising and not paying attention to me."

"One. Two. Three. Four…" Slater counted his squats.

She pouted at the camera. "*Sla-ter*, if you don't start paying attention to me, then I'm going to—"

Slater snuck up behind her and swept her up off her feet, cradling her in his arms. "I won't be able to do things like carry you around, if I don't exercise."

"But it's our honeymoon," she whined.

While her bottom lip jutted forward into a seductive pout, he carried her back to the area he marked off in the sand for exercising on his channel. His balls ached to make love to her, to send more seed into her body and make more babies. But he liked his channel and the money it made, and he helped people think about exercise, and some even exercised with him online. His channel changed lives for the better. His channel helped balance the heavenly scales toward good. He'd told her all these things, but the chaos living inside her pulled her in two different directions. The healthier she became, the more powerful her gifts of love and seduction grew. The chaotic tug toward good remained strong within her, but with the development of her gifts, a darker desire awoke in her wings of chaos that could swing the judgement scales to good or bad, depending on her mood.

"I still need to stay fit and healthy, and so do you," he said. "Squats are done. Now, lay in front of me while I do burpees. Each time I kiss your belly, you shout out the number until I get to fifty."

"Fine," she said.

"Thank you." He placed her on her back on the sand and gazed into the camera. "We're going to end this after the burpees. My lovely wife is feeling neglected, and I need to make it up to her." He dropped down into pushup, kissed her belly, and breathed in her sweet, sugary aroma.

"Fifty," Fin shouted. "We're done for the day!" She rolled over, away from him, and jumped up. She sprinted to the camera as Slater chased her. "We'll see you later tonight or tomorrow or maybe in a few days. Love you." She blew a kiss to the camera and pressed the button to stop filming. "Wenzel, no more filming today. No training. No testing. No arguing. No ordering me or Slater around. You can leave food, and we'll cook ourselves. I do not want to see anyone else until tomorrow around lunch."

"You can't take a day off, Finley," Wenzel said.

"I need a day off," Fin shouted at him. "It's vacation. It's *my* honeymoon. I want to run around naked with my husband. I do not want him telling me I have to *put on clothes*. Not today. So, go and do something, anything else, just don't do it where I will see you."

Wenzel held up his hands in surrender. "You get the rest of the day off. Enjoy it. I'll be around if you need me."

"I won't," Finley screamed. "I won't need you. You're making me unhinged."

Wenzel backed away. "I love you both. I think maybe two days off would be reasonable. I'll make sure there's food for a few days. I'll be in my house on the opposite side of the island and give you a call before I come back."

"Call Slater, not me." Fin pivoted and smiled at Slater. "I'll be waiting for you to take off my bikini just out of reach of the waves."

"I'll be there in a minute," Slater said. "It's going to be just you and me for a few days."

"Better be," she mumbled. "I want my honeymoon."

The second she walked out of range of hearing, Slater hugged Wenzel. "Put a note on the channel that I'll be back for more live footage in a few days."

"Already done. It took a lot of control to not laugh at Fin just now. The viewers love her. I'll have Aurora manage the channel for the next couple days. Finley does need some extra-attention from you. You've been distracted.

"Her father keeps showing up, unannounced," Slater said.

"He appears outside her classes and takes her to her favorite coffee shops or for lunch. He takes her to baby boutiques and buys her anything she wants. She knows who he is, but she's a love angel. She loves, even him." He gazed at his wife, near the water…with her father wearing a black speedo. "Speaking of the devil." *I've got to keep myself together and not start an argument with the man. I can't believe I married the devil's daughter.*

The two men strode to Finley.

"Luci," Slater said. "I thought you weren't going to visit us while we were on our honeymoon."

"I wasn't, but then I saw your live broadcast and my daughter looked upset. You're not paying enough attention to her, and I'd like to have a private conversation with you about the appropriate way to treat *my daughter*."

I want to pound you into nothing. Grind your bones into dust…

"Dad, stop." Finley placed her hand in Slater's, squeezing it lightly, lovingly, calming the fury inside him. "You're pushing boundaries, and you know I don't like that. Slater and I were teasing one another. Go home, or I'll call Rager and Logan and Liam and Daniel and all those angels you dislike so much to start harassing you. I'll tell them all where to find you."

"Rager isn't an angel," Lucifer said.

"He's been anointed by God and not afraid of you. Please don't push me, Daddy," she pouted. "I love you and enjoy our time together. But this is my honeymoon. I've already had to have a talk with Wenzel. I don't want to go away with Slater for the rest of our honeymoon where no one will find us."

"Baby girl," Luci cooed. "I missed most of your life. I don't want to miss any more. I love you."

"You need to miss the honeymoon," she stated. "Slater and I haven't had near enough alone time together and some of that is because you keep popping up everywhere I am. And yes, I see you. I feel when you're near and no matter how hard you try to hide, I can find you just as easily as you can find me now, too."

"You've made your point," Lucifer said. He gazed at Slater. "Love angels aren't warrior angels. They're defensive angels. They aren't aggressive or the first to start a fight. They protect. They only protect."

"That's enough," Finley shouted. "I'll learn anything I want to, including how to protect myself, my children, and those I love. I'm going to attack when I feel it's the right thing to do. And right now, I'm getting very angry with you, Father. Leave, before I bring out my wings, given to me by my family, my entire love angel family and start a real conversation, *one about chaos*."

Lucifer grinned at Finley. "I'll see you next week. I am going to take you to a new boutique where I saw the cutest cribs for—"

"Liam, Daniel, and Logan, the law angels, are making the furniture for our children, including the cribs," Slater said. "My mom is making the linens for the cribs."

"And what do you think about that, baby girl?" Lucifer asked in a sugary sweet seductive voice.

"Considering I asked if they would, I'm thrilled they were all willing to do it," she said. "Dad, I love you. Now it is time for you to go. Slater is here and Wenzel won't leave until you do. So, leave me alone so I can have a freaking honeymoon with my husband. It's not too much for me to ask."

"Fine," Lucifer huffed just like Finley did whenever she didn't get her way. "See you Tuesday for lunch." He kissed her forehead. "I love you, even though you make me crazy."

"Back at you," she said.

Lucifer walked into the ocean and dove under the water, disappearing.

"I'll see you two in a few days." Wenzel opened his wings and flew to his side of the island.

"We're finally alone," Slater said.

"I know why my family lived in a type of hiding," Finley said softly. She rarely ever spoke about her family or the memories that had surfaced since her healing.

"Why?" The scrolls about love angels never gave reasons as to why the special angels remained isolated from everyone else.

"Everyone, angels, demons, and humans, want to be near me." She slid her hands around him and pressed her body against his. "I just want to be with you. Alone. No one else anywhere near us. Is there anywhere on earth we can really be alone?"

"Yeah, but it's not a place I ever like going."

"Where?"

"Daniel Hutchison's house in Exorcise, Texas. He has to invite you inside, and if you break any of his thousands of rules, you find yourself outside the county limits naked. The only way to get back into the city is walking through the woods to the main road and waiting for him to escort you back inside. He's an original fallen angel, one that came to help humans and angels follow God's laws."

"He's in love with Aurora," she said. "He doesn't need me coming into his house and messing with his emotions. I know I do that without even trying, and I don't want to do that to him. I guess, we need to stay here with my father lurking in the ocean to see what we're doing and not doing, while Wenzel devises strategies to circumvent my father's attempts to pull me into his world." She rolled her eyes. "Like I'd ever do that."

"You love him," he said softly.

"I love," she whispered. "It's what I do best."

"Mmm," he mumbled.

"Can we go to your place in Georgia? Maybe have breakfast at your restaurant? Stay in a different hotel every night? Have Wenzel be our private chauffer and pilot?"

"Anything you want," he said. "I'll have Wenzel set up our itinerary and we'll be surprised everywhere we go."

"Let's do it." She rose up onto her toes. "Please make it happen quickly. I am so hot for you and I don't want to have sex where my father can see us. The sooner Wenzel can get us out of here, the better."

She didn't have to ask him twice. In a flash, he opened his wings, held her in his arms, and flew to the other side of the island, where a small army of warrior angels waited for them on the tarmac.

Wenzel stood at the front. "Cloak and fly, above and below, in front and back."

"This is my move," Slater whispered. "It's so much fun."

As one unit, the warrior angels opened their wings, facing each other in pairs and rose into the airstream, as they hid her and Slater in the middle. One moment, they were up in the air, and the next, they were across the world on a balcony overlooking a vineyard in need of harvesting in Italy with no one around.

"This is one of my vineyards," Slater said. "It's in need of some love."

"I have a feeling this year's wine will get all kinds of awards." She pulled him inside the bedroom and closed the doors. "Now, do with me whatever you want, because I want it all."

"Let's start with getting this bikini off you…"

ALSO BY ANNA LORES

Contemporary Romance

Billionaire 42 (Streaming Lovers series) Book 1

Billionaire 43 (Streaming Lovers series), Book 2

Billionaire 44 (Streaming Lovers series), Book 3

Billionaire 45 (Streaming Lovers series), Book 4

Ella's Triple Pleasure (Sinfully Hers series), Book 1

Evangeline's Power Trio (Sinfully Hers series), Book 2

The Horse List, Book 1

The Horse List Challenge, Book 2

The Horse List Unveiled, Book 3

Unexpected Love: Chase Allen

More coming soon

Contemporary Romance Short (er) Stories

Milk and Honey series

Blade's Fertile Virgin, Book 1

Stetson's Fertile Virgin, Book 2

Greg's Fertile Virgin, Book 3

Evan's Fertile Virgin, Book 4

Brandon's Fertile Virgin, Book 5

Maverick's Fertile Virgin, Book 6

Denver's Fertile Virgin, Book 7

Bastian's Fertile Virgin, Book 8

Quinn's Fertile Virgin, Book 9

Malcolm's Fertile Virgin, Book 10

Brianna's Fertile Virgin, Book 11

Blade's Second Fertile Virgin, Book 12

Nash's Fertile Virgin, Book 13 will be here soon

More on the way…

Urban Fantasy Paranormal Romance

Werewolves and Vampires

Cursed to Love

One Night of Love

More coming soon

Fallen Angels and Demons Series

Logan: Law Angel, Book 1

Slater: Warrior Angel, Book 2

More coming soon

For more steamy stories and to join Anna's VIP Lounge, visit
https://www.AnnaLoresAuthor.com

ABOUT THE AUTHOR

An avid romance reader, Anna Lores started writing steamy romance novels as a by-product of insomnia. One night, with a nudge from her husband to write a book, Anna borrowed her son's laptop and set about breathing life to her very own characters. After a month, she was surprised with a new laptop of her own to pursue her dreams of writing sensual happily ever afters.

The desire to fill her world with wonderful stories she and her close friends could not just talk about but gush over keeps Anna's fingers racing to keep up with her imagination. As the rest of the house is sleeping peacefully, Anna sheds her title as Supermom of Three to write sexy love stories

Sleeping might still be a battle Anna hasn't conquered, but armed with a B. A. in English Literature and all the hot men in her mind calling for their own story, she stays busy during those midnight hours writing her next international bestselling spicy romance.

Visit http://www.AnnaLoresAuthor.com/ for more information and to sign up for Anna's VIP Newsletter.

facebook.com/AuthorAnnaLores

bookbub.com/authors/anna-lores

x.com/AnnaLores

instagram.com/AnnaLoresAuthor

goodreads.com/annalores